ELEMENTAL CLAIM

WAR OF THE MYTH
BOOK ONE

MIRANDA GRANT

BY MIRANDA GRANT

WAR OF THE MYTH SERIES
Elemental Claim
Think of Me Demon
Tricked Into It
Rage for Her
Wish of Death

FAIRYTALES OF THE MYTH STANDALONES
Burn Baby Burn
The Little Morgen
Bjerner and the Beast
To the Devil's Tune

DEATHLY BELOVED SERIES
Death Do Us Part
For Better or For Worse

THE FOUR RIDERS SERIES
Immortal Hunger

What People Are Saying About Elemental Claim

"I absolutely love, love, love this book. At the first chapter Miranda Grant had me hooked."

"This is easily my favourite Paranormal Fantasy I've read all year. It was unique and brilliant, well written and fast paced with characters to die for (and a romance that I adored)."

"I want to hear more of their story so bad that I'm literally crying."

"Elemental Claim starts with a bang and doesn't stop! I loved every bit of the mythology she weaved in this story, gods and goddesses, vampires, elementals, hellhounds, and so much more!

"This was an unexpected read. I saw my friend reading it and thought why not since I was in a slump. So I bought it and as soon as I got to reading it I was stuck."

"Omg!!!! So hott and exciting im def putting this in my top 5 Sexy as hell"

"loved it. I couldn't put it down, starting #2 now."

"This book doesn't disappoint. It's her first and Miranda starts with a bang!"

ELEMENTAL CLAIM

Edition Two

This is entirely a work of fiction. Names, characters, places, and incidents are all products of my imagination and should not be seen as having anymore credibility on reality than fake news does. Any resemblance to actual events, locales, organizations, or persons, living, dead, or stuck in purgatory, is entirely coincidental.

https://www.facebook.com/warofthemyth/
https://www.instagram.com/authormirandagrant/
https://www.tiktok.com/@authormirandagrant
authormirandagrant@gmail.com
www.mirandagrant.co.uk

ISBN: 978-1-914464-56-0

Cover and chapter headers designed by MiblArt.
Edited by Writing Evolution.

To Delentia, you crazy goddess:

You hijacked my entire mythical world and made it so much better. Thank you for not shutting up about how awesome it would be if you were in it.

TERMS

Angel – A winged creature of 'purity'. They can tell when someone is lying, cannot lie themselves, and can shoot a blinding light from their palms that has the power to burn the souls of demons.

Archangel – Six black-winged angels who are tasked with policing the gods and holding order and justice in the Seven Planes. Light cannot exist without darkness.

Ascension – "Puberty" for creatures of the Myth. This is when they get their powers and their bodies become capable of healing themselves.

Berserker – There is only one family of berserkers and Tegan Jólfrson's family, which consists of him, seven older sisters, and his parents, is it. Once they enter a Rage, they will kill anything and everything they see.

Craving – Severe bloodlust that makes one mindless with the need to hunt. Made vampires broken during their change and werewolves under the blood moons are the most at risk into falling under the power of the Craving.

Descendant – A child whose parents are both gods, but is not a god themselves. They were made infertile by the archangels.

Echidna – A monster/killing machine that speaks using a mode of telepathy. Due to this, their human forms are mute.

Elementalist – A person with the ability to control one of the four elements: water, earth, air, or fire. If strong enough, a person can control their element in all its forms, but there isn't a single person that can wield more than one element.

Elv've'Norc – A mythical special ops organization tasked with protecting the Seven Planes. It was founded by Tegan Jólfrson three and a half thousand years ago, when Sebastian the Ancient Destroyer and Rakian the Call of Ragnarok had started their war. A member of the Elv've'Norc is called an Elv've'Nor.

Phasing – Teleporting, regardless of distance. A person must either know the place they're phasing to or be told of it in great detail. Other people can be taken with them, though they suffer side effects such as headaches, nausea, and occasionally death. Most people with this ability can only phase from inside a plane, but those strong enough can phase from one plane to another.

Pulsing – When a powerful creature undergoes their ascension, their powers lash out uncontrollably at random intervals. For a short time after pulsing, they become vulnerable.

Telepath – One with the ability to communicate through their mind. They can also force people to do as they command, as well as create bleeds in the brain.

Trickster – A creature capable of creating illusions and shapeshifting. Their objects of illusions are just that – illusions. They mimic an object in every sense, but they do not have a physical body.

Scrolls of Atlantis – A book of unspeakable power, written by Prometheus, who stole the wisdom from the well of Mimir, the same well Odin sacrificed his eye to in exchange for knowledge. Its pages don't just hold the secrets of life. They *are* the secrets of life. It can only be read by Atlantians.

Seven Planes – The seven worlds where creatures created by the gods live. They are: Earth, Gaera, Halzaja, Persic, Blódyrió, Konistra, and Alazul.

Vampire – There are two types: born or sired. A born vampire is able to walk in direct sunlight with only mild discomfort and has the ability to phase. They are also stronger and faster. Sired vampires are created by born vampires through a biting and exchanging of blood ritual. They are infertile and their bodies 'freeze in time' at their point of rebirth. They awake in a frenzy and will kill whoever is nearby in their need to feed.

Werewolf – A bipolar monster roughly resembling a wolf. Their bite is poisonous to vampires. Their ability to follow a scent is unmatched.

CHARACTERS

Delentia – A sightseeing fury known as the Incarnation of Madness.

Elizabeth – A descendant with the power to kill with a single touch. She's working with Sebastian.

Emma – Elizabeth's older sister. She'll do anything to save the only family she has left.

Gabriel – An archangel who has a long history with Xeno.

Hunter – A tech whizz curious about everything. Member of Rogan's team.

Jack – A trickster who never takes anything seriously. Member of Rogan's team.

Lucille – A young vampire Sebastian cares for.

Rakian – The last descendant to have walked the Seven Planes before Elizabeth and Emma.

Rogan – Head of the Retrieval Elv've'Norc team. The mission always comes first. A water elementalist.

Sebastian – A sadistic, clever vampire who wants to destroy the Seven Planes. He has just stolen the *Scrolls of Atlantis*.

Tegan – Head of the Elv've'Norc. A berserker with the weight of the Seven Planes on his shoulders. He will sacrifice the good of the mission in order to save his agents.

Xeno – An angel in the midst of her fall. Once she loses her wings, she'll never get them back. Member of Rogan's team.

ONE

Peering through the windshield, Emma stared at the dark clouds closing in, not at all surprised her shitty day was about to get worse. She had already been pissed on by everything else: work, her younger sister, a small yappie dog (literally). Why not God too?

It's not like the bastard had ever been there for her before.

"No chance of rain, my ass," she muttered, her scowl deepening as she ducked her head to peer further up at the sky. She'd believed that forecast, had even peeked out her window this morning and seen clear blue skies. What she hadn't done, was take her jacket when she'd left this morning. *For fuck's sake. Can this day get any worse?*

A sudden sharp bark right beside her head caused her to swerve. The front wheel hit the curb, then bounced back onto the road. Heart racing, she half twisted to shove the massive black head back into the backseat.

"Stay!" she commanded, trying not to gag over the smell of death emitting from the animal. The dog must have rolled in a deer carcass. Or an elephant's. Something big for sure because its entire body smelled like six-day old roadkill.

Giving a small whine, the massive dog settled back away from her. It wasn't far enough to help with the smell, but at least he wasn't drooling beside her face anymore. Wiping her palm hard on her thigh to get the stench off, Emma focused back on the road.

The last thing she needed was to crash, even if it would be ironic. She'd stopped to save the massive canine off the highway a few minutes ago. If he caused her to die, at least she'd go out laughing.

Well, screaming more like. But laughing on the inside.

With a soft shake of her head, Emma pulled up to the curb outside her sister's house. Stepping out of the car, she slammed the door behind her. When it bounced back open, she slammed it again. One of these days, she was going to get that fixed.

Liar.

Ignoring the judgmental, unhelpful voice inside her head, Emma peered into the backseat. The black beast was already scratching at the door, begging to be let out. Mud (and hopefully nothing else) was being pushed into the gray upholstery with every stomp of his paws. But at least *he* hadn't peed on her.

Yet...

Trying not to think about how much she smelled, not having had the chance to change after work, she held up her hand in the universal command for "stop." She locked eyes with the massive mangled mess she suspected was part, if not entirely, wolf and told him to stay.

He barked louder, pawed harder, but Emma held firm.

She wanted to be in and out in five minutes before the storm hit, not getting drenched as she chased after a semi-wild animal determined to mark every fence post as his and his alone.

"Stay...um...Max? No, Rex. No... Oh, I'll figure out a name for you later. Just stay. Okay? Stay." She waited until he finally admitted defeat by plopping his butt down. Satisfied he wasn't going to whine the whole time, Emma made her way to the front door of the house.

She left it open behind her in case the dog *–Wolf? Horse? Bear?–* had separation anxiety. Heading through the open-floor kitchen, she made her way to the master bedroom. A large bed with red satin sheets dominated the area, rubbing it in Emma's face that she was still a virgin. You'd think if her sister could get laid, then she could too given they were freaking identical twins.

But nope.

The furthest Emma had gotten was to second base. And that was when a customer had reached past her to grab the salt.

Sticking her tongue out at the bed, Emma scooted around it to get to the walk-in closet.

"Oh, hey," she said in a mimic of her sister's voice. "You know how you've been working fifty-hour weeks to go back to college? Yeah, well, I have a better idea on how to use your savings."

Rolling her eyes, she shoved the dozens of dresses and crop-tops aside.

"You just need to book a *very expensive* last minute flight to England so you can courier a box for me. That'll set you up for life."

She dragged boxes of shoes around. Picked up glittery bags and shook them upside down. "And no, you can't just mail it. It's *important* you come with because I need it *in two days*."

Stepping back, Emma placed her hands on her hips and

glared at the now messy closet. *Where the fuck is this thing?*

Her flight left in six hours and she still needed to go home and pack. Not to mention, shower and change. And drop off the dog at a shelter. Closing her eyes, Emma had half a mind to leave the box behind. Granted, it was the whole reason she was going to England in the first place, but screw it. She'd already bought the tickets and she could use the vacation. Except...

She was a freaking sucker when it came to telling her sister no.

Ever since their mom had died, Emma had struggled to deny her sister anything. It didn't matter that she was only older by a mere twenty minutes; she was the eldest and had mentally promised not to shirk her sisterly duties to a dead mom and an unknown father.

She just wished that said "duties" didn't involve her catching an expensive last-minute flight to Manchester, England, in order to deliver a mysterious box and its extremely important contents.

Contents, Emma realized as she finally located it at the very back of the closet, that she knew absolutely nothing about.

Her sister could be asking her to transport drugs or blackmail secrets or other illegal items. Liz liked to party into all hours of the night and sometimes, even into the morning. Not to mention, she occasionally kept company with a few extremely suspicious characters, like weed dealer Eric and whose-car-is-that Reese. So really, who knew what criminal belongings could be lurking inside this box?

Biting her lip, Emma raised her fingers over the lid. On one hand, she'd be invading her sister's privacy; on the other hand, she *could* be unknowingly ferrying something illegal...

She had just grazed the underside of the lid when a crack of thunder destroyed the silence. As the dog went off like a bloody fire alarm, she rolled her eyes and headed for the door, wishing she'd grabbed a coat this morning.

She stopped in the hall with the thought of grabbing one of her sister's, only to immediately continue. The car wasn't far and she couldn't be bothered going back.

Instant regret. She stared at the open door dryly; it was raining like a bloody monsoon. Letting out a heavy exhale, she hunched up her shoulders before stepping out. It didn't help.

Turning to lock the door, she hollered over her shoulder, "Quiet...dog! It's just a bit of – mmmmfh!"

The hard grasp of a hand smothered her yelp. A masculine arm locked around her waist and jerked her backward, dragging her across the wet ground. She tried to move, to throw an elbow or dig her heels in, but her body was frozen. Panicked. *Weak.*

I don't want to die!

"Hurry!" His voice quivered.

Emma's eyes widened. Why would *he* be afraid?

Maybe he wasn't as strong as he felt.

Maybe he knew someone was close enough to help her.

Desperately, she rammed her head back. Felt his nose crack beneath the pressure. Howling, he relaxed his grip, but it wasn't enough to free her.

Biting down hard on his hand, Emma stomped on his foot, then twisted free. A tornado of expletives exploded behind her. Stumbling forward, she spat out the blood in her mouth. Heart in her throat, she ran.

When a rough hand locked around her wrist, she kicked out at her attacker blindly. Her heel slammed into the unprotected cushion of his balls. Ripping her arm free, she scrambled toward her car. The dog tore up the backseat, scratching and barking and growling.

As she slammed into the gray sedan, grasping for the handle, she prayed that he wouldn't bolt. Fear for her own safety wouldn't allow her to wait for him for long.

"Stay," she pleaded as she wrenched the door open and chucked her sister's box inside.

But before she could climb in, he dashed into the front seat and leaped for freedom. She barely managed to dodge his bulking frame. Just as she was about to yell at him to get back in, a terrifying scream claimed the silence.

A knot formed in Emma's throat as she spun around. Horror twisted her stomach. There was so much blood. As the dog ripped the man's hand to pieces, a tube of plastic flew free and landed in the puddle at her feet.

Heart hammering, time freezing, she looked down.

A syringe glistened in the water.

What? Why!

But then the entire situation came crashing down on her in mind-warping clarity. They weren't here for her. Well, they were, but not really. They were after her mom. Her mafia-upsetting mom who had struck a deal with the FBI when she was pregnant. She'd turned in some head honcho in exchange for witness protection.

Protection that clearly wasn't very good.

Screaming out in feral frustration, Emma kicked her attacker hard in the stomach. "She's dead, you moron!" She kicked him again just because she could.

Dammit! This was *not* how she had planned her day to go when she'd forced herself out of bed this morning! First, she'd woken to find her sister had left an urgent voicemail the night before, requesting her to use up *all* of her savings. Then, when Emma had requested emergency time off work, she had been fired on the grounds of not giving them enough notice – *after* having just worked a double shift! And after having been peed on by a 'therapy dog!'

And now – *now!* – she was being attacked by a group of men all because of something her dead mom had done long before she was even born!

Screaming, she punctuated her frustration with another kick.

The man cursed, but whether it was over her or the dog, she didn't know. Probably the latter though given the half-wolf was now lunging for the man's neck.

She raised her leg to strike again. But just as she started to swing, a sudden movement off to the side had her stumbling forward. Grabbing the dog by the scruff of his neck, Emma hauled him back.

She screamed at the sound of gunfire, then again when she noticed the blood pouring out of the man's head and mixing with the rain. His blank eyes stared up at her in accusation as she vomited onto his legs.

A sharp bark sounded behind her. Turning toward her car, she saw the dog –*Tank? Bulldozer?*– waiting inside expectantly. On shaky legs, she climbed in. With even shakier hands, she somehow managed to throw the car into drive.

A bullet slammed into the trunk. As the tires screeched beneath them, her hand automatically groped for the safety of her seatbelt.

Frantically glancing in her rear-view mirror, she saw the three men still alive running toward a black SUV as another car screamed around the corner. Bile threatened her mouth once more at the confirmation that they had indeed been waiting for her. With a hard swallow, she managed to keep it down. Barely.

Emma had known this day might come eventually. She

had even been trained for it ever since she was a child. But having lived for twenty-two years without so much as a peep from the mafia, she'd never believed that they would actually find her.

Otherwise, she sure as hell wouldn't have slacked off on attending her self-defense classes. The only training she had kept up with was her breathing exercises. And given her current hyperventilation and scattered mind, she should probably ask for her money back.

But how had they found her? She had habitually kept her head down and her roots adrift even though her mom wasn't around to force her to constantly be on the move. Was Elizabeth in the same danger? Did the mafia here have ties to the family in Italy? Was that the truth behind her sister's unreasonable request? She'd said, "I love you," and Liz never –

A sharp bark broke into her thoughts, causing her to jump. She jerked her eyes away from the mirror. A mounting horror filled her chest. A young dark-haired man stood in the middle of the road, looking straight at her.

As she slammed on the brakes, Emma screamed and jerked the wheel. The car spun uncontrollably. The dog barked wildly. A flash of river passed her window, her windshield, the passenger's side...

And then she was plunging over the edge of the bridge.

Screaming.

Her hands gripping the wheel.

Her heart dying.

Her mind racing.

For fuck's sake, why did I never learn how to swim?

TWO

As the car flew off the bridge, Rogan moved his hands through the air, controlling the water surrounding his target. He tightened his hands into fists, solidifying the rain around the door handles into ice.

His power flowed through him, reaching out to touch every drop of water. His lips tightened. The gods had actually answered his prayer for rain.

Fifty-seven years, Rogan had been an agent of the Elv've'Norc, hunting the worst of the worst in order to protect the Seven Planes, and not once had the gods ever answered his prayers. The fact that they did now, when he was after a descendant, a forbidden child of theirs...

Fuck. He hoped that didn't mean they were planning on getting involved. The last thing he needed was childish idiots with massive fucking egos getting in the way of his job. His team was already one member down, their communication expert having not answered the call this morning, and Rogan did not have the patience to deal with any more shit.

Shit like the two SUVs trailing after his target.

Eyes narrowing, Rogan swept his arms through the air. The flow of the river heeded his command, swallowing the car and anchoring it exactly where he wanted it. He rolled onto the balls of his feet. His hands flicked out. The ice he'd coated the road with a second ago melted back into rain.

Stepping back from the edge of the bridge, he increased the mist around him, blocking himself from their view. When he caught sight of one of the drivers, a bitter smile pulled at his lips.

The tattoo on the man's neck, a flaming sword in front of angel wings, marked him as a member of the Warriors Against Lycans and Lessers. They were a brutal group that had started off raping and killing their own kind before "advancing" to become the "protectors of Earth" by killing the werewolves, witches, and vampires too stupid to hide their presence here.

Rogan's fingers twitched. His smile widened. Their deaths wouldn't count as casualties.

As they braked hard in front of him, right beside the broken railing, Rogan reached for the water bouncing off the road. The feel of it seeped into his body, merging with his power and connecting them as one.

Nine men, all heavily armed and dressed in black, piled out of the cars. Rogan's gaze instantly locked onto his target – a dark-haired man with three triangular dots under his left eye, the sign of a leader of the WALL.

"Light her up!" Three Dots shouted, lifting his assault rifle.

With two deft movements of his left hand, Rogan raised the water from the road and wrapped it around the men's weapons, holding them still. Lifting his right arm lifted, he rotated his hand in a circle. The rain around

Three Dot's head formed into a sphere. Closing his fist, he turned the outside of the ball into ice, leaving the man to drown.

Before the others could do more than scream, Rogan launched a tidal wave up over the railing. One of the men twisted his gun free from the wall of water and fired off a wild shot. Ignoring the ping by his feet, Rogan dashed forward with two knives of ice in his hands.

Dropping to his knees, he slid across the road as the wave crashed into his opponents. He sliced through their calves as they fell backward, but their screams were drowned out by the sudden water filling their mouths. Their bodies hit the road and were instantly swept into the river.

Spinning to his feet, he tossed a blade into one of the men's stomach. The assault rifle that had just been aimed at him clattered to the ground. Snapping his leg out, he kicked the last man in the chest, sending him over the railing. The water claimed yet another soul.

If such men even had souls.

The things he had seen WALL members do. They vivisected vampires to see how fast they could heal. They forced werewolves into changing so they could bet on which one would win in a fight. They raped the young witches, not caring that a twenty year old was still seen as a child across the other six planes. They called themselves protectors, but all they were were hateful imbeciles.

"Please, have mercy!" someone shouted from below. Peering over the edge, Rogan saw a man struggling to hold on to the railing. The river flowed violently beneath him. Merciless.

Ignoring him, Rogan pushed his power out into the suburbs, searching for the water signatures of his team. Nothing.

He frowned. They should've been here by now. Their target was here. This had been their agreed upon grab point.

His gaze turned to the water, his seventh sense to the car held at the bottom of the river. Rakian, the last descendant to have walked the Seven Planes, had taken on armies on his own. He had single-handedly wiped out entire cities. Destroyed monarchies that had ruled for centuries. Had nearly wiped out Rogan's race completely, along with the fey. And yet, this descendant hadn't even left its car? He could still feel it there, sitting. Waiting.

"Please, help me!"

A feeling of unease twisted Rogan's stomach. If the descendant's partner Sebastian the Ancient Destroyer was here –

"I can't hold on anymore!"

Rogan's head snapped up in the direction of the suburbs. His feet itched to take a step forward, to help his team. Xeno, his second-in-command, was nearly fallen, her angelic power a weak flame of what it used to be. Hunter was an excellent marksman, but a gun wouldn't stop Sebastian. And Jack was barely a hundred years old; his power, as strong as it was, was nothing in comparison to a nearly five thousand year old vampire.

And without Galvanor, their missing telepath, there to give them the power to communicate as one, to fight as one, Rogan's team would get slaughtered.

His fists tightened.

The urge to step forward consumed him.

But if he didn't complete this mission, if he didn't grab the descendant and force it to tell him where the *Scrolls of Atlantis* was, his team would just be a small number in a sea of deaths.

And Xeno would never let him live that down.

Facing the river, Rogan dived in.

As soon as his hands cut through the surface, he shot a jet of water up behind him. It wrapped around the WALL member's legs, pulling him into the river. His scream vibrated through the water, only to be quickly silenced forever.

Mercy, Rogan knew, would have only led to more deaths.

Emma jumped with a small scream. A dark-haired body floated outside her car window. Her now *underwater* car window. *Oh God, did I hit him?*

She wanted to shout at the dumb fucktard for having stood in the middle of the road. She wanted to tell herself, and oddly, her new dog, that she wasn't at fault. But then the man reached a hand toward her and she just wished she'd hit him harder.

He's coming to finish the job!

Desperately, she yanked at her stuck seatbelt. Her fingers clawed at the fabric strap, then the buckle. But as before, neither would budge beneath her frantic pulls.

She glanced over at –*Mastermind? Chewie?*– as he continued to gnaw through her shoulder strap. He was half-way through it now, but Emma feared it wouldn't matter. Water had been pouring in nonstop from all the little holes everywhere and it was just about up to her waist. Even a clever dog like hers wouldn't be able to breathe underwater, meaning death was imminent.

And although the thought of dying in her dying car had made her laugh hysterically before, all it did now was make her cry.

"Oh, to hell with it! Let the mafia man outside come in and kill me or open my door and drown me faster! What does it matter anymore? Dead is dead is dead! Oh, I'm so sorry, Sam!" she wailed as she twisted in her seat to hug her wolf of a dog. "I should have let someone else save you, but now you're just gonna d-d-die with me! I-i-it's not f-fair and I'm s-so s-s-sor– *Ow!*"

The sudden sharp sting of canines froze her into silence.

She stared with wide eyes at the ungrateful mutt. "I rescued you!" she sputtered.

He grinned.

Grinned!

She was sure of it. His tongue lolled out from between his teeth and everything.

She opened her mouth, then closed it again, certain she was going mad. There was no way he could understand her. But his eyes shined a bit too bright and her stomach fluttered with uncertainty.

She opened her mouth to dumbly ask, but all that came out was a hoarse cry as the window behind her shattered.

She swung around to face the onslaught of water with the impossible idea of keeping it out of the car. But as she raised her hands, she was confronted with the gorgeous face of an angel, and all she could do was blink.

His electric-blue eyes seemed bright even in the darkness of the river. She fell into the sheer intensity of his gaze, her mind going straight into the gutter and rolling around in all the muck.

A wave of thick black hair wandered down to the base of his neck, framing his blue eyes to make them seem near luminescent. A five o'clock shadow textured his strong square jaw, and his olive skin beckoned to a part of her that had never been touched before.

For fate to let her meet a man like this and then have her die...surely even it wouldn't be that cruel?

So when he reached for her through the shattered window, she didn't fight him as she had her other attackers. Instead, she merely closed her eyes with a throaty moan, having finally come to the only conclusion that made sense.

Water wasn't filling up her car through the broken window.

The dog seemed to actually understand what she was saying.

Clearly, she was dreaming. They always felt so real until she awoke. Heavens only knew how many times she had experienced the unbearable pain of gnawed off limbs and the practices of sadistic serial killers before. Or the amount of times she'd smelled and tasted the delicious foods that would render her poisoned in one fashion or another. Why she couldn't have normal dreams without all the bloody awareness was beyond her, but that was just the hand she'd been dealt. *So to hell with it all*, she thought with a last bit of rage.

She was going to enjoy this dream. It was her nightmare, and if she wanted it to turn into a wet dream with her mafia hitman as the star, then it bloody well would.

Or not.

As his arm breezed across her breasts, his hand aiming for somewhere else entirely, Emma groaned. She opened her eyes to see where it had landed, only to immediately wish she'd kept them closed. Wanting to die now, she watched with sickening horror as he pressed the button on her seatbelt that she had completely forgotten about in her panic.

The dog made a noise that sounded oddly like laughter. But before Emma could shoot him an evil look, she was wrenched backward for the second time today.

This time, though, she didn't slam her head back in defiance. She was too busy – first, inhaling a sudden gasp of air so she could survive the long swim to the surface; second, with frantically twisting her legs out from under the steering wheel in time to the hitman's pull; and third, clinging like a madman to the only person capable of reaching the blissful air that her lungs already craved.

So what if he was most likely going to finish the job of either killing her or kidnapping her to be killed later? Right now, she needed him because unfortunately, she had come to the harsh conclusion that she wasn't dreaming at all.

Fucking.

Dammit.

THREE

The effort Rogan needed to pull his package to the surface was of no little feat. He had quickly realized that she – it couldn't swim, but every time he tried to arrange for a more comfortable carry, she – *it,* dammit – fought frantically to cling to him in the most inconvenient of ways.

Ways that were making it extremely hard for him to keep thinking of her as an it. A package. A threat that would not be able to sway him from his mission.

Her legs were wrapped around his waist. The softness of her inner thighs were pressed hard against his hips, sliding with every stroke of his arms, with every kick of his legs. Her small, palm-cup-sized breasts were pressed against his chest, the wet fabric of her shirt doing a very bad job of acting as a barrier. But it was her lips that were killing him. They trailed across his neck, rubbing back and forth as she shook her head in fear.

But even though he knew this was most definitely a ploy, that she was using some sort of power to control him, to make him react and bring down his guard, it didn't stop his cock from twitching over every graze of her lips. Didn't stop it from swelling every time she rocked a bit too close to it.

Gritting his teeth, he focused on making it to the surface. He stopped just below it, pushing his powers out to feel the touch of rain on anyone standing nearby. The storm had already quieted to a light drizzle, but he only needed a drop to tell him if anyone was there.

Satisfied there wasn't going to be any witnesses, Rogan swam up the rest of the way. He allowed his target to suck in a few ragged breaths before clamping a hand over her mouth. Ignoring the trembling of her lips against his overly sensitive palm, he headed for the shore.

But her fearful tremors were doing odd forgotten things to his gut. Things that he had buried decades ago in order to do what needed to be done.

He was an Elv've'Nor, he reminded himself.

He did not have room for sympathy or mercy.

"Bloody hell, stop shaking," he ground out as soon as they reached land. Unsurprisingly, the trembling didn't stop. "Are ye cold? Is that it?"

Not waiting for an answer, he drew the water off her, leaving only a well-padded ball around her right hand. Though it took more effort to contain as a liquid, an ice cage would be too easy for her to smash. She had the power of two gods running through her veins, and one of her neat little tricks was to kill with a single touch of her right hand.

As her eyes flicked to the ball of water, Rogan readied himself for a fight. Instinctively, he pulled on the power of the river behind them.

Her eyes widened, then immediately rolled back into her skull. When she fell completely limp, he was left in a state of sheer disbelief.

"Do ye take me for a fool?" he asked.

He wasn't surprised when she did not answer. Only an idiot would give up pretense after a single question. Although, she *had* forgotten to press the button on her seatbelt... Then again, those not used to adrenaline often made moronic mistakes before they grew into seasoned veterans like himself.

But...wasn't she supposed to be hardened? Cold? The target they'd been briefed on had been deadly. She'd massacred dozens of people, many of whom had been trained since birth to fight. She'd nearly taken out an entire Elv've'Norc team on her own. She should've been able to take on the WALL squad, as well as him, with one hand tied behind her back.

And yet, the woman in his arms, the supposedly same woman, was acting like a green recruit. Nay, like a complete civilian.

And Sebastian did not recruit civilians.

He forced them to go through rigorous torture sessions before even considering them as bottom-tier members. They had lost many agents over the years trying to infiltrate the group, and yet, this woman, his supposed package, was supposed to be the vampire's right-hand man?

For the first time in a long time, Rogan felt the tendrils of unease winding deep inside his stomach.

Something isn't right.

He shook his head, hardening himself against his doubts. She was an exact match to their target. He could read her water signature; he knew she wasn't human. He needed to 'wake her up' and interrogate her, needed to know if Sebastian was in the vicinity.

Not get tricked by whatever magic she was using.

And yet, despite knowing what would make most captives – male, female, or sexless – stop the pretense of being unconscious, he found himself hesitating. His pulse quickened ever so slightly, but it was enough to throw him off balance. Scowling at his lack of control, Rogan forced the cold feeling of indifference back into his body. Swiftly, he placed his lips on hers.

It was such an impersonal kiss, one that he had performed thousands of times to rouse faking captives – whether it was with shock, distaste, or even pleasure. The movements of his lips and tongue were all calculated with the sole purpose of pulling a sudden unwanted reaction from his target. Not from him.

So why was his heart pounding so hard in his chest? Why was his breath coming in short erotic gasps? Why was he disheartened when her tongue stayed still beneath his but not for any reason that concerned the mission? He wanted her simply as a man and nothing more and that primal thought was enough to jolt him back into aloof professionalism.

He severed the intimate contact between them. Then berated himself for thinking it was intimate at all. She could kill with a single touch and bring back the dead. She was a weapon of Sebastian's. A danger to the Seven Planes. As a child of a god of death and some other deity, she had more power than he'd ever come across. He had to remember that whatever he felt for her, whatever she was making him feel, was nothing but lies.

A falsity to make him lower his guard.

Shifting her in his arms, Rogan put a bit more space between them. He'd just dug a hand into the pocket of his jacket with the intention of calling his team when a low growl erupted behind him.

Adrenaline spiking, he spun around to face the new

threat. He felt slightly guilty using her as a shield against her own pet, but the thing was more wolf than dog. And probably of a dire wolf line rather than anything from Earth.

It easily stood up to Rogan's waist, which was no easy feat given his 6'5" frame. With the dog's sharp white teeth fully bared and its solid black coat stretching over nothing but packed muscle, Rogan wasn't taking any chances. He might be able to control water in all its states, but many an elementalist had fallen to the jaws of a dire wolf.

Forcing himself to stay completely still, he awaited the wolf's assessment. Any movement that could be taken as a threat would end with blood, and he wondered why he hadn't just drowned the thing when he'd had the chance.

A threatening growl had him demolishing the thought immediately. A feeling of dread took its place. His heart rate increased.

"So yer a god's companion, aye?" he asked warily. "Or was it mere coincidence yer growl and not a reading of my mind?"

The wolf yawned as if it didn't even consider him worthy of an answer.

Rogan's uneasiness grew exponentially. If the animal truly was a god's companion, then it had most likely been sent down by one of the woman's parents. And although he didn't want to kill her, he couldn't exactly claim he had her best interests at heart. He was trying to see her forever imprisoned inside Damaculus, a place where only the most high-profile and dangerous of criminals were kept. Given the link that all godly companions had to their masters, the wolf would know which side he was on and thus, what his mission entailed.

Rogan touched the river with his magic ever so slightly, careful to keep his face expressionless.

He wasn't surprised when he was warned again with a growl. His disconnection to the water, though, caused him to shiver. He felt as if he'd lost a piece of himself. Of his soul.

Unable to stop himself, Rogan flicked a glance at the river. It was a soulless black rather than a murky brown.

"*Fuck*."

The beast smiled at him. A full toothy smile that did nothing to set him at ease.

When the water turned back to its rightful color, his connection to it returned. The monster trotted past him – not a dog, not even a dire wolf, but a full-on monster.

Cerberus.

Guard of the Underworld.

And messenger to Hades, the Graeca God of the Dead.

As a heavy dread filled his stomach, Rogan shifted the woman into a more comfortable carry. His toes dug into the dirt, scratching a quick code into the ground before he dutifully climbed up the bank.

He didn't know if his teammates were alive, didn't know if Sebastian had managed to make a deal with a god, but he did know one thing.

A war was coming, and this time, the gods and goddesses were playing.

FOUR

"Padraig!"

Smoke filled my lungs as soon as I inhaled. Coughing and wheezing, I struggled to take a breath deep enough to scream. Flames licked the walls around me, searing my throat and eyes. I covered my mouth with a hand as if that could keep out the smoke as well as keep down my fear. I was choking on two fronts, assaulted on all sides.

I just needed my baby.

Stumbling down the hall, I rushed toward his room. "Padraig, pumpkin, we have...to go!"

He was always up at this time. He would bounce onto my bed, begging me to wake up. His small hands would cup my face and he'd lean in until his nose touched mine. I didn't think about why he hadn't done so this morning. Refused to give such thoughts a voice.

Agony pierced my heart, affecting me more than any flame. Falling to my knees, I struggled to carry on.

It's just a dream, Emma told herself, fighting to wake up. She could feel the rocking of a car through the solidity of the nightmare. Could sense that giant of a man somewhere close by.

Her heart rate spiked.

Her breaths turned shallow.

Furrowing her brows, she struggled to find her way free.

"Padraig..." I reached out a hand, dug my burning nubs into the floor, and pulled myself forward. My stomach dragged across the charred ground. My vision narrowed. My lungs burned so sharply I could barely breathe.

But just as I started to lose all hope, just as I started to get consumed by what I would find by the time I reached his room, a strong hand wrapped around my ankle. Relief flooded through me. Sobbing, I tried to turn around to my savior, tried to tell him about Padraig.

But his words stopped me cold.

"Don't worry, Ciara. I'm here."

Tears ran down my face. No!

We'd divorced.

I'd changed the locks.

Had taken out a restraining order.

He shouldn't be here. He shouldn't be here. My stomach twisted. Why was he here?

There was a bed beneath her now. Emma tried to hold on to that feeling, to use it to pull herself free, but his hand caressed her ankle, then skimmed up her calf.

"I told you we'd be together until we died, luv. All three of us..."

Twisting away from him, I tried to dig my hands into the floorboards. Tried to claw myself away to safety. "Padraig!" I screamed, only to cough and gag and sob.

His hand slid up my thigh. "Don't worry, luv. I already got him."

No!

Snapping awake, Emma tossed her head side to side, struggling to breathe. She could feel her lungs still burning. Her utter despair as she realized her child –

No. Not my child, she told herself. *It wasn't real. None of it was real.*

She squeezed her eyes shut, only to immediately open them again, not wanting to see the flames. Not wanting to smell her burning flesh nor hear the crackling laughter of her husband. *Ex-husband.*

Not my husband...

Focusing on the ceiling above her, she searched for the crack in the corner, a glimpse of familiarity. Something to ground her to the present.

When she didn't find it, her entire body froze. Even her breath held still as she finally realized that this was not her bedroom. It wasn't anywhere in her house. She jerked upright – or at least, had tried to, but a sharp pain erupted across her shoulders. Her hands were tied above her head.

Heart hammering, she tried not to panic. Tried to figure out what was happening. The last thing she remembered, she was being rescued from the river and then –

The ball of water!

Jesus Christ, what is he?

Lifting her head, she looked around the room. It didn't take her long to find him. Sitting in the only chair, he stared at her as if he could peer into her soul. His icy blue eyes looked a bit too bright now. Otherwordly. Devilish, even.

Thrashing against her binds, she kicked her legs and arched her back. "Help!" she screamed as she banged her feet against the bed. "Somebody help!"

With every passing second of silence, Emma thrashed harder. Banged louder. She twisted and jerked and kicked and screamed until her throat grew hoarse. And still no one came.

Wriggling on the bed, she moved it back and forth, smacking the headboard against the wall.

Thud.

Thud.

Thud.

Thud.

But it was drowned out by the answering silence.

"Enough."

Trembling, Emma slowly stilled. Her chest heaving, she struggled to remember the breathing techniques she'd been taught. She didn't want to faint again. She didn't want to wake up somewhere new. Live through another nightmare that fucked with her reality.

And hyperventilating always made them worse. Made her dreams come on stronger until she passed out, leaving her defenseless.

She squeezed her eyes shut, needing to find her calm. Tears blistered her cheeks.

Not blistered, she whined. *The fire isn't real. It isn't real.*

Sobs wracked her. She drew in a ragged breath. Her chest tightened. Her lungs burned. Letting the air out in a rush, she dug her nails into her palms.

I am calm. I am in control.

"Oh, Hades' fire."

Standing, the man walked toward her. Her eyes latched onto him automatically in her need to concentrate on something – *anything* real to keep her grounded.

And he just so happened to be here. That was all.

But as he started to close the distance between them, she became intimately aware that her clothes had shifted in her struggle. A button had popped loose between her breasts. His eyes flicked down her body, lingering for half a beat before rising again. Desire pooled between her legs even as she trembled in fear.

This was insane. Her feelings were insane.

And confusing.

And delicious.

And *insane.*

She closed her eyes, hoping that if she couldn't see him, she could think past this sudden primal lust. Then she could concentrate on what was really happening. Could try to figure out how the hell he'd managed to pull off the magic trick at the river.

"Open yer eyes, lass, and look at me." His deep tone sent shivers down her spine. There wasn't any bite to his words, just a thick accent – Scottish maybe? – that caused her to want things only a fool would want. "I promise I doona wish ye any harm, love. So open yer eyes and look at me. Please."

She didn't want to believe him. Her mother would call her a fool for daring to even hope he might keep his word. He'd kidnapped her. Was most likely part of the mafia. A hitman or something. *Who could control water.*

She shook her head.

This was insane.

And that was coming from *her*. A girl who'd grown up on the run. A girl who fainted into nightmares where she could feel every bloody sensation.

And yet...a part of her trusted him. Really trusted him.

God, I need therapy.

Taking a deep breath, she opened first one eye and then the other and was instantly sucked into the most beautiful, most gentle gaze she had ever seen. For a moment, the world stopped. All that existed was his eyes. His promise to keep her safe. A promise she trusted.

But then he blinked, and when his lashes lifted, a cold sea had replaced the summer lake of his gaze.

Fearful once more, she swallowed.

His lips tight, he took a step back, giving her the space she hadn't even known she needed. She sucked in a sharp breath, trying to sort through all her thoughts. All her emotions. But before she could even begin to untangle that mess, he started to talk.

"We know ye are helping Sebastian."

Who?

"And why ye attacked Xi'aghn."

What? Or is that another who?

"We know yer real purpose there had nothing to do with the armory – that was a mere added bonus."

Wait, armory? What armory?

"Nay, ye stole Artifact ZX796 – a weapon of mass destruction that only a handful of people even know about. I need to know how Sebastian discovered it, what his plans for it are, and where we can find every member of his ragtag team."

She blinked rapidly, trying to make sense of what he'd said. An armory? Like at a military base? Or a nutjob's house?

A bubble of laughter formed in her throat. She was a waitress, an ex-waitress, at Oriental Dragon for crying out loud! The most illegal thing she'd ever done was not charge a returning customer for fountain drinks. She made sure all of her bills were paid on time. She volunteered at the animal shelter twice a week and tutored underprivileged kids in three different subjects.

Yet, he was telling her that she had been shot at, almost drowned, and kidnapped all because some idiots had mistaken her for a crazy lunatic bent on setting off a WMD! Had this not been her own life falling apart, she would've died in a fit of laughter over the insanity of it all.

Instead, she just shook her head. "You – you can't be – You don't actually – This isn't serious?"

If she thought ice couldn't get any colder, she was wrong. His gaze hardened considerably until she thought even the fires of Hell wouldn't be able to warm it.

"Oh, I'm serious, lass. Ye will tell me all I desire."

The unspoken 'or else' hung in the air with such honest ferocity that Emma wished he had just gone out and said it. Then he would sound so cliché and she could dismiss the phrase as wannabe tough talk instead of a real threat with real repercussions that made her stomach clench and her lungs stop in a world of overwhelming fear.

"I – um – I –" Her attempts to explain only made sense in the internal workings of her mind. Knowing the man towering over her was truly dangerous, though, she fought to express herself clearly.

"I –"

For fuck's sake. Why does my stammer always come back at the worst bloody times?

"I –" Her eyes misted with frustration. She could do this; she just needed to breathe.

On her next attempt, her lungs collapsed and any chance of being coherent died right along with them. Then again, as she stared into the hard, unmoving gaze of her abductor, she doubted anything she'd said would've been believed anyway.

"I've no time for patience, lass."

A jolt of fear arched through her. His eyes were without mercy, telling her without a doubt that he'd killed before. Her spell of silence was broken by a strangled sob. She was going to be tortured for information she could never give all because of a stupid case of mistaken identity. Why couldn't she have just left her credit card somewhere and suffered from afar?

She wondered how he was going to kill her. With a knife? A garrote? His bare hands? He had large hands. He could just kneel over top of her, his thighs crushing her chest, lean down, and strangle her.

Gasping for breath, Emma couldn't fight the images of her last moments. Of her tongue lolling out, her eyes bulging. It wouldn't be pretty. She was an ugly, horrible crier. And this god of a man would be the only witness.

And for some reason, the idea of *that* just made her cry harder.

At the feel of a sudden pressure on the bed, most likely his knees, she struggled to dry her tears. She wanted to see what was happening so she could make an attempt – however pathetic – to stop it. Or maybe she just wanted to die with a bit of dignity.

As she wiped what snot and tears she could off on her bicep, a furry head nudged her side, filling her with a wave of relief. Her puffy eyes locked with the dog's gentle ones, and she found her breath eventually dropping into a normal rhythm. After a few calming exhales, she turned her attention back to her capturer and swallowed.

She winced at the raw soreness of her throat, but she quickly lifted her chin. She didn't want to be one of those fairy tale damsels in distress who sat around waiting to be saved by a knight she'd never met. She wanted to be strong. She wanted to explain his mistake. And then she wanted to leave.

"You've –" She hesitated as she worked out the best way to handle this. The fear of him being one of those men who turned violent when they were told they were wrong stopped her from blurting out how stupid he was being. What if he killed her out of spite? "I mean, I – I think there's been some sort of mistake? Did you see me at...um...Zi Uhn...yourself?"

"Nay, but we have photographic evidence of your presence there."

His words were void of all feeling, but his anger over being questioned was unmistakable. This was a man who took clear pride in his work; she needed to tread carefully if she was to convince him to let her go instead of, say, killing her to hide his mistake.

God, she really hated her overly active imagination. Surely, he wouldn't kill her for that. Would he?

Not wanting to dwell on it unbiased, she cleared her throat and tried again.

"May I see this evidence? Do you have it here?"

"It is pointless, lass. It is ye in the photos; even a blind man could see the resemblance."

"Please." She tried to keep the returning terror of hopelessness from breaking up the word, but she wasn't sure if she'd succeeded. "I'll tell you everything if you j–just let me see them."

A flash of wary confusion cut through the double glaciers of his eyes, but it was gone quicker than she could understand it.

"Very well. I will show ye, but then the games end, aye."

Captivated by his slow approach back to her bedside, Emma could only nod.

He seemed to stalk toward her like a big-game hunter who knew the rules of the game could change at any second. It was such a ridiculous level of caution that she almost laughed before remembering he thought her to be extremely dangerous. Though to what extent, she didn't know. Could this woman he was after escape from such a helpless situation as hers? Fight a man of his strength and ferocity and actually come out the winner? It didn't seem feasible.

But as his hands reached for her head, she had a fleeting wish that she was such a talented woman. Flinching in fear, she closed her eyes.

His hands were on her then, cradling her head as his thumbs rested over both of her temples. She was about to tell him to get off her when a blinding series of images ripped through her brain.

Bodies, men and women both unarmed, laid on a cold concrete floor. Their eyes stared up at her with an overwhelming blankness. Blood splattered the walls around them, having been flung from their victims, who had been cut down like wheat at harvest time.

A woman crouched in the distance with long dark hair and auburn eyes, who looked as different as she did familiar. No longer were her features smiling with youth and bold innocence. Now they were drawn grim with cold determination in destroying everything around her. No longer was her skin flawless and her body sculptured by curves. Ugly bruises marred every other inch of exposed flesh, and her once radiant skin hung from nothing but a bag of bones. But even with all of the heart-breaking changes, Emma recognized her instantly.

The image was so real, she instinctively opened her mouth to call out in aid. But it was a gasp that escaped, Elizabeth's name smothered by the horror of yet more wretched images.

Her sister was now standing in a hallway, her hands lifted in the air with an unspoken order of command. A feeling of horror settled deep in Emma's stomach at the realization of what was happening. *Is she raising... Are those fucking zombies?*

The image morphed again. Her twin stood over a fallen warrior, his accusing eyes proving her guilty beyond a doubt. Eyes that Emma had never seen but could decipher all the same.

Elizabeth ran down a narrow pathway, her hand hugging her right side, blood seeping through her fingers. An unseen man chased her, and then Emma's brain was awash with confusion and anger at the sight of a solid dead-end that shouldn't be there.

"There's yer proof, lass. Now tell me the answers I wish to know."

The deep Scottish voice acted like an anchor, pulling Emma free of the chaos flooding her mind. She took shaky breaths as she fought for composure, but they did little to quell her internal screams of frustration and denial.

There was a reason for all this, a drug she had been given to make her see all of those horrid lies. But even as she ordered herself to believe it, she somehow knew it wasn't true. The images had been too real – as if they had been taken from someone else's memories with all five senses and emotions attached.

That had been her sister, her little, lovable sister, responsible for all of those deaths.

No, there's another explanation for this.

Liz would never do something as heartless as what this man claimed. She had a temper, sure, but who wouldn't when they had a childhood like theirs? Her twin was not a murderer, and she most definitely wasn't in possession of a deadly weapon with the intent of actually using it.

It was crazy to even think that! She was in Europe for goodness sake! Enjoying beaches and the sun and the Colosseum and guys and baguettes and castles and all that other cliché tourist stuff.

But even as she reminded herself of all this, Emma had an undeniable sense of fear for her sister's safety. She was supposed to look out for her; she had promised, and Emma Sterling never gave her word lightly.

"Okay," she said, fighting back her tears. "I'll tell you everything you want to know."

FIVE

Rogan knew his mask of indifference had broken in the way of genuine surprise, but he was too shocked to control it. He had expected days of interrogation before she gave him anything. Sebastian demanded loyalty above all else, often to the point of suicide. If the bottom rung of his soldiers would choose death over his wrath, then why was it that his right-hand man – or woman, in this case – would want to give everything up without a fight?

"Where is Sebastian now?" he demanded.

"Europe."

"Aye, because that's such a wee place to search."

She grimaced. Her eyes darted up and to the right, a clear indication she was either lying or stalling. An unwanted flare of disappointment caused his lips to tighten. *So the little dragon is loyal after all.* The only question now was what was her end game?

"England. Manchester, England."

His gut tightened as she began talking with conviction.

"He's been there for a few days. I was going to head

there to meet him tomorrow morning actually, but –" She shrugged as if to say, 'Here I am instead.'

"How long is a few days?"

She sucked in a ragged breath, struggling to breathe through the snot in her nose. She looked awful. Terrified and frantic. Her eyes were red and puffy. Streak lines stained her cheeks, and the occasional tear still slipped free.

She was a damn good actress, he'd give her that.

"What?"

"How long has he been in Manchester, England?" he demanded, ignoring all the parts of himself that wanted to trust her.

"Um..." She sniffled and wiped her face on her bicep again. "Three. He's been there three days."

"Where at precisely? It's a big city and I doona wish to run around with no destination in mind."

"Um...well...uh..." It was like a solid punch to his chest when her eyes lit up in a moment of Eureka. "He moves around every few days out of paranoia, you know, so I'm not sure exactly where, but he was going to pick me up at the airport. So if we go there together..." She faltered as she looked into his cold dark eyes. Fury radiated off him.

"So is that yer plan, lass? To lure me over there so ye can reunite with yer lover while bringing him the gift of an Elv've'Nor? Tell me true, did ye really think I'd fall for something so simple?"

Her eyes widened. "L-lover? Seb and – I mean, you think Seb and I are lovers?"

His eyes narrowed. "Ye deny it then?"

Another feeling of unease snaked through his desire to paint her as guilty. Worse, it was joined by an easing in his chest that felt suspiciously like relief. He didn't like the thought of her with Sebastian, but he shouldn't have an opinion at all. She was the enemy, and whatever spell she was working on him, he was stronger than it.

"Well – I – uh – No, no of course not. Yep, lovers. Sebastian and I are definitely um, lovers. Of the most passionate variety too."

She winced as soon as the words left her mouth. Had her hands not been tied, he was certain she would've smacked herself on the forehead. Instead, she settled for digging her nails into her palms.

He was leaning half-way across her before he even realized what he was doing. The idea of her marring her delectable skin, of anything hurting her...

Disgusted with himself, he glared down at her. "Stop it," he growled. "Ye will release me this instant."

Her eyes widened. She was no doubt surprised he was able to detect the spell she was weaving over him. Rogan had been attracted to many targets over the years, had even slept with a few to sate his thirst, but he'd never come close to being swayed into actually helping them.

When his magnetic pull to her lessened, he knew he'd been right about the spell. Odd then, that that knowledge only added to his frustration.

Scowling, Rogan reached for the hem of her shirt. She yelped and jerked beneath his touch, but he quieted her protests with a glare. Trembling, she swallowed in fearful obedience. Knowing exactly where her mind had gone, he was overcome with the need to explain. "I'm not goona hurt ye, love. I merely wish to check yer wound. It looked like an ugly one in the photos, and to be honest with ye, ye have been blabbering away like an idiot that I'm almost certain it's infected."

He wasn't sure what was more troubling: his attempt at humor or the smile he was currently giving her. Had he not already discerned she was casting some sort of spell on him?

But when she returned a small, hesitant smile back, all thoughts left him. His eyes locked on to her perfect lush lips as a wave of desire overtook the functioning of his brain. With more difficulty than he cared to admit, Rogan lowered his eyes to her stomach. He paused only briefly on the soft mounds of her breasts. Pushing her shirt up to the underside of her bra, he was careful not to touch her bare flesh with his own. And yet, his pulse still quickened at the mere proximity, then increased again at the sight of black lace.

"Ye've..." He cleared his throat, forcing himself to focus. "Ye've healed completely."

Which should've been impossible. Cariad had sliced her with a skaoa blade, a weapon made out of a rare dwarfish steel. It was crafted to rebuff the healing effects of immortals until the person that had dealt the blow either relieved them of it or died. Even a descendant shouldn't be immune, but against all odds, she had recovered in only a matter of days.

"I – uh – I saw a really good doctor? Sebastian paid for it?"

A straight-up lie if ever there was one. Sebastian might be foolish in his pursuit of total domination, but he wasn't so foolish as to alert humans to their existence. Better to keep them completely ignorant right up until his moment of invasion, which Rogan suspected was coming all too soon.

So then why had she lied?

In fact, why was she still tied to the bed when she had the power to put up a damn good fight?

None of it made any sense. She could act with the best of them, crying and sobbing on demand; yet, she couldn't lie? She was eagerly answering his questions; yet, she didn't seem to actually know any of the facts? She had a god's companion by her side and the water signature of a non-human. She was definitely the descendant they were looking for...

And yet, his gut said she wasn't.

He had long honed his sixth sense, had learned to trust it completely, but he also could not deny she held power over him. She had been manipulating his emotions from the start, but despite knowing that that's what she'd been and was still doing, the urge to untie her, to believe her was almost too powerful to resist.

Digging his fingers into the hem of her shirt, Rogan struggled between his two desires. But as always, his duty to the Seven Planes won out. He would do whatever was necessary to break her. Whatever was necessary to get the information he needed about Sebastian and the *Scrolls*.

There were simply too many lives on the line for him to fail.

But just as he started to heat the water in her blood to boil her one section at a time, the god's companion lifted its massive head and growled. Silently cursing, Rogan released his hold on his powers.

If the dog wouldn't let him interrogate her, then he'd have to find some other way of getting his answers – like baiting her into attacking, letting her win, and then seeing what questions she asked him once their roles were reversed. It was a dangerous plan, but given the dog hadn't killed him on sight, that meant whatever god it was working for wanted him alive.

Hopefully.

Lowering her shirt, Rogan let his features relax into that of careless indifference. "Ye'll be taken to Elvanisia tomorrow, where ye'll be tried at the Royal Courts."

Her eyes widened as she shook her head frantically.

"Ye will then most likely be sentenced to life in Damaculus for endangerment of the Planes – or maybe they'll make an exception to their centuries old rule and execute ye."

Her face twisted into one of despair. He ignored the urge to soothe her. He resisted her devilish attempt to control him. "Either way, I'll be rid of ye tomorrow and good riddance."

"But – but you need me! Seth – Seb won't approach the airport if he doesn't see me!"

"Nay, I doona. I need a shower, aye A good night's sleep, aye. But ye? Nay. Ye, I only need to be rid of so I can go about capturing that brutal lover of yers. Maybe I'll even get the privilege of killing him m'self. It's against protocol, but –" He shrugged. "For him, I'll make an exception."

"You – you –"

Retrieving the black gag he'd left hanging over the headboard, he tied it around her mouth. The damning promise of her glare as he gave it a tightening tug had him stilling in anticipation. But when she didn't attack, he stepped back and headed into the en-suite.

Dropping his clothes onto the floor, he let her hear the sound of his belt clinking against the tiles. He then turned on the shower, and as the water spewed out a steaming mist of relaxation, he double-checked the bathroom door was unlocked.

Stepping into the shower, he prayed the god really did want him alive. Otherwise, he'd be dead within seconds.

SIX

So much for convincing him I'm innocent...

As Emma wiped her nose on her arm, she told herself the man was a brute. An unreasonable, moronic brute who wouldn't be able to see the truth even if it smacked him on the ass. The fault wasn't on her. She'd tried her best.

But funny how that didn't console her in the slightest. He was going to throw her in jail. Her sister was going to get into even more trouble, and there was nothing Emma could do to help her.

Overcome with hopelessness, she wanted to curl into a ball and pretend life hadn't just fucked her over. How had everything changed so drastically in the course of a few hours?

Not too long ago, she'd been at her sister's house. Safe. About to go on holiday. With no idea that magic and whatever he was existed.

No, not magic, she tried to convince herself.

There's no such thing as magic.

And he's just a man.

I can take on a man.

She'd managed to get the upper hand on the men at Liz's house and there had been three of them at least. She could do the same with him. *I can.* But first, she had to figure out a way to escape her binds.

She gave them a testing tug and wasn't surprised when they held firm. Despite his utter inability to discern the truth, the man seemed to be a freaking master at tying knots.

A sudden unwanted image rose into Emma's mind. Her chest rose and fell rapidly as she thought about being tied down by him in a different way.

A hot way...

A stupid way, she corrected herself.

Her body did not seem to care.

Her throat suddenly dry, she forced herself to focus on the items in the room. There had to be something she could use to escape. But a quick glance around told her the only thing she was likely to find in this generic hotel room was a Bible. And assuming he wasn't a vampire, which she doubted, it probably wouldn't be of any use anyway. Especially since she wasn't even sure if vampires were scared of Bibles. Was it all Christian relics or just crosses?

Shaking the thoughts away, she sucked in a deep breath. The snot in her nose blocked one nostril, but the other was semi-free. She hoped it stayed that way so she didn't suffocate while gagged.

Wincing, Emma shoved those thoughts away too and returned her attention to the room.

In front of her was a wooden dresser and on top of that was a flat-screen TV. A remote controller lay at the edge of it. She briefly wondered if it would even hurt him were she to use it to whack him upside that bloated head of his.

Hoping to find a better weapon, she turned her gaze to the chair. To her dismay, it wasn't one of those simple desk chairs that were always used to knock someone out in the movies. Rather, it was the common comfort chair, made out of fake leather and too awkward of a shape to wield threateningly. Not to mention, it looked heavy.

Telling herself not to lose hope, she focused on the dark blue jacket settled across its top. There was nothing much to see where it itself was concerned, but it was the only item of his in the room. And a man like him, surely, he'd have a weapon?

As hope flared for the first time, Emma scrambled to think of a way to reach it. Maybe if she unplugged the alarm clock beside her with her feet, passed it over to her hands, and then miraculously turned it into a lasso, she'd be free?

Or maybe...maybe she could just use the alarm clock as a weapon?

You're an idiot, her little voice said, always the helpful optimist.

She exhaled roughly, trying to think of another plan. If only she had a secret ally hiding away somewhere or a trained pet monkey or –

She slyly turned to the animal stretched out beside her. "Mmphmmpfmmoomph."

Bloody freaking blasted piece of crap ignorant jerk of an – arrrgh!

Clenching her fists above her, she breathed hard. On the exhale, she rotated the knots in her shoulders loose, wincing only slightly at the uncomfortable pinch of pain. On the inhale, she brought her knees up so the flats of her heels rested on the mattress and then shimmied up the bed until her head knocked into her hands.

As she worked blindly on the knot keeping her gagged, she prayed that the man really liked long showers. By the time she managed to free her mouth, Emma was spitting with rage. Muttering promises of pain and torture on her kidnapper, she twisted her entire body around until she was lying on her stomach.

"I am going to kill him, Rex," she growled as she scooted up the bed. "Just you watch. I don't even want your help anymore because I want all – *all* the pleasure for myself. I – What the hell are these?"

Her eyes wide and her mouth full on open, she stared at her otherworldly cuffs. The gold chain was as thin as a necklace, nowhere near strong enough to hold her.

No. *Otherworldy-looki*ng cuffs, she quickly corrected herself. There was no such thing as 'other worlds.' He must've drugged her when she'd been passed out, making her see all those horrible images with Liz. He was crazy, deranged. Probably an escaped mental patient.

Who saved you from the mafia, the little voice said.

Emma snorted. *I would've saved myself had I not fishtailed into the river.*

And then remembered to unclip the seatbelt, it offered. *And suddenly learned how to swim.*

Fuck off.

So maybe he had saved her a little bit.

But big freaking deal. Whatever goodwill the man had warranted had been completely canceled out when he'd abducted her! It didn't count as a rescue if someone took you out of the frying pan only to drop you into the fire – even if that someone did have the most captivating eyes she had ever seen.

No! Bad Emma! Shaking the rest of her traitorous thoughts away, she turned her attention back to the very important matter at hand: escape. Using her best oh-aren't-you-just-a-cute-dog voice mixed with a stern dose of I-am-your-god-like-master-so-you-better-listen-to-me-or-else, she addressed her pet once more. "Go on, boy! Go get mama that jacket over there. Go on. Go! Aren't you a good boy! Yes, that one right on top of the chair! Aw, what a good dog!"

Excitement flooded through her as the dog bounded up onto the chair and sniffed the jacket in question. She flicked her eyes worriedly to the bathroom door. When it didn't burst open to reveal a hot, angry warrior, she turned her attention back to her dog.

"Come on, boy. That's it. Just bring it over here for me. No...no, bad boy. Bad. Bring it here. Now."

She knew she'd failed to sound stern enough when he curled up inside the deep comfort of the chair. With a mocking yawn, he laid his giant head down upon crossed paws.

"You – you ungrateful mutt!" she finally managed to spit out as he gave another yawn of contentment. "I am going to name you the most – the most – the *worst* name you can ever imagine! Like Mr. Peewee or Hotdog! Or – or Buttercup or Bella or Tinkles or Snuffles or –" Her eyes narrowed in glee at the sight of his teeth. "Snuffles, come."

He growled at her then, but his ears weren't flat in true warning, and she was too frustrated to care even if they had been. She was getting well pissed off after having been abducted, tied to a bed, interrogated like she was some Hitler-terrorist hybrid – which, she just realized that Hitler would've been labeled as a freaking terrorist, so it would be more of a sub-category and that just didn't cut the level of rage she was feeling – and then ignored by the freaking dog she had bloody well rescued! That was it! She was going to kill someone!

Right after she got out of these damn cuffs.

"Here, Snuffles." She was pretty proud of the command she'd managed to issue. The dog seemed to be impressed with her too given he finally leaped off the chair.

Only, he forgot to grab the jacket.

Telling herself he was only a dog and she should be lenient given his lower intelligence, Emma opened her mouth to coo him back toward the seat. But as soon as the first breath of air left her, her words morphed into a scream – and sadly, it was not one based on sensual pleasure despite the dripping wet, smoking hot, totally toned naked man suddenly in front of her.

For he looked like he wanted to kill her.

SEVEN

Get out.

Rogan cursed at Hades' intrusion into his mind, but he didn't dare ignore him. Ignoring the woman's scream, he focused instead on the dog. Its eyes were glued to the door, but its teeth weren't yet fully bared, which meant there were a few seconds before whoever it was attacked.

Given they weren't planning on coming through the thin walls, they had to be either amateurs, human, or a creature forced to use doors. He doubted Sebastian would choose either of the first two to take on an Elv've'Nor, which meant a horde of made vampires was about to break through the door.

Trusting the dog's ability to have his back, Rogan pulled a stream of water to his side as he dashed toward the window. He yanked off its blinds in one smooth movement, letting the light from the streetlamp outside pour inside their room. As soon as he smashed the glass out with his elbow, a shadow barreled out of the darkness of the night and through it.

A man with elongated fangs formed in front of him. In the blink of an eye, he was a blur again. Drawing on the holy water in his jacket, Rogan flung up a new ice window to keep the others out. Hisses of frustration met his ears, but all of his attention was on the blur heading toward Emma.

Shooting a whip of water forward, Rogan felt neither pride nor pleasure when his weapon found its mark, just a singular sense of calm. As he twisted the water into barbs of ice, a shrieking howl of pain mixed with a feminine shout of fear, but they were both drowned out by the crashing of the hotel room door. Half a dozen attackers advanced on the dog in his peripheral. Growls and shrieks of pain erupted in the room while screams erupted down the hall.

Focused solely on his target, Rogan diced at the vampire with frozen blades. The bloodsucker tried to defend himself with his hands and feet, but the ice cut into his pale skin. Snarling, he launched himself at Rogan

Pulling his arms back to his waist, Rogan twisted his hands around each other, then shot one arm back out. He shifted to the side, his eyes cold. Merciless. Before he'd finished his step, the vampire's head rolled across the floor and his body started disappearing into ash. The rotating blade of ice Rogan had flung out melted back into a whip of water, then flew to his jacket and brought it to him. Only then, did he turn toward the door.

As he watched the remaining intruders get ripped apart by a terrifying display of teeth and claws, Rogan donned his jacket. Clearly not needed by the dog – which was most definitely *not* a dog given it had grown to the size of a horse – he turned his attention to the woman everyone seemed desperate to have.

Her eyes found his, terrified and glistening with tears.

A solid punch to his gut nearly floored him. In three quick strides, he crossed over to her side. Holding his hand over the golden chain, he commanded, "Cotealos."

It slid off her, and with barely a thought, he sent it into a random pocket of his jacket.

Realizing the sudden danger he was in, Rogan's eyes flew to hers. He stilled, ready for her to grab him with her lethal hand and then make a run for it over his dead body.

But all she did was lie there in frozen shock.

Deciding he was going to have to give her the benefit of the doubt, Rogan reached for her.

She immediately wrapped her arms around his neck and pressed her head against his chest, trusting him to protect her. Heat flared through him. Little bolts of electricity arched off her body and burrowed into his soul. Faltering a step, he tightened his arms around her. He wanted to hesitate, to take the moment to tell her everything would be okay, but he didn't. Time was not on their side, and if he looked into her eyes again, seeing her blatant trust, he knew he would break.

And until he knew for certain which side she was on, he couldn't risk it.

And even then... She was a descendant. Her very existence was a crime.

Striding over to the window, he shifted her across his chest so he'd have one arm free. She looked up in confusion, then horror, no doubt having just remembered they were on the third floor.

"Wait!" she yelped.

But her protest came too late and he didn't care. With a flick of his wrist, he shattered the makeshift window. Shards of holy water flew off in all directions. Shrill hisses rang in his ears as the ambushing vampires were forced to flee.

Holding her tight, he jumped. A jet of water pushed up from the ground, softening their landing. He morphed it into a whip, but it didn't transform fast enough. A blur of anger collided into them, knocking him off his feet. His grip tightened on the woman. Twisting in midair, he formed a bed of liquid to break their fall. Water splashed out around him. His back banged hard into the asphalt. Gritting his teeth, he pushed himself to his feet just in time to see three vampires charging toward them.

Drawing the woman tight against his chest, he spun around to take the bulk of their attack on his back. Her fingers dug into his skin. Her breath hitched in her throat. As he pulled on the holy water in his jacket, a vampire grazed his shoulder. He stumbled from the impact, but the pain of being rammed into wasn't anywhere near as harsh as he'd expected it to be.

Hardening the holy water into small shards of ice, all that would be needed to slow them down, he pivoted to face the vampires head on. A shrill hiss ruptured his ears as a golden-haired vampire was dragged back by a massive beast. The god's companion, now the size of a small elephant, tossed him into the air with a jerk of its head. It opened its mouth and swallowed him whole, then looked at Rogan with a smirk. Exhaling sharply, the dog shot a cloud of ash out of its nose.

Nodding at his furry ally, Rogan tossed his package over his shoulder and then bolted across the carpark. Mixing the holy water with that of his whip, he lashed out with an artist's precision at every shadow that charged them.

After decapitating another vampire, he yanked open the door of his Jaguar XJ and threw the woman into the backseat. A bark sounded behind him as he climbed in behind the wheel, but it didn't stop him from throwing the car into drive and flooring it. He controlled the machine with the same expertise as he had his water. He dodged every pissed off vampire in case one had the brilliant idea of grabbing hold of the vehicle and ripping their way inside.

As Rogan aimed for the exit, he spotted the god's messenger running bloody and huge off to the side. He didn't bother doing any calculations before flinging open the passenger's door. He was certain that by the time the dog leaped inside, he'd be back to his previous relatively small shape. Hypothesis correct, he banked hard to the left. The energy slammed the door shut with a definite bang.

"What in Hades' name is going on?" he demanded aloud despite expecting the reply to form within his mind.

No magic. She'll follow.

Gritting his teeth and going against every grain of his being, Rogan released the water from his hold. It ran down his naked form to puddle on the floor beneath the pedals.

"This isn't happening," Emma said hysterically from the backseat. "This is *not* happening. It's just a dream. A bloody long dream. Because there's no such thing as monsters or men that can control water or make you see things in your mind that aren't true or giant fucking dogs that can change size to even bigger dogs. So logically, this has to be a dream. Just a fucked up dream, and I'm going to wake up any minute. Any fucking minute."

Ignoring her despite his urge to pull over and make sure she was okay, Rogan asked the voice inside his head, *Who sent them? Who's she?*

And why hadn't he been briefed this morning about a third party involvement? And where in Hades' realm was Sebastian? Why had he and the descendant split up in the first place? Was she pushing for her own agenda? Had she lost her memories? Could she even lead him to the *Scrolls of Atlantis*? There were far too many questions and not nearly enough information.

Contact your team.

Of course the god wasn't talking. It was just like one to ignore any direct questions.

Opening its blood-stained mouth, the dog grinned beside him. Shooting it a glare, Rogan fished his mobile out of a jacket pocket and pressed the speed dial for his second-in-command. Before the first ring could finish, it was answered.

Relief filled him from knowing his team was okay.

"Flying south," Xeno said. Her voice was completely professional with no hint of friendliness despite their three decades of acquaintance. Some would call her cold, but Rogan knew her better than that. He had been there before she'd changed, before she'd walled herself inside, welded the lock shut, and thrown away the key. But despite a bit more than a decade having passed since then, he couldn't shake the unease in his stomach every time he heard the monotone drone of her voice. She'd used to be so happy. So carefree.

"Werewolves sing," he replied, giving the code phrase to let her know he wasn't compromised.

"The area has been swept and a package retrieved. We might have a Mission Gemini and are checking for confirmation."

His grip tightened on the wheel. His eyes flicked to the woman in his rear-view mirror. "What's the evidence?"

"Photographs in the target's house. A lot of them. Hunter is making sure they haven't been tarnished with magic, but none of us think they have been."

He bit back a curse even as a feeling of relief washed

through him. She was a Mission Gemini – a twin. A fucking twin. Which meant she wasn't their target. She wasn't the evil woman they were hunting. She was –

Still a descendant, he reminded himself. A person he would have to bring to the Royal Courts to stand trial. A person he would be damning to a lifetime in Damaculus just because she existed, just because her parents had committed a crime.

"The WALL leave behind anything of use?" he asked gruffly, focusing his eyes back on the road.

"No, but the SCU is going through their vehicles now. They'll collect their bodies from the river over the next few days, and Hunter's sister will call us if they find anything we need to know."

He rattled off the address of the hotel they'd just left. "Have the SCU send a clean up team there. They'll need wipers." Although Rogan had been too preoccupied to notice any witnesses, he doubted the chaos they'd caused had gone undetected. And if humans relearned that the Seven Planes existed before the right time, there would be a war. So the SCU wiped any and all minds, as well as deleted any visual evidence.

Turning the wheel, Rogan merged onto the motorway. He only half-payed attention to Xeno's confirmation. The other half was attuned to the woman in the backseat. She was still shaking in denial. Her ash-colored eyes were still wide, and her mouth still moved in soft mumbles.

"Did ye get my message?" he asked Xeno.

The dog growled low beside him, causing him to look in every mirror. Once he was certain they weren't being pursued, he dismissed the monster's unrest.

"Affirmative. How do you want it handled?"

A snarl of teeth was as clear an answer as any. Despite the frustration of working with one hand effectively tied behind his back, Rogan heeded the order. "We don't," he said. "He wants this kept quiet."

Xeno's second of silence spoke volumes.

"It's not my call," he explained. "I'm just a knight in this game."

A sudden ball of lightning flew across the sky. The dog's tongue lolled out of its mouth as humor lit its eyes. Many people sought the gods' attentions, and he himself had welcomed it when it had brought him rain. Now, though, he was quickly growing tired of the constant surveillance.

Another ball arched, a clear sign some sky god was laughing at him. He ignored it.

"You do know queens are sacrificed when they play?" Xeno warned.

A smile tugged at his lips but grew no further. "Aye, but not when they're protecting the king."

Another second of silence. "Plan unchanged?"

"Aye. Going dark. Activating Bastet."

"Will convey the message."

Xeno clicked off and Rogan slipped the phone back into his pocket. He took the exit into town. His eyes once again flicked to the rear-view mirror.

"Wake up. Wake up, wake up, wake up. Please...just wake up!" She pushed her palms into her eyes.

"You're awake, lass. Accept that and it'll be much easier for ye."

"Wake up. Wake up."

Knowing from experience he'd get nowhere with mere words, Rogan sped up to 70mph. He took a sharp turn into a parking lot and then slammed on the brakes, parking perfectly in an empty space.

The feminine scream was a welcome change to the non-stop ranting.

Unclipping his seatbelt, he twisted around to face her. She stared at him with wide eyes, her mouth still open but now silent. The stark terror on her face ripped at his heart. "It's all goona be okay," he murmured, his voice a deep soothe. "Ye can trust me. I did not allow them to harm ye, did I?" When she didn't answer, he pressed again. "Did I, love?"

Her mouth closed slowly. Her fear, though it didn't disappear completely, faded into the background. She gave the slightest shake of her head.

"Nay, I did not. Ye're alright and it's goona stay that way. I swear it."

"Wh-what were they?"

He judged it in a second. Whether she was ready to hear the truth of what they were or if it would shove her back into her chantings of denial. Whether she was strong enough to go forward; whether she had latched herself onto him enough to believe anything he said and follow anything he commanded. Whether she would understand just enough to accept it or get distracted by all her questions and not be able to complete the task he needed her to. He had years of experience judging the outcome of people and events in less than a second.

But the one question that nagged him, that made his decision take a full second to decide, was whether or not he wanted to be the one who flipped her world upside down. Nay, the one who destroyed it completely and tried to convince her that the ashes that remained were just as beautiful as the life and people she once knew.

"I will never let them hurt ye," he murmured.

He waited as she looked out the window, her eyes staring into the darkness. As the silence stretched, Rogan became acutely aware of how much he wanted to hear her answer. He wanted to hear her say she believed him. That despite being abducted, tied up, and interrogated by him, she trusted him to keep her safe. His jaw clenched slightly at the idiocy of it, but that didn't stop the want inside him from seeping into his lungs.

Turning to him, her eyes dipped low, she asked, "Why are we at Walmart?"

Wanting to put her more at ease, he grinned. "Because I'm as naked as the day I was born. With exception to me jacket, aye."

Her face heated immediately at the word 'naked' and only flushed further from there. His blood heated sharply in response, surging hotter as her eyes did a quick dart to his crotch. Or rather, to the area of the seat covering it from her view.

"R-right," she stammered, her eyes still downcast. Then she emitted a sharp gasp as she realized what she was still attempting to stare at. Her eyes jerked up to his, mortified and way too cute.

He pretended as if he hadn't noticed. As if his cock wasn't currently standing at attention. "So I need ye to go in, love, and buy me something to wear. I'm a thirty-nine at the waist and a double XL in shirts. Size thirteen and a half shoe. Nothing denim nor restricting, aye."

He glanced down at her hugging black jeans. "Same goes for ye. We need to be able to move easily. And quickly." Digging the wallet out of his jacket, he pulled out a solid black card. "This will cover whatever you want."

She reached for it, but she didn't take it. Her fingers on the hard plastic, she peered into his eyes. He watched as she searched inside him, looking for that inkling of trust too many captives tricked themselves into seeing.

He hated that she thought she'd found it.

Hated himself more for not correcting her.

But the mission always came first.

With a deep breath, she twisted the handle and stepped out of the car. He readied himself to grab her as she was fully faced with the freedom of escape. Even if she now trusted him to keep her safe, captivity was a dirty way of life and he couldn't fault her for trying.

But she didn't bolt. On shaky legs, she took a step toward the store. Her next one was stronger.

Needing to make sure she wouldn't run, he lowered the car window. "Trust me, love, and we'll find yer sister together."

She didn't turn around, but then she didn't need to. He had given enough barely veiled threats over the years to know of the fear now pinching her face.

Rolling up the window, he pushed down the guilt eating at his gut. It was just a spell she was weaving, a trick to get him to do what she wanted. She might not be the descendant that had killed Cariad's team, but she was still a threat to the Seven Planes.

And Rogan would do whatever it took to complete his mission.

He could not – he *would* not fail.

EIGHT

Emma's heart thrashed wildly inside her ribs as she approached the double doors of the store. The familiarity of the place left her mind a disheveled mess. She felt like she was entering her childhood home, only to find it was no longer her home. As if she was meeting up with her first innocent crush, only to discover he was nothing like she remembered. Her legs trembled. Her resolve nearly crumbled.

But feeling that man's eyes on her back, she found the strength to keep walking. He would help her find her sister...and if he didn't, then *she* would. Liz was counting on her, and Emma would do whatever it took to save her.

As she walked through the double doors, a mother scurried out with a cart of toys and three small children surrounding her. The two women locked eyes. Emma held her breath, wondering what she would say if she was asked if she was okay. Could she convince her to call for help? Would the man kill her if she did? Just like he'd killed all of those...*people* back at the hotel?

But in the end, the woman didn't say anything.

And Emma wasn't sure if she was relieved or not.

Placing one foot in front of the other, concentrating on one step at a time, she made her way over to the women's clothing. She ruffled through a few racks before picking up a pair of slim fitting black slacks. She headed to a mirror and held them up to her waist for judgement.

She might be running for her life and fighting for her sister's, but there was no reason she couldn't look good while doing it. Besides, she needed a little pick-me-up right now, and Liz always swore by a sexy outfit being just the thing.

Not that I'll find anything smoking hot in here...

But she could at least pick an attire that highlighted the natural flair of her hips and the tight curve of her butt.

She looked up to find the changing rooms, but her gaze was snagged by a pair of tights on the sports rack beside her. They were a blue denim that looked exactly like jeans.

Her heart pounding, she slowly walked over to them.

Her fingers trailed across the fabric, each brush of her hand sending jolts of electricity down her arm. This was a bad idea. He could get so mad... And yet...

She didn't care.

She didn't. Fucking. Care.

He'd kidnapped her. Was holding her captive. Had killed dozens of...people in front of her. If he wanted to kill her, he would've. But he needed her alive, however annoying she was. So fuck it.

Grabbing the 'jeans,' Emma marched over to the shoe aisle. Her eyes were instantly snagged by the pair of black strappy heels she'd been eyeing for weeks. Then she paired them with a killer red thong with a black bow at the front and its matching bra. Not for the prick, of course, but for her own self esteem.

To prove it, she picked out an unflattering long baggy t-shirt and a plain brown jacket that spoke more of comfort rather than appearance.

Feeling marginally better about her whole messed up situation, Emma made her way over to the men's section. She thought briefly about choosing him a size too small, but decided she'd much rather stay alive than be able to laugh at his discomfort. Besides, she'd already spotted the rack of bad puns and cartoons that would do the job of making her smile – something she desperately needed in order to stay sane.

After flicking through all the different options, she settled on a shirt that said, 'CSI, Can't Stand Idiots.' He was probably part of some sort of organization like that anyway. His conversation on the phone had seemed less mafia and more government.

He mentioned gods.

Unable to deal with that knowledge right now, she ignored it.

After grabbing a plain pair of black cargo pants, a packet of superhero boxers, and dark leather boots in his size, she headed toward the pharmacy. She wanted a few sleeping pills in case she needed to create an escape. She doubted she'd actually get the chance to drug him, but she wanted to be prepared if the possibility ever arose.

Thoughts going in a similar direction, she added a switchblade and some pepper spray to her shopping cart. At the checkout aisle, she grabbed a handful of chocolate bars. And then another.

Pocketing the card, she headed into the disabled restroom in order to change. She took a moment to admire herself in the well fitting lingerie and black heels. A boost of confidence filled her, but it quickly waned as her eyes focused on all the parts of her she didn't like.

Turning away from the mirror, she kicked the shoes off and shimmied into the denim tights. She threw on the shirt and jacket, laced up her old sneakers, and shoved the pepper spray, knife, and sleeping tablets into the inside pocket of her jacket. With a deep exhale, she headed for the door, but when she glanced at the mirror, she stopped.

An unfamiliar woman looked back at her. Not even twenty-four hours ago, she never would have had the courage to face the nightmare her life had become. She was a bookworm who occasionally fought monsters through a console or from around a table full of D&D figurines. Emma didn't have Elizabeth's spunk or her fearlessness of the outside world. She had grown up afraid of the dangers their mother and the constantly violent news had warned her about. Emma hadn't even been strong enough to stand up to her boss when he'd unjustly fired her after years of always being able to count on her.

She'd even babysat his kids once for crying out loud.

And even they had run all over her...

But the woman in the mirror... That strong, confident woman would've ripped her boss a new one and left a horrible but honest review on how he treated his staff. She would have traveled with her sister to Europe in order to experience the world she had always craved to know. She would give the man outside a flamboyant middle finger and then kick him in the balls the second she had the chance.

Probably.

Maybe.

After he was drugged for sure.

Emma's lips curled into a small smile. Unable to put off the inevitable any longer, she headed outside.

As soon as she was back in the cold night air though, she stopped. She couldn't recall what the car looked like, but then she remembered it had been parked near one of the trees. Certain she knew the way back to that spot, she headed over with strong strides, only to be redirected by the small honk of a horn.

Her brows furrowed. Then relaxed at the sight of his obvious irritation as he glanced at her legs. She was about to flick him the physical bird to go along with her mental one when the light above her flickered out, and all her bravado exited on a silent scream.

Her chest tightened with stark terror as she vividly recalled the smashing of the window. The monsters trying to push inside. Them nearly grabbing her as they hit the ground. Her throat closed at the memory of the blood and body parts flying about, of a head being decapitated by a whip of freaking water. Her legs froze solid at the reminder that the man and the dog waiting for her were even more dangerous than whatever 'things' had attacked them back at the hotel.

Sweat broke out all across her body. Her legs trembled as if there was an earthquake erupting beneath her. Her breathing grew shallow and quick. Faster and faster until the whole fucked up world tilted on its side and then went completely dark.

Rogan cursed as he climbed out of the car. Lunging forward with a burst of inhuman speed, he caught her just before her head hit the ground. The bag of shopping spilled out at his feet. A frown pulled at his lips.

She'd been fine a second ago, a look of defiance in her eyes. And then she'd dropped like a stone, her face now twisted in pain and terror. Worried she'd seen something, Rogan glanced around the carpark.

But it was empty. He didn't detect any creatures hiding

in the shadows either. Still on high alert, he carried her to the car. Cerberus was curled up in the backseat, snoring loudly. Seeing the monster at ease made Rogan relax a little but not by much.

Sliding her into the passenger seat, he hurried back to grab the shopping. Whoever had sent the made vampires, might be closing in. Or it could be Sebastian himself. Even if he was where the woman had claimed, the vampire had the ability to phase anywhere on a single plane. He could jump from England to here in a split second and back again.

Grabbing half a dozen chocolate bars off the ground, Rogan shoved them into the bag, then froze.

When had he stopped wondering if *she* was playing him? She could've pretended to faint so she could steal the car.

Swearing, he turned around at the start of an engine.

But it was a different car pulling out. A silver one, whereas the one he'd just stolen was black.

Still, he never should've put himself in a position to be taken by surprise like that. He needed to stay on his toes around her, even if it was her sister doing all the crimes.

Even if he felt like he could trust her...

It's just a spell. She's probably of the succubus line. They could convince nearly anyone to care for them, to protect them. And with the powers she undoubtedly had, even a seasoned Elv've'Nor trained to resist such magic could be at risk if they weren't careful.

Turning, Rogan picked up the next item. He opened the packet of boxers and slipped one on. Then the pair of cargo pants. He looked around for the shirt. His eyes narrowed when he found it. Even with the light out, he could see the design. Hunter and Jack were going to tease him mercilessly for it, but at least Xeno would keep her mouth shut.

As soon as he pulled the shirt on, his eyes snagged on a single black heel lying in the next space over. A sudden wave of desire slammed into him. Images of her in them and them alone filled his mind.

Cursing, he wrenched his eyes away. She must have spelled them inside the shop. Whatever magic she'd used was strong. His cock was hard and thick, and the pants she'd grabbed for him already felt too tight.

Fuck.

Now all he could think about was how she'd wrapped her legs tight around him in the river. How her lips had brushed across his neck. How her breasts had felt pushed against his chest.

His fist tightening on the bag of shopping, he quickly grabbed the leather boots she'd purchased for him and headed back to the car. The heels he left.

But they stayed in his mind as he threw the car into drive and headed for the highway. Even knowing she had to be the daughter of some love or sex goddess, Rogan struggled to fight her power. His cock wouldn't go down and the damn heels wouldn't get out of his fucking mind. What had been her plan anyway? To seduce him, then kill him? Had she bought lingerie to go with the shoes?

His eyes darted over to her, taking in the ugly brown jacket and skin-tight jeans.

His grip tightened on the wheel. *It doesn't matter if she bought lingerie. She spelled the shoes...*

But what if she'd spelled the lingerie too? What if he was struggling to concentrate because she was wearing them now?

Fuck.

Shifting in his seat, Rogan accelerated faster.

Taking off the lingerie would be what a logical agent

would do. Throw out the magical items so he could regain his control.

But the thought of undressing her was only making things worse.

Seeing the neon light of a hotel, Rogan pulled off the highway and swung into the carpark. Trusting the dog to look after her, he headed inside.

"I need a room with two beds," he told the woman at the counter.

Glancing up from her phone, she smiled at him. She popped a bubble with her gum, then leaned forward and moved the mouse of her computer. "Long night?" she asked sweetly.

That was one way to put it. He nodded.

"I've had a few of those myself." She sighed as her eyes darted to the top right of her screen. "I have another five hours to go."

"So do ye have a room?"

Her smile widened. "Yep, but there's only one bed. You can buy an extra set of bedding for ten bucks." She popped another bubble.

Fuck.

Digging a hand into his jacket, he pulled out his wallet and grabbed a card. He slid it over to her.

"Sorry, hun, but we only take cash."

Slipping the card back into the wallet, he put it in his jacket. Its pockets were spelled to give him whatever he wanted. "How much?" he asked.

"A hundred and twenty. Thirty with the bedding."

Ignoring the strange look she gave him when he pulled his wallet back out, he withdrew the exact amount of cash. When she handed him the key and extra bedding, he nodded and left.

His eyes roamed around the dark and quiet carpark

before landing on their car. The woman sat in the front seat, her arms wrapped around herself. Seeing she was awake, he walked over to her door.

"Come on," he said, gesturing her out. "We're in room twelve. Second floor."

When she stumbled out of the car, clearly exhausted, he automatically grabbed her before she could fall over. She glanced up at him, her eyes heavy with sleep, her lips parted.

"Cut it out," he snapped.

Her brows furrowed, then relaxed as she shook her head. "I'm too tired for this right now. Get on to me in the morning."

"If ye are too tired, then stop it. It's draining yer energy."

She stepped back, pulling her arm free; he let her go. "No, *you're* draining my energy." She waved an arm in the air. "This whole *night* is draining. Now can we please just go to our room and sleep?"

His lips tightened. He pushed out with his own power, feeling the water in her veins, the beat of her heart. It was calm.

But that didn't mean she wasn't lying.

"The stairs are over there." He stepped out of her way so she could go first. Without so much as a glance at him, she slid past. They climbed the stairs in silence, Cerberus taking up the rear.

Opening the door to their room, Rogan stepped inside and looked around. The single bed called to him like a beacon. Ignoring it, he headed over to a spot on the floor and dumped the extra bedding down.

"I'm not sleeping on the floor," the woman said as she shut the door behind them.

He refused to think about sharing the bed with her. "I

didn't ask ye to."

Taking off his jacket, he slung it over the chair, then sat down and pulled off his shoes.

The bed creaked behind him.

He did not think about her in it.

With a heavy thud, Snuffles jumped up beside her, effectively killing the thoughts in his head. The last thing anyone would want was a god's messenger anywhere near the act.

Not that he was thinking about any kind of acts.

Scowling, he laid out the blanket.

"Snuffles, down," she whispered, her voice wavering just a little.

And that single phrase caused his chest to tighten. Turning on instinct, he watched as fear flitted across her face, and every part of him wanted to soothe her worries away.

It's just a spell.

Giving a low whine, 'Snuffles' hopped off the bed and settled in front of the door.

Rogan started to turn back around when she flicked him a glance. Their eyes caught each other's, a magnetic pull he couldn't break.

Her lips parted.

She swallowed.

His gaze dipped to her neck.

Why had he ever thought he could resist the magic of a descendant? Decades of training or not, decades of never losing control, he didn't have the strength to fight power like hers.

So why was he resisting?

To save billions of people.

The last descendant had nearly wiped out his entire race. What used to number in the hundreds of thousands was now barely a thousand strong. Atlantis, and all its people, had been wiped off the map. The portals to Earth had been forced to close in order to stop total annihilation from occurring here. Gaera, Rogan's home plane, was slowly dying, the primordial elementalists having been slaughtered during the Great Extinction. And Persic was an absolute mess, the plane having literally folded in on itself due to the release of the Duesychosis Plague.

Not to mention, Rogan told himself as his eyes trailed down her body, the woman's birth had broken a Holy Blood Contract between the gods. After Sebastian and Rakian had finally been dealt with, all of the mythical species had banded together for the first time in history. They'd forced every god and goddess to sign a Holy Blood Contract concerning the birth of another child – an oath that could not be broken without severe punishment.

So taking the woman's side wouldn't just be selfish, it would be suicidal. He had to keep resisting.

Clenching his jaw, shoving down all thoughts of her in his bed, Rogan ripped his eyes away from her and laid down. He just needed to sleep. Just needed to make it through one night. Then he could meet up with his team and foist her onto someone else.

Someone like Xeno – an angel who actually had the power to resist the magic of a god.

It was a good plan. A solid plan.

So why was the idea not sitting well in his stomach?

I just need some fucking sleep.

NINE

He couldn't sleep.

Four thirty-nine in the fucking morning, and he was still staring at the ceiling, listening to her murmurs, her thrashing. The dog was asleep. Their neighbors, who had woken up an hour ago with lots of moaning, were back asleep. The whole fucking town was probably asleep. And yet, he wasn't because she wouldn't stop talking.

"Don't touch me..."

Grabbing the pillow out from under his head, he put it over his face. If he suffocated himself, at least he wouldn't be able to listen to the raw torment of her nightmares.

With every word she uttered, it felt as if a thousand red-hot knives were being rammed into his chest. She had been begging and pleading all night, her desperate words leaving him shaking.

Her powers had clearly wrapped around him, urging him to help her, to care for her. To save her. And every time he refused, he felt as if he was being carved open and ripped apart.

"Please..."

Fuck.

Tossing the pillow away, Rogan climbed to his feet. She was twisted in the blankets, her pillow clasped to her body as she laid in a fetal position. Scowling, he leaned down and shook her shoulder. "Ey, wake up," he snapped.

She jerked away from him, then curled in on herself even tighter. Cursing, he reached for her again. This time, he shook her harder.

She whimpered.

"Fuck."

Glaring over his shoulder at the dog, who was snoring loudly, Rogan thought about waking him. But what could he possibly do? Bite her? As far as he was aware, Snuffles didn't have any powers other than being able to disguise himself as a regular dog and communicating with Hades.

"I loved you..." A choked cry escaped her, breaking up the words, sending each shard into his chest one piece at a time.

Her fucking magic was driving him mad.

"Ey," he said strongly, shaking her again.

Reaching up, she grabbed his hand. She held onto it with a grip like iron. Like desperation. Trembling as she slept, she held it tight to her chest.

Clenching his teeth, he tried to pull his hand free. She clung to it harder.

The thought of smothering her crossed his mind. As a descendant, it wouldn't kill her...

It might even be a mercy given whatever nightmare she was stuck in...

His eyes glanced from the spare pillow to her face, only to realize that the lines between her brows had smoothed out. The rest of her started to relax.

Thanking the gods, Rogan started to pull his hand free

so he could finally go to sleep.

But her grip tightened.

And the worry lines in her brow came back.

He groaned. *Fuck.*

It was just a coincidence, he told himself. She hadn't relaxed because he was touching her. *And if she did,* he reasoned, *it was most likely a ploy.*

But for what gain?

If she wanted to kill him, she could've done so already. She had the power of two gods running through her veins, and her sister could kill with a single touch.

It didn't make any sense.

Unless...

He stilled as he remembered the heels. His cock twitched.

She had wanted to seduce him.

Succubi could control the people they slept with. If her mother was a sex goddess, then perhaps she had a similar ability?

Cursing, he ripped his arm away.

She reached for him, pain twisting her face, but he steeled himself against her magic. Clenching his jaw, he took a step back. And another.

He would not fall into her trap.

Marching over to his spot on the floor, he laid down.

"Please..."

He turned over and closed his eyes, trying to drown her out.

"Don't hurt me."

Her soft crying wouldn't get to him. He knew what she was doing, and now he could resist.

"Stop...Please, just stop..."

Cursing, he was back on his feet and over by her side. Telling himself this was just so he could get some fucking sleep, he crawled into bed beside her. If she needed something to hold, then he'd let her use him. They were both clothed. And he was a trained Elv've'Nor. He could resist temptation for one fucking night.

Exhaling sharply, he laid on his side and pulled her into his arms.

She rolled into him immediately.

The warmth of her magic seeped through every part of him, making this feel right. Making her feel right in his arms.

Clenching his jaw, he fought it.

But then she wrapped a leg around his hip and sighed against his chest.

Fuck. This was a mistake.

As she burrowed against him, getting comfortable, her body brushed against his cock. He tried to scoot back, but she just followed him until they were on the edge of the bed.

Cursing his stupidity, Rogan stilled. His cock hardened. His pulse hammered. His breathing became labored.

But at least her desperate murmurs had finally stopped.

Closing his eyes, he focused on the silence. On his exhaustion.

On how right she felt in his arms...

Holding her close, he breathed her in.

And finally fell the fuck to sleep.

For the first time in her life, Emma woke up feeling safe. There weren't any lingering nightmares hounding her brain. There weren't any screams or the smell of blood assaulting her senses.

She was just cocooned in a blanket full of warmth –

Her eyes popped open.

Her kidnapper was in the bed.

His arms were around her. His cock pressed against her stomach. His breath whispered across the top of her head, slow and even as he continued to sleep.

And she *wasn't moving*. Worse, she had one arm wrapped around him and the other was –

She jerked back as she whipped her hand off his cock. Or at least, that's what she *tried* to do.

In reality, she laid there frozen, acutely aware that what was pressing into her stomach were her knuckles and what her fingers were wrapped around was his fucking hard penis. Inside his boxers.

Shit.

Let go. Let go. Let go.

But instead, her dumbass hand gave it a small squeeze.

A groan escaped him. His hips bucked, moving his cock through her fingers.

Her mouth watering, Emma glanced down between them. But all she saw was her arm disappearing into his waistband. Praying he wouldn't wake up, she slowly unwrapped her fingers and slid them out of his boxers. Then she scooted back. Then off the bed entirely.

Oh God.

Hurrying into the bathroom, she went to wash her hands. As she splashed water onto her face, she tried to rub off the feeling of him pressed against her. Tried to ignore the thoughts of what he would feel like *in* her.

He kidnapped you, you dumb idiot.

Also, he's most definitely not human.

Shaking her head, she pressed her palms to her eyes and took a deep breath.

How was she ever going to look him in the eye now that she'd had his cock in her hand? Now that she'd felt him slide through her fingers and heard that delicious deep moan he'd made?

Fuck.

As soon as she escaped and found Elizabeth, she was enrolling the both of them into therapy. Lots and lots of therapy.

Taking a shaky breath, knowing she couldn't put it off any longer, Emma opened the bathroom door.

He was sitting on the edge of the bed, bending over to tie his shoes.

"Morning," she croaked, feeling hot all over.

He lifted his head, his bright blue eyes pulling her in like a bug to a lamp.

Her breath caught.

Her palms grew damp.

"So where are you forcing me to go today?" Emma blurted, needing the reminder that he'd kidnapped her. Regardless of how hot he was, regardless of how nice it'd felt to wake up in his arms, he was the enemy.

Silence lingered as he ducked his head and finished tying his laces. Rising off the bed, a tent still in his pants, he grabbed his jacket and slung it on. She drank in the sight of him, his hard lines, the lethal way he moved.

Only when he'd crossed over to her, did he answer. "Manchester, England."

Her heart stopped as she craned her neck back to look at him. She opened her mouth, then closed it again, struggling past all of the emotions clogging her throat. Finally, she managed, "You're not taking me to stand trial? We're really going to find Liz?"

She silently begged him to say yes. Well, no, then yes.

His head dipped just the slightest.

"Aye," he murmured. "Now put on yer shoes, lass. We have a wee drive ahead of us."

TEN

An hour into the ride, Emma was still staring out the window, thankful for the silence hanging thick in the car. She needed more time to herself. Time to think, time to process everything she'd seen. Everything she'd touched. She wiped her palm on her leg. Her thighs clenched as she thought about him touching her there. Hell, everywhere.

She'd woken up in his arms.

With her hand in his boxers.

She'd heard him groan.

Felt him move.

Flicking him a glance, Emma let her eyes roam down his body. Even with the ridiculous shirt, he gave off a deadly confidence that made her shiver. The hard lines of his chest combined with the flat surface of his stomach, set match to a fire inside her. She had lusted after a great number of men, mostly from afar, but never had she felt a pull like this.

Which was crazy. And stupid. And... *He's not human.*

A chill raced down her spine as she recalled the

'things' that had attacked them at the first hotel. Things that shouldn't exist. Things like him.

When he glanced at her, his eerie blue stare capturing hers, her breath hitched. His eyes darkened under her quiet assessment. He held her captive for a second, then two, before sliding his attention back to the road.

And finally, she could breathe again.

Swinging her gaze to the windshield, she cleared her throat. "So I'm Emma. What's your name?"

He didn't answer for a heavy few seconds. "Rogan. And yer sister's?"

Her chest tightened. The thought of Liz dealing with something like this all alone brought her to the edge of tears. Not ready to talk about her, Emma blurted out something random. "Do you have a girlfriend?"

She winced, not wanting to talk about this either.

"Nay."

Her pulse kicked up a notch. "Why not?"

She felt him glancing at her, but she refused to look at him, knowing she'd burst into a ball of flaming horror and embarrassment if she did. She shouldn't be asking him such personal questions. She shouldn't want to know the answers.

"When's the last time ye saw yer sister?"

"Is it because of your work?"

His grip tightened on the wheel. Her gaze fastened onto the curve of his fingers. She recalled all too well what her fingers had been curved around barely more than an hour ago. Shifting in her seat, she forced the memory down.

"If I answer, will ye tell me when ye saw her?"

Recalling all the bruises on Liz's face, Emma frowned and turned to look out the window. She no longer felt like testing him. "Those...images you showed me," she said softly, "were they real?" Her mouth ran dry as she waited for his answer. She didn't want to know. She didn't want to hear him say –

"Aye."

Her heart broke. Something terrible had happened to Liz in Europe and Emma hadn't been there to save her. Because she'd been too scared to leave the country. Too weak to handle the stress and anxiety of a trip...

Her throat worked hard against the lump quickly forming. The irony wasn't lost on her and that just made her hurt all the more. She *could've* gone with her. She could've... She didn't know. But she could've done something because she'd managed the last few hours well enough, and surely, a backpacking trip around western Europe couldn't have been harder than that.

"This Sebastian guy you mentioned..." She didn't want to ask because she already knew the answer. She didn't know how she knew, but her gut screamed he was bad news. "Are you going after him too?"

His hesitation scared her.

"Nay."

"Why not?" She recalled the ragged bones her sister had turned into. The bruises on her body. "He hurt her. He's twisting her, forcing her to do these things. I know it. Liz would never... She'd never..." Tears burned her eyes and she angrily brushed them away.

"All I need is for ye to tell me where she is."

"But I don't even know what's going on!" Her chest tightened, restricting her air. She fought to keep her breath even, her panic down, her head level. She would not fucking pass out again. She needed to focus, to stay in the present so the nightmares couldn't grab her and wrench her back under. Digging her fingers into her palms, she murmured, "What's going to happen to her after you find her?"

"She'll stand trial at the Royal Courts."

"And then sentenced to life in prison, right? In Damas or whatever you called it?"

He didn't answer. But then he didn't need to. His 'aye' hung heavily in the air.

She felt sick. Even if she helped her sister, she'd be damning her still.

"Is there anyway ye can get in touch with her? Ask her to meet ye somewhere and turn herself in? If she does that, they might be more lenient."

Emma shook her head in near overwhelming distress. "Elizabeth got a new number for her travels, but I don't remember what it is. And yesterday, she called from a blocked number. I remember not being able to call it back, but that was probably Sebastian's number, right? You can trace it?"

Then she remembered where her phone was, and what little bit of hope she had just garnered died a quick and brutal death. Her pulse jumped into her throat as she fought to ask the one question she really didn't want to ask. "Is he...is he like th-th-those...those c-creatures?"

A sick feeling of dread pooled deep in her stomach. Sweat beaded along her brow. The tendrils of a new nightmare started to rise.

"Aye."

She closed her eyes, fighting back the grief wanting to consume her. Her head grew dizzy. She raised a hand to her forehead. *Please don't come on now. Please.*

But she knew her condition wouldn't listen. Her heart was pounding too fast. Her blood pressure was rising too quickly. If she didn't concentrate on her breathing, if she didn't start to relax...

But she needed to know.

Clenching her hands, she focused on the pain of her nails, using it to ground herself.

"What are they?" Emma whispered. Her vision started to blur. The edges became black. And the nightmares that always assaulted her whenever she closed her eyes banged at the door of her consciousness. Soon they'd overwhelm her.

"Please. I need to know."

"They're vampires," he said, glancing at her. "Or at least they were."

Her eyes felt really heavy. She nodded. Or at least she tried to. But her head only went down and it didn't come back up again.

And the only sounds she heard were the nightmarish screams of a dying child.

ELEVEN

You are not to leave the compound without me.

The command wrapped itself around Elizabeth like a physical chain, tightening around her legs and chest. She struggled to breathe as she fought the power holding her back. The outside world beckoned to her, mocking her with how easily it would be to reach. She wasn't guarded. The doors weren't locked. If she could just get out, she could run away and hide. She could be free...

But despite how much she wanted it, she could not take a single step forward.

You are not to leave the compound without me.

She clenched her hands and jaw as she willed herself to move. But as with her every attempt to do so before, she could not walk past the mantel. His words bound her, a magic spell she was hopeless to break.

For now.

Every day she was growing stronger, more able to defy his commands. *One day*, she vowed, *I will walk out of this damn door.*

Her toes twitched inside her shoes.

"Pathetic," Sebastian said as he came up behind her, his presence chilling her like the touch of death itself. "Every morning you stand here, looking out over the fells. And for what? You cannot leave."

Elizabeth desperately wanted to pretend he wasn't here, but her ribs still ached from when she'd done that the last time. Ignoring the sick twisting of her stomach, she turned to face him.

"I just enjoy the view, my lord."

"Then look at it," he said with a wave of his hand.

His blatant dismissal of her ability to escape set the embers inside her to light. He thought her so weak and compliant, not even worthy of a guard watching her. *Well, the joke will be on him*, she thought bitterly. *A time will come when I grow strong enough to resist his commands. And then I'll set this damn place on fire.*

"I guess it's not a terrible view," he agreed, his voice a purr as he pressed against her back.

Elizabeth's heart hammered high in her throat. Her fight vanished at the sound of his tone. She hated it. Had learned to fear it. Trembled against it now.

"Would you like me to take you?"

Elizabeth drew on all her strength to keep herself from flinching at his words. She had long learned that he craved her fear, fed off it like a sick psychopath, and she would be damned if she gave him that victory. So she stood as still as the stone, her eyes solidly fastened on the magnificent view. She stayed strong even when his hands came around her to squeeze her breasts. But when he gripped them harder, she couldn't stop a sharp cry from escaping.

He had bruised them terribly last night, and despite her new ability to heal faster these days, they were still painfully sore.

"I'll take that as a yes," he breathed in her ear, and she struggled with the urge to vomit.

His hands gave her breasts a final squeeze before trailing down to her waist. One slipped under the hem of her shirt, then up to cup her bare flesh. He pinched her nipple sharply, pulling an uncontrollable whimper from the very bottom of her soul. She sagged against him on instinct, flinching away from his hand.

But then she felt his erection against her back. The movement of his other hand as he undid the button of her pants. He pulled down the zipper slowly, drawing out the horrible anticipation until it left her weak with nausea. After a few more seconds of torture, he slipped his hand into her underwear.

Desperately, Elizabeth focused on the beauty of the hills in front of her. She ignored the glide of his fingers, their sweep across her labia. She cast her mind away from the acts he was doing to her body, away from the sharp pain as he pushed inside, and instead imagined herself out there smelling the flowers and listening to the sweet song of birds.

But then came the agony of his fangs as he bit deep into her neck, and she couldn't hold the comforting illusion any longer.

His fingers moved faster. She bit the inside of her cheek hard. As he rubbed himself against her, he groped her breasts, squeezing them and twisting them until she could not feel anything other than the assaulting pain.

He tore at her neck with his teeth, making it hurt, punishing her, but it was better than when he made her enjoy it. When the scrape of his teeth felt erotic and pushed her to the edge of orgasm.

Clenching her fists, trying desperately to smell those

flowers, Elizabeth waited until he was done. Her strength slowly left her, drained from her neck. Her vision began to narrow. And still he drank.

Only once she was on the verge of passing out, did Sebastian let her go. He removed his hands and kicked at the back of her knees. She collapsed to the cold floor, hitting it with a loud thud, unable to garner the strength to break her fall. Her tears threatened to burst through when the open wound in her side screamed in agony, but she fought them back like there was no tomorrow. She would die before she ever let him see her cry again.

The sick bastard could go fuck himself.

His feet filled her vision. Terror filled her lungs.

He never lingered after a feeding. The last time he had...

The bile came up quickly as she recalled the deaths he had forced her to deal. She vomited down the side of her face, thankful she was already on her side.

His foot slammed into her stomach. He hated it when she was sick. Knowing she was about to be kicked again, she closed her eyes. She didn't bother trying to block it, to protect herself. All that would do was warrant another kick, maybe a break of her fingers as he stomped on them again.

"Sit up."

His command wrapped around her broken and bruised body, forcing her to roll into a sitting position despite the pain. She wiped at her mouth with the back of her hand. She looked out at the view behind him, but the colorful fells had already lost their beauty. They were tainted by a horrendous memory she'd never be able to shake.

"I'm very disappointed in you, Liz. You didn't tell me you had a twin."

She froze. Her entire world shattered into a million

pieces from that single sentence. Her eyes snapped to his as she struggled to form words of denial. But looking into his triumphant gaze, she knew nothing she would say could convince him she was an only child.

A tear slipped down her cheek. "Leave her out of this," she begged.

Another one fell as he smiled wide.

Emma, I'm so sorry!

But her silent apology would mean nothing. She never should've included Emma in her escape plan. Because now... now Sebastian had her in his clutches.

As he told her what he wanted her to do to Emma, her tears broke freely from the dam she'd kept them behind. She couldn't defy any of his orders. Whatever he told her to do, she was forced to carry out. And as she listened to his grand plan, every inch of her broke.

Soon, she would be reunited with her sister in the worst of ways.

Oh, Emma... she cried.

I'm so sorry...

I'm so fucking sorry.

TWELVE

For fuck's sake. If I pass out one more time, I swear I'm going to get a vivisection.

As the last remnants of her nightmare finally faded, Emma opened her eyes. The hacked up face of a child stared back at her. She flinched, cowering in her seat as she pressed her palms against her face. The scent of blood filled her nose. Shuddering, she dropped her hands.

She could still feel the cold metal of the knife in her grip though. Could still hear the screams she'd inflicted on that little girl before turning the blade upon herself.

Twisting to face the man beside her, Emma drank him in. She knew it wasn't healthy to use her kidnapper as an anchor, but she'd do anything to make the images stop. Twenty-two years and they never got any easier to handle.

His eyes flicked to her, holding her, helping her breathe even though he didn't know it. She wondered if he'd let her use him if he knew what she was doing. Or if he'd prefer to let her suffer, keep her panicked and off-balance so she'd be easier to manipulate.

As if he needs to do that to get you to do what he wants, her little voice said, and Emma mentally flipped it the bird.

Touching the bottle of mace through her jacket, she assured herself she was just waiting for the right moment to escape. She needed to learn everything he knew about Sebastian first. Try to think of a way to save her sister when all she had was a passive-aggressive attitude and a cheap ass bottle of mace...against a vampire with fangs and superhuman strength...

Fighting down the panic, she pressed her palm against the bottle, but the hard plastic wasn't anywhere near as reassuring as she'd hoped it would be.

"There's food in the bag," Rogan said, his voice a shiver down her spine. That mysterious urge to trust him again resurfaced, and she stared at the takeaway bag he must've purchased while she was 'asleep.' Leaning forward, she grabbed the bag off the console between them without a thought to it being poisoned.

It wasn't until the third bite that she stopped, the egg and cheese sandwich in her mouth only partially chewed, and worried about dying a horrible death. Her throat suddenly dry, she had to work it a few times before she could swallow. Telling herself that if he wanted to kill her, he would've done it already, she forced herself to take another bite. She needed her fuel.

And to not be so bloody paranoid.

But a life on the run would do that to a person...

A small smile graced her lips.

Getting caught by the mafia didn't seem like such a bad thing anymore.

"What's Sebastian wanted for?" she asked softly, her heart starting to pound again as she imagined the worse.

Though really, what could be worse than being a vampire?

The blood drained from her face.

"Will he turn Elizabeth?" Her words came out on a breath of air. If Rogan hadn't glanced at her, she wouldn't have been able to tell if she'd spoken loud enough. All she could hear was the rapid beat of her pulse banging around in her skull.

Clenching her fists, she shoved the nightmares down.

"Nay," he said. It was one word, one small little word, and yet, it had the strength to ground her.

Exhaling shakily, she forced her hands to relax. The crumbled wrapper of her sandwich dropped onto her lap. "How do you...kill a –" She swallowed. "A v-vampire?"

"Ye not goona eat anymore, lass?" he asked, nodding at the bag of food.

She shook her head. Everything left had meat in it, and knowing what it felt like to be decapitated and chewed on, she couldn't bear the thought of doing it to anything else. Besides, she didn't have the stomach to eat anymore.

Before she could press him about vampires again, they turned onto a runway. She looked out the window, her eyes wide. Her pulse spiked as every human trafficking movie she'd ever seen jumped straight to mind.

She was half turned around in her seat, her fingers about to grab the handbrake in a desperate attempt to escape, when the car slowed to a stop. Looking up, she found herself in front of a private jet.

But it wasn't the mechanical beauty holding her gaze.

It was the three people standing outside of it. All tall, built, and undeniably dangerous...

She wasn't escaping anywhere.

THIRTEEN

Rogan had barely managed to put both feet on the ground when a masculine voice called out in laughter. “Dude, what in the gods’ names are you wearing?”

He tried for a glare, but it was in such stark contrast to the rest of his team’s expressions, that it looked almost comical – more like a friend who was being mercilessly teased and unable to do anything about it.

Hunter, with his dark skin and short tight curls, was flamboyantly alight with a wide grin across his face. The corner of Jack’s mouth was upturned in a small smile, stretching the scar cut diagonally across his lips. Even Xeno had the inkling of humor found at his expense. Not that anyone who didn’t know her could tell.

Her face was a porcelain mask, but her eyes were as blank as a black hole – a clear indication she was hiding some sort of emotion because normally they screamed, “Don’t fuck with me. I’ll gut you with extreme pleasure.”

“It’s courtesy of our new friend here,” Rogan said dryly. He flicked his eyes across the top of the car to Emma, but she was too busy gawking at his teammates to notice.

When Hunter turned to her with a smile, Rogan had a strong urge to pull Emma to his side. To claim her as his. He'd been fighting the desire all morning, since he'd woken up to her fingers sliding down his stomach, to her body pressed flush against his. He should've woken her, but by the time he'd managed to fight her spell enough to move, she'd slipped her hand into his boxers and ensnared him all over again.

And the tendrils of that snare had yet to leave him. Every breath he took smelled of her. Every shift she made had him glancing over, acutely aware of every inch of her.

Even now, with the car between them, he could feel the heat of her body wrapped in his arms, sliding against him like a cat in heat.

It was driving him mad.

"You did wonderful." Hunter winked at her as he gave her a once over.

Rogan's jaw locked. His desire shifted hard into jealousy. Hating how easy she was able to control him, he forced himself to breathe. *Hunter's just doing his job, building a profile like always.*

"Thanks." She gave Hunter a warm flash of teeth.

Rogan's glare hardened into daggers. *It's just a fucking spell,* he tried to remind himself.

But it didn't fucking work.

Especially not when Hunter's smile turned flirtatious.

As it always does. His job was to get their captives to relax so they were easier to interrogate and manipulate. But that reminder also didn't help. All he wanted was to waterboard the guy.

Slowly.

"Now that that's all answered," Rogan snapped as he stepped between them, "can we move on to the important matters at hand? Because in case ye've forgotten, there's a war brewing and we're stuck in the bloody middle of it."

He silently dared them to say something else. When no one did, he made his way inside the plane, and the rest followed.

He could hear Hunter already charming their captive behind him. His hands itched to clench into fists.

Was Hunter just being Hunter or was she controlling him too?

The thought left a dry taste in his mouth.

Scowling, he figured her mother was probably a goddess of chaos, like Eros...or Loki when he was in one of his moods.

Or Artemis, who despised men and wanted to see them make fools of themselves.

Holding tight onto his control, Rogan forced himself to carry on into the cockpit, away from her, where he waited for Xeno and Jack to join him. Once the door was shut and his second-in-command was seated in the pilot's chair, he asked, "Ye mentioned a package?"

He needed to get his mind off Emma. He needed to stay focused on the mission. The last twenty-nine had all been a success and he was determined to make it a solid thirty.

Going through her checks in preparation for take-off, Xeno said, "There was a black box on the floor of the Sedan. Inside was a dead rat and below that were numerous pictures and a few trinkets. In some cases there were two of our target in the same image."

"Why a rat?"

"Unknown. Hunter has a theory given his knowledge of the humans' history."

"He thinks it signifies the Black Death," Jack said, his green eyes locked onto the horizon as Xeno directed her attention to the runway. She was more than capable of multitasking, but Jack had a not-so-slight fear of flying. It was a mystery as to why, considering he could change into a bird on a whim, but he wouldn't say and none of them felt like prying.

"It wiped out a third of the population in Europe within a handful of years," Jack continued. "And even though it traveled through human flea populations, rats have taken the blame."

As the engine whirled and the plane started to incline, Jack swallowed nervously. The blood drained from his already pale face, making it nearly white. Clearing his throat, he added, "He thinks it might have something to do with them planning on infecting this plane and then the others with their own special disease.

"Given who their father is, we also think it could carry a message should it be resurrected. However, that requires the aid of Package B in order to be confirmed." His words came out less strained toward the end due to the plane leveling out.

"Any pictures of significance?" Rogan asked, a frown pulling at his lips. He had a hard time believing Emma wanted to infect the Seven Planes. He'd seen the horror in her eyes when he'd killed those vampires. She'd left all of the meat products at breakfast too. He doubted she had the stomach for mass murder, especially on that scale. Whatever was about to happen, he wanted to believe she had nothing to do with it.

But until he had evidence of that, he couldn't let her convince him of her innocence.

"Unconfirmed."

"And the trinkets?"

"Same as the photos. Just childhood memories, really, but without either of their cooperation, we can't be sure."

Rogan nodded. What might seem meaningless to him and his team could be of utmost significance to the two descendants. "Keep them away from her until we can be sure."

He tensed, silently reprimanding himself for his slip of tongue. Jack shot him a quick look, but neither of them commented on his referral to 'their package' as a 'she' and not an impersonal 'it.' Slowly, he relaxed – well, as much as he could when in the middle of a war between the gods.

Cutting through the silence, Rogan informed them, "Her name is Emma and her twin is Elizabeth, but I've yet to discover their last name."

"It's Sterling," Xeno supplied. "There was a driver's license in the car with an address a few counties over. We searched the package's house and found further evidence of a Mission Gemini. There aren't many photos of our targets over the years outside that box, and Hunter has been unable to find any social media accounts linked to them.

"However, given the impersonal nature of their homes, we believe they move every few years and live as if they're on the run. We have not been able to confirm whether or not they knew of their true nature before now."

"It's hard to say," Rogan supplied. "She's had numerous chances to kill me and escape, but she hasn't. She doesn't seem to know anything about the Myth, and her panic attacks seem real, but –" He hesitated, remembering the feel of her in his arms this morning. It'd felt so right, and saying what he was about to say would mean he'd never get the chance to hold her again. Xeno would make sure of it.

He cleared his throat. "She's been using magic since I grabbed her at the extraction point."

Xeno turned her head to look at him. "Even when

asleep?"

He nodded.

"What kind of magic?"

"Emotional and physical manipulation."

There was a second of silence before Jack burst out laughing. "You mean she gave you a boner. You, Mr. Always Serious and Always About the Mission." He wheezed. "Are you sure it's not just because she's hot?"

His eyes narrowed. "Aye." He had gone up against a harem of succubi before and hadn't fallen under their power. Emma's magic was different. She wasn't just making him sexually attracted to her; she was weakening his resolve, making him feel as if he could trust her, as if he should protect her above all else. And although succubi made people subconsciously not target them in a fight, Emma's power was making him want to give her the world.

Still laughing, Jack headed for the door, no doubt not wanting to leave Hunter alone with someone so powerful. Although he might joke around all the time, he was actually a damn good agent.

"I'll let Hunter break her in first," Xeno said as the door shut behind Jack. "He brought her some clothes and personal items. Once she's relaxed, I'll interrogate her."

He frowned. Xeno had never needed someone to be relaxed before interrogation. Her power had always been strong enough to coax the truth out of anyone, even ancient demons. He wanted to ask her how she was holding up, if her powers were waning along with her wings, but he bit his tongue.

Past interactions had taught him she would avoid the answer. And Rogan didn't have the heart to kick her off this mission, not when Sebastian was the one who had tortured her for three years. Not when this mission could finally allow her to heal.

"Any idea who its parents are?" Xeno asked.

"Hades." After telling her about the river and Cerberus, he added, "And there's some sky god, but I doona know which one. As for who we're fighting against...I have no idea."

The silence spoke volumes, but neither of them had the courage to voice their thoughts aloud. They would wait until they were on the ground to question if they were batting for the right side. A god was fickle at the best of times.

Although they'd mellowed out a lot over the years, telling someone they were prettier than Aphrodite or more fearsome than Odin was a pretty surefire way of getting the both of you killed. Or cursed.

No, they would wait until they were on the ground before holding a proper discussion. Nothing like the feel of false security to loosen a few tongues.

Emma found herself surprisingly at ease as she talked to the man called Hunter. He might technically be one of her kidnappers, but he had such an easy smile, and the stories of his insane adventures across six other worlds were too captivating to resist.

"And that, my dear," he finished with a wise lift of his brow and a slow nod, "is why you should never upset a woman from Vira."

She laughed good heartedly at his reckless tale of misguided love, then told him he had definitely deserved it. He pretended to be wounded, but his exaggerated pain was quickly replaced by a grin that had her shaking her head in glee. At first it had been weird hearing herself laugh in her situation, but his easy manner had eventually worn her down, and now she chuckled easily.

"So you're all agents of the Myth, but what ah..." She trailed off, blushing madly as she realized her words could be considered extremely rude.

Hunter laughed. "What are we? It's a polite enough way to ask."

Emma gave him a nod to continue as she leaned forward, perched on the very edge of her seat.

"Well, Xeno, that's the lady, she's an angel, but I bet you already guessed that."

He gave her such a playful wink that Emma wasn't sure if he was joking or not. She might have only met the woman a few hours ago, but she was struggling to picture the blonde bombshell with a halo and wings. Weren't all angels supposed to be friendly, heartwarming, and lovely? The woman Emma had seen was as cold as ice and looked as if she sided more with death than with life.

"But – but where are her wings?" she asked in clear bafflement, not daring to voice her other objections.

"She keeps them hidden unless needed. Can't exactly go walking around with wings growing out of your back if you don't want to be dissected."

Emma tilted her head to the side as she looked toward the cockpit. Although that sounded logical enough, she still wasn't entirely sure if he was pulling her leg or not.

"And the others?"

"Well, Rogan – he did tell you his name, didn't he?" When she nodded, he quirked an eyebrow in exaggerated surprise. "He's a water elementalist."

"What does that mean?"

"He can control water in all its states."

She recalled the ball of water he'd put around her hand, then the whip he'd used to cut into the vampires. His eyes had been so cold.

Swallowing, Emma looked at Rogan. He was facing away from her, talking to a man of smaller stature with bright red hair and green eyes. They'd exited the cockpit some time ago, but not once had Rogan looked over at her.

Not that she was counting. Shaking her head, she asked, "And the guy he's talking to?"

"That's Jack. He's a trickster. Think Loki from *Thor* but with the ability to transform into animals and way less flair for the dramatic."

"And not as good looking, I would say," she teased as she finally managed to tear her eyes away from the dark-haired agent.

"Really? I always thought he was kind of hot." He blew a kiss to the trickster, and Emma laughed when Jack pretended to catch it and then smack it on his ass. She gave him a wave.

Her hand stilled when Rogan turned to look over his shoulder. His blue eyes snagged her, choking the air out of her lungs. As her breath caught in her throat, Emma quickly turned her attention back to Hunter, hoping her discomfort wasn't too obvious.

Hoarsely, she asked, "And what about you?"

"Me? I'm the best thing here." He paused for dramatic effect, but it was lost when he wiggled his eyebrows. "Why, I'm a hundred percent human."

She laughed first in good humor and then in full delight when he pulled a face of great offense.

"Oh, come on, Hunter; you're joking!"

His hands flew to his chest as he winced in mock pain. "Why, my dear, I would never joke about the great human race. We might not have any fancy abilities, but the best of us can outdo them anyway. That clearly makes us the better species."

A snort came from Jack even though he looked deep in

conversation with his leader, and Emma couldn't help but laugh.

"So is that all there are? Tricksters, angels, vampires, elementalists, werewolves, and witches?"

"Not by a long shot." He leaned back in his seat. "There are also telepaths, demons, fairies, shifters, astralists, echidnas, fey –"

"Echidnas?"

He grinned. "Not the little furry things you're thinking of. No, these are full on killing machines you do not want to mess with."

"But...echidnas?" She struggled to contain her laughter as she tried not to picture a little marsupial challenging Rogan to a duel.

Before Hunter could answer, a cold voice interrupted them. She didn't have to look over to know who it was, but that didn't stop her from doing so anyway. While his attention was focused on his teammate, Emma took the opportunity to appreciate the hard lines of Rogan's body. His jacket hid the majority of them, but they still bulged beneath it. Her eyes trailing down, she recalled his other bulge. His morning moan...

Squirming in her chair, she bit back one of her own, her hands and cheeks growing hot.

"Ye're needed in the cockpit," Rogan said gruffly. "I need to talk to Xeno."

"You can't just talk to her in there?" Hunter wondered. "I'm having a wonderful time getting to know the lovely Emma." He grinned. "Also, you seem to be scaring her. She was all relaxed before you came over."

Emma nearly choked as she angled her gaze to the ground. Her 'discomfort' had nothing to do with fear and everything to do with a sudden flair of sensitivity.

"If that was possible," Rogan said slowly, "then I

wouldn't be here, now would I?"

"Ah, I get it." Smiling, he leaned forward as if to share a secret, and Emma instinctively followed suit.

In a voice you could hear across the plane, Hunter whispered, "Boss is sweet on an echidna. Probably doesn't appreciate her being compared to a cute ball of fluff."

Sweet on... Her chest tightened. So it was definitely his work keeping him from having a girlfriend because there was no way in hell anyone he was interested in wouldn't return the attraction. The man was a walking god of good looks and masculinity. Not to mention, the hard feel of his cock would have a fasting nun desperate to eat...and be eaten.

Dear God, my therapy cannot come fast enough.

Winking at her, Hunter rose to his feet. He gave Rogan a grin despite the man's icy gaze. When he finally headed toward the cockpit, an awkward silence lingered in his wake.

Rogan needed to walk away. He shouldn't have even come over here. And he sure as all of Niflhel shouldn't have the urge to explain that the echidna in question was a fierce warrior whom he felt nothing but respect toward. Even friendship would be stretching it. Dominix wasn't cold like Xeno; she was just indifferent. To absolutely everything, and that made any kind of relationship with her nearly impossible.

She was simply a loyal comrade and a damn good fighter, and she'd saved his life more than once.

But if he told his captive that, it would be admitting he cared enough to explain. Which he didn't.

In an attempt to convince himself of this, Rogan turned on his heels and left without a word to her. But he could still hear her laughter, could still see the smiles she'd directed at Hunter.

And they ate at his gut something awful.

It's a fucking spell.

"You wanted to speak to me?"

As Xeno appeared beside him, Rogan stilled. The hasty excuse he had used to get Hunter to leave Emma's side seemed to be biting him in the ass already. He was trying to think of something to tell her when Xeno cut in for him.

"You want me to read her feelings."

With that single sentence, Rogan's chest tightened. Oh, aye. He wanted to know if she felt the same elemental claim he did. If she felt that somehow they were connected, their fate written together by a hand not their own.

But, of course, that would be stupid. Spellcasters never felt the pull of their own handiwork.

"Concerning the truth of her claims, as we discussed earlier," Xeno added not so subtly.

Crossing his arms, Rogan glared at her. "Aye. What other reason would there be?"

He refused to think about Emma nestled against him. Refused to pretend that his crossed arms were holding her to him. He had to keep fighting her spell. If she got him to attack his teammates out of jealousy, it would kill him.

Lowering her voice, she said, "I'm more than capable of taking point on this mission if you've been compromised."

His jaw ticked. Turning away so Emma wasn't even in his peripheral vision, he snapped, "I haven't."

But he didn't quite believe it.

FOURTEEN

"Hey."

"Hi. Xeno, right?" Emma asked as the tall leggy blonde claimed the seat Hunter had just vacated. She looked less scary now that Emma knew she was an angel.

Well, slightly. Very very slightly.

She swallowed.

"How are you holding up?"

A nervous laugh escaped her. She pressed her palms against her thighs. "Well, I was shot at, kidnapped, rudely interrogated, attacked by vampires, and have just been informed of the Myth – a whole other world, sorry, worlds of supernatural creatures that nobody ever knew existed. So good."

God, she wanted Hunter back. He would've laughed at that, helped her to relax.

But the woman in front of her was a mask of cold indifference. "Actually, there are quite a few humans that know of our existence," she said as she crossed her legs. "The WALL for instance."

When Emma frowned, Xeno elaborated, "The people at your sister's house."

So they weren't the mafia?

But then why...

Leaning forward, trying to make sense of all the thoughts running around her head, she asked, "What did they want with me?"

There was a moment of silence between them.

Trying not to fidget under the angel's cold blue stare, Emma dug her fingers into her thighs.

"They hunt supernatural creatures," Xeno said at length. "They were given an anonymous tip saying you were one."

Emma gasped. *What?* She hadn't even known these other worlds *existed* less than twenty-four hours ago! She didn't have any inhuman powers and had lived her entire life being one hundred percent human. A weird human, sure, with a bit of a weird lifestyle, but a hundred percent human nonetheless.

She had gone to public school, had gone on to amass a ridiculous amount of debt for a degree she hadn't even been able to use, and had gotten a shitty, low-paying job where she was treated like crap. That was all very typically human! She hadn't been like Liz who –

Oh God, Elizabeth!

How had she forgotten? She was only in this mess because of her sister. No one actually wanted plain old, boring Emma.

But then they were twins, so did that mean...?

She paled.

"My sister...what's wrong with her?" Her words were hoarse with trepidation. Liz must have been bitten. Or eaten a radioactive piece of bologna or got injected with –

Her heart stopped as she remembered the syringe the

man had tried to use on her.

Trembling, she squeezed her eyes shut.

"Mommy!"

Wrenching her eyes open, she dug her nails hard into her thighs so she wouldn't see whatever nightmare was waiting for her. She wouldn't pass out again. She wouldn't let her dreams –

Her throat tightened.

What if they weren't dreams?

What if they were something else?

Something more? Something otherworldly?

She shook her head.

No, they were just dreams.

Where I feel everything, taste everything... Where I know everyone, can recall a whole lifetime of memories...

They're just dreams.

Dreams that had the power to suck her under any time she let her guard down.

Dreams that fucked with her ability to tell them from reality.

Xeno's voice was cold and uncaring, ripping into her thoughts, giving her a bit of a reprieve. "Not sure. She popped up on our radar only a couple days ago."

"Mommy, don't leave me!"

"B-because of the attack on Zi-ann?"

When Xeno nodded, Emma forced herself to breathe. She instinctively searched around for Rogan. Her nails pressed into the thin fabric of her leggings.

When her eyes locked onto his, her breath caught. The pull of her nightmare faded. Her pulse started to calm. Swallowing, she kept her eyes on him. He stood with his arms crossed, his back against the wall of the plane. His attention was fully on her, his lips a thin line across his handsome face.

The air finally settling in her lungs, she exhaled slowly, then blinked. He took a step toward her before sharply turning away.

Collapsing back into her seat, Emma breathed out harshly. She felt as if she'd run a marathon. Or been beaten up by a MMA fighter.

Shuddering, she clenched her fists tight. She needed to stay calm. To think.

Xeno had said her sister had only popped up on their radar because of the attack on Xi'aghn. Maybe it hadn't been that bad. Maybe they'd just been mistaken, just like they and the WALL had been mistaken when they'd targeted her. Or –

"She must've been drugged or spelled or something?" It felt weird blaming magic already, but this whole situation was weird. Vampires existed for crying out loud! And angels. And – Her eyes flicked to where Rogan had been. Water elementalists with eyes that almost seemed to glow.

"She helped massacre dozens of people, including children," the angel said coldly. "She will not escape punishment."

Emma swallowed hard.

No. That couldn't be true.

With the burn of bile high in her throat, Emma surged to her feet and ran to the bathroom. Slamming the door shut behind her, she sagged against it, trembling with one hand to her mouth. How could it be that every time she thought things couldn't get worse, they did? What she wouldn't give to go back to her sister's house, running in a panic from the mafia.

"Mommy, come back! I promise to be good!"

Clutching her head in her hands, she willed the nightmare to leave her alone. For a moment, she wished Rogan was in here with her. But she quickly killed that thought. He wanted to imprison her sister for life. He wanted to take the only family Emma had left.

She couldn't ever trust him.

Crossing over to the shower, Emma wished she had grabbed the bag Hunter had been kind enough to pack. She needed familiarity right now even if it came in something lame like an old t-shirt. Needing to get under the soothing spray of hot water, Emma frantically grabbed at her shirt, tugging it up.

Hey, sis.

As Liz's voice cut through her mind, Emma froze, the shirt halfway off. Great, she was going crazy now. The first step was hearing voices. The second was –

It's really me.

Blinking rapidly, Emma struggled to comprehend.

What?

How?

"*Liz*?" she whispered feverishly. Her eyes darted to the bathroom door.

Shh. Don't speak. Just think and I can hear.

Emma's mouth opened and closed and opened again. Everything was moving too fast. When the hell had telepathy entered the chat?

Where are you? she thought, a heat creeping across her neck at the absurdity of it all. *Are you okay? Why can I hear you in my head? And why were you standing over that man with – with so much blood? My God, what is going on?*

Oh, Em, there's so much you need to know...

Rogan sank into the seat beside Xeno as he kept his eyes on the bathroom door. "So is she genuinely at a loss?" he asked.

"Yes."

A bittersweet weight settled in his chest at the proof of her innocence. But that also meant he'd dragged her into the deep end, flipped her life upside down, and destroyed any safe places she might've had. He couldn't imagine what thoughts were whirling in her head. He hadn't liked the panic in her eyes when he'd caught her gaze earlier.

"What else did ye feel?" he asked Xeno, telling himself he needed to know for the mission and not because of a primitive need to know she was okay.

"Terror and frustration."

Stop her! The god's voice was in a near panic, and Rogan was up and over the seat before Hades had finished his command.

"Xeno, the door!"

Reaching forward, the angel ripped it free of its hinges. A scream sounded in front of them, and every horrible thought about why flooded Rogan's head.

But no, she looked safe. Shivering in terror, but safe.

Jack, Xeno, and Snuffles crowded behind him, but he barely noticed. His attention was focused solely on the near heart attack before him.

"What are ye doing?" Rogan demanded, knowing her father wouldn't have warned him without good reason.

"I – I'm –"

"Well, spit it out!"

"Rogan, dude, you just scared the shit –" Hunter began as he came running out of the cockpit.

But before any sense could be made, Snuffles lunged past Rogan and sank his teeth into Emma's leg. She screamed in agony as her head fell back. Collapsing to the ground, she sat in a pool of blood.

No!

Pulling water from the toilet, Rogan shaped it into a

knife and slammed it into Snuffles' left eye. A terrifying howl shook the plane.

Stumbling around, Snuffles slammed his head into the side of the bathroom. His muscles rippled beneath his fur, and Rogan had a brief feeling of regret as the dog snapped and snarled so close to Emma's form.

Reaching down, he tried to haul her into his arms, only to jump back as the dog started to grow.

Screaming again, Emma curled up tight against the wall. Frantic, Rogan twisted a whip of water so he could grab her ankle, but Hunter was already reaching in past all the snapping teeth. Snagging her wrist, he yanked her out of the bathroom.

You fool! Get off the plane! Now*!* Hades command was barely heard over the rapid beat of his own pulse.

Wrapping an arm around Emma, Rogan turned toward the exit. Jack was already at the door with her box in his hands. As Hunter moved to join him, the plane lurched sideways.

Thud!

A growl of pain and fury filled the cabin, along with another strong *thud* that left Rogan chilled. Glancing over his shoulder, he saw Snuffles shaking his head and ramming his body into the shower. Broken glass littered the floor beneath him, but he didn't seem to notice the shards embedded in his paws.

As Snuffles' head split into three, five eyes looked over at Rogan. He growled.

Fuck.

Directing his whip of water at the side of the plane behind Jack, Rogan slashed across an aluminum rib. Xeno shouted behind him in an ancient tongue. Her toned body rammed into his shoulder as she leaped past. The side of the plane ripped open, the panel bending outward from the change of pressure. His eyes on Hunter, Rogan cursed.

And then he was being sucked out of the plane along with everyone else.

As they tumbled through the air, Emma screamed against his throat, her lips vibrating across his skin. He held her tightly as he looked around for Hunter. The man was only human. He wouldn't survive the fall unless Xeno grabbed him.

He's at seven o'clo – Fuck! Rogan shouted inside his head as soon as he remembered that Galvanor, the team's telepath, wasn't here. He hadn't answered the call to arms this morning and had yet to catch up with them.

Cursing, Rogan shoved a hand inside his jacket and pulled out a vial of bright pink water. He popped the lid and whipped the water through air, aiming it for Hunter. He wrapped it around the man's body, marking him for Xeno to find through all the rubble.

A chunk of debris hit Rogan on the shoulder. He gritted his teeth against the sharp stab of pain and tightened his arm around Emma. She might be a descendant and would undoubtedly survive the crash, but the fall would still hurt her. And the idea of her in pain, especially because of him... Everything inside him rebelled.

As they tumbled through the air, he struggled to keep the water wrapped around Hunter. His concentration was broken every time a piece of debris cut across his body. Every time Emma's scream reverberated against his neck, her lips pushing against his skin as she trembled in his arms.

But Rogan would run himself into the ground before letting one of his agents die. Twisting in the air, he closed his eyes and concentrated on the water around Hunter. As sweat beaded along his brow and his magic pulled at every one of his muscles, weakening him, weakening his hold on Emma, he forced the water to slow its descent.

Ice started forming around the man. Hunter's heart rate slowed; his body shivered. Throwing everything he had into his magic, Rogan forced the ice back into a warm liquid. Blood dripped from his nose from the overuse of magic. His consciousness started to wane.

But just as the darkness closed in, he felt Xeno break through the water barrier and wrap Hunter in her arms.

With a shudder, Rogan released all of his power. The world went black.

And Emma slipped from his arms.

FIFTEEN

Screaming, Emma fell through the air as the debris of the plane rained down around her. Blood rushed to her head and then down to her feet as she tumbled end over end. She was falling too fast, just like Rogan now was. Struggling against the wind, she spread her arms and legs out, hoping it would slow her descent.

A piece of debris slammed into her arm. She screamed as she curled her bleeding limb against her chest. Tears running down her face, she forced her arm back out again. She needed to slow down first. Everything else would have to wait.

But just as she started to slow, something grabbed her from behind.

She screamed as she started to rise. Looking down at her chest, she found a large scaly talon wrapped around her. Another scream ripped free as she looked up at the massive bird it was attached to.

It was going to eat her. It was going to peck her alive, rip her up limb by limb, and then regurgitate her for its babies.

Oh my God, just drop me.

"Emma!"

At the broken sound of a masculine voice, she looked over to her left. Rogan was there, held in another talon.

She reached for him instinctively, trusting him to save her. His fingers clasped hers and squeezed. He tilted his head in a single nod, telling her it would be okay.

But how the fuck was it going to be okay?

Everything was just getting worse.

Yesterday, the worst thing that had happened to her had been getting pissed on by a small yappie dog. That evening, she'd been attacked by what she'd thought was the mafia. Then she'd been kidnapped from them by a man who could control water and wasn't even human. Her dog turned out to be a three headed monster –

Her eyes widened.

Cerberus.

Oh my God. Does that mean Hades is real? All the other gods? Fuck. Is it too late to not be an atheist?

She groaned and started to pray. *Hades, I'm so sorry for never believing in you, but I believe in you now. And if you let me survive this, I swear I'll...* She stopped, having no idea what she was supposed to offer him. Did they still accept live sacrifices or had they grown up from that? She really hoped they had because she didn't think she could bring herself to kill a virgin.

My child, I've waited so long to speak to you.

Eyes widening, she screamed. She hadn't expected him to actually reply.

But now is not the time. His deep baritone moved through her skull, soothing and freaking her out all at once. *You will survive the fall. Trust the man beside you until you find Elizabeth.* He paused, and the silence that followed was heavy.

We'll speak soon, he continued, *but first, I have a few things to attend to.*

And then he was gone, leaving her trembling in the air as she struggled to keep hold of the mess her mind and life had become.

What the ever loving fuck?

As soon as they landed, Emma collapsed to her knees and vomited all over the ground. She cradled her bleeding arm to her chest, hoping it wasn't broken. Shakily, she looked up at Rogan.

He crouched down beside her, his lips in a grim line. "Let me look at it, lass." When he reached forward, she let him take her arm. A sharp hiss escaped her lips as tears blurred her vision.

"I doona think it's broken. Ye should heal in a couple hours."

She blinked. "Wait, what now?"

He frowned, studying her in a silence that made her shiver. "If ye're not using magic, then what are ye doing to me?" He whispered it so softly, she almost missed it.

And by the time the words registered, he was back on his feet and striding away.

Blinking rapidly, she turned to follow, needing answers to all the questions flurrying around in her skull. But when her mouth opened, it was only for her jaw to drop to her chest.

An angel.

Xeno is an actual fucking angel.

Her wings were spread out behind her, white feathers glowing softly, like the sun behind a cloud. But they were crooked, and –

Emma gasped.

Broken. They were broken. Patches of feathers as wide as a dinner plate were missing. Blood seeped from large open wounds. Emma would've thought the damage had occurred today if not for the puss oozing scars. This was old damage that wasn't healing.

"Want to do the honors, here, boss?" At Hunter's easy tone, Emma snapped her gaze away from Xeno. Her cheeks heated. She hoped no one had noticed her staring.

Walking over to him, Rogan grabbed his left arm and shoulder. There was a sickening pop as Hunter's shoulder clicked back into place, but the only one that seemed bothered by it was her. Even Hunter didn't seem phased, rotating his arm as if he was warming up for a game of baseball rather than from a dislocation.

"Did anyone see where Snuffles fell?" Rogan asked.

The giant bird that had saved them ruffled its feathers. Then it dropped to the ground, twisting in agony as it shifted into a naked Jack. Emma's mouth opened further.

Cracking his neck side to side, Jack said, "If you're talking about that thing you stabbed in the eye, it fell that way." He rubbed his jaw, pain still lingering in his eyes as he pointed.

"Is it wise to call him Snuffles?" Hunter asked.

Oh fuck. Her blood chilled. The blood drained from her face. *He's going to kill me for naming him something so stupid.*

"Aye," Rogan said sharply.

Her eyes flew to his. *What a lying bastard.* "He already has a name, doesn't he?" she asked, not yet ready to say his name aloud. Not ready to admit that Hades' personal guard dog was by her side.

Or rather, wherever he was now, having landed far away from them. *Thank God – or Hades, or whoever I'm supposed to thank.*

Rounding on her, looking her dead in the eye, Rogan said, "Aye, it's Snuffles." Turning to Jack, he asked, "Mind carrying her? Her leg could use the break."

My leg?

Emma looked down, then immediately collapsed at the sight of all the blood. Pain ricocheted up her leg, pulsing from the large bite mark Snuffles had given her now that the adrenaline had worn off. Feeling queasy, she wrapped her arms around her stomach and groaned.

Dropping down onto all fours, Jack's body twisted and cracked unnaturally. A few seconds later, he'd shifted into a brown and white painted horse. His head towered half a foot above Rogan's, and his mane was pristine white. Flicking his hair out of his green human eyes, he neighed once and then flashed his teeth.

Emma blinked.

Then swallowed hard.

Shaking her head, she refused to let the panic drown her.

Rogan stopped in front of her, then leaned down to pick her up. Gritting her teeth against the pain in her leg and arm, she held on as well as she could. Just as he'd settled her on the horse that was Jack, three bloodcurdling howls shattered the air behind them. She turned and saw a bolt of lighting whip down from the sky somewhere in its direction.

Hunter's mouth turned up in grim humor. "I vote we go that way," he said, pointing in the opposite direction.

"Aye," Rogan agreed. "I saw a small village a few miles away. We'll grab a car and drive to the closest hotel."

Jack tossed his head in agreement.

When a thick blue blanket was handed to her, pulled out of Rogan's dark blue leather jacket, Emma took it without a word. 'Impossible' didn't seem to have much meaning anymore.

A crazy laugh bubbled up in her throat. *Don't lose it now.*

Swallowing down her urge to break, she wrapped the blanket around herself and held on tight to Jack's mane.

Liz had spoken to her.

That meant she was alive.

And she was the only thing that mattered.

SIXTEEN

Hades clenched his fist, wanting to kill the dumbass Elv've'Nor for being so stupid. As he sat on his throne in the Graeca Underworld, he rotated bright blue fire in the palm of his hand. It twisted through his fingers, feeding on his emotions to hold the color of sadness and pain, of torment and loss, of guilt and shame.

His jaw tightened as anger flared inside him, painting his fire red. One of his daughters was being tortured by that sadistic vampire, Sebastian, and the other had just given away her position to him. He could be there in a second, grab her, and disappear before that *dumbass Elv've'Nor* even knew what hit him.

Cerberus was supposed to stop that from happening, but the beast had turned out to be a fucking *pussy cat.* After getting one little stick in his eye, he'd thrown a massive hissy fit. The useless fucker.

The flames roared higher, turned a darker red.

And thanks to the fucking Holy Blood Contract he'd been forced to sign, Hades couldn't go save her himself.

He was stuck in this blasted hole for another 488 years as per the terms of his punishment. The next time he was topside, he was going to kill every direct offspring of the bastards who had forced him to sign the HBC.

The flames turned black, the color of regret. If he killed all those people, he'd have to bring some down here, and he really didn't want any more souls in his kingdom. Perhaps, he could just torture them for an eternity on the Seven Planes...

Yes, that was an idea.

Closing his fist, he snuffed out the flames. Taking a deep breath, he forced himself to relax. His daughters, being descendants, couldn't truly die unless they were killed by a godslayer, and there hadn't been talk of one of those in a millennium.

The most lethal thing Sebastian could do to them was send their souls to one of the underworlds, as he'd done with Rakian. But as Hades knew all too well, there were many things far worse than death.

As his flames flickered a bright blue, he wondered if his children experienced Dethros, the vivid reliving of a soul's last moments before they needed to be guided to the Underworld. He'd had since the first death to get used to the agony each one brought, and now few registered in his mind. Only the most torturous deaths whispered inside his skull these days, but even those he barely noticed.

How would Emma and Elizabeth fare, born straight into a time where thousands of people died in a single minute across all of the Planes?

The flame turned yellow with hope that maybe they had not inherited the skill that made him an ideal ruler of the dead. Maybe for once, Fate had been kind...

Blue light once again flickered across his face.

In a sudden roar, lightning crackled around the room.

Strikes flew out from every direction. They burned so fiercely they left scorch marks on the walls, which were made out of cooled lava. One skipped by Hades' seat, sizzling his black pants due to its close proximity.

The Lord of the Underworld didn't so much as twitch.

He was well used to his brother's flamboyant arrivals and knew that each bolt, despite the seeming chaos, was meticulously controlled. Not that Zeus wouldn't direct one straight at him, he thought warily as he remembered all too well the half dozen times his brother had done just that.

Still, he didn't move when another arced close by. He merely snuffed out the green flames in his hand, not wanting to leave an open view into the workings of his mind. With a patience that killed him, Hades waited for the theatrics to stop.

Zeus always had been a show off.

"Brother!" A solid shape eventually formed in the blinding middle of the lightning. If it wasn't for the regal arrogance in the newcomer's stance, no one would think the two of them were related.

Zeus was built like a linebacker with a taste for the extravagant. His white tailored suit crackled with tiny sparks of electricity and his tie held the very essence of a sunrise. Upon his head sat a crown of gold made of such craftsmanship even Aphrodite (or Zeus' shoulder length, beach blond hair) couldn't compete with its beauty.

And then there was Hades. Dressed in black jeans and a casual gray shirt, he clearly didn't put much effort, if any, into his appearance. His black hair was cut short and nothing adorned his head. How the two weren't even half siblings was beyond him.

Grinning like the fool he was, Zeus spread open his arms in greetings. "I'd tell you you look like shit, brother, but that would be offensive. To the shit."

"Always a pleasure to have your company." Hades' sarcasm was unmissable and yet, Zeus still seemed to miss it.

"It is, isn't it?" the Graeca God of the Sky smirked.

Hades barely stopped himself from rolling his eyes. They might not get along at the best of times (mostly because he found his youngest brother to be extremely annoying), but when push came to shove, they always had each other's backs. Well, except for that one time in Kyravic...

Though, really, who could blame them? That woman had put Helen of Troy to shame with her deep red hair and silver eyes. Zeus, in his desire to show off, had shot a lightning bolt at Hades' crotch. Unfortunately, very very unfortunately, the sky god had actually managed to hit a bullseye that time. Then the Underlord had retaliated.

Which was unfortunate for Poseidon given the amount Hades had had to drink.

They had been so consumed by their brotherly battle, that none one of them had noticed the lady in question was robbing them blind. Their manly pride and bodies had been hurt, names had been called, and some very harsh things had been said by the Sea God. Eventually, however, they'd made up.

Or rather, Zeus and Hades had made up. Poseidon was still very much pissed given his Trident had been stolen. Instead of helping him retrieve it, the two Olympians had brilliantly drank in order to 'forget his harsh words' until eventually, they had passed out drunk. Come the next day, her very memory had vanished from everyone's minds except theirs.

Five thousand years later and no one had ever seen her nor any of the trinkets she had stolen. Losing his Trident had left Poseidon vulnerable to attack – or it would have done if his rage hadn't stepped up to the plate. Not even his powerful brothers thought to visit.

Shaking the memory away, Hades focused his thoughts back on the present. "So what have you found out?"

"Always to the point." Zeus sighed as if that was an insult. "There are whispers of a war brewing unless the goddess you put with child comes forth."

"No one knows who she is?" Hades nearly rose from his throne. The gods gossiped about every little thing, regardless of whether there was any fact to it or not.

"Well, no. There are probably three people who know. Her, given she was the one who gave birth." He cocked his head to the side, a smile teasing his lips. "Unless she bears child like a bear, where they just appear and she has no actual idea if they're hers or not, but as far as I know goddesses don't do that."

Hades clenched his jaw but didn't interrupt. If he did, Zeus would take it as an excuse to spout even more irrelevant facts about bears.

"You, but you claim not to remember –"

"I don't," he gritted out, his eyes smoldering with red flames.

Zeus merely dismissed his defense with a wave of the hand. "And whoever is helping her. She broke a Holy Blood Contract. For someone not to have noticed her punishment, she must be having help from someone very powerful indeed."

Hades' eyes grew cold in calculation. "And a less obvious punishment," he growled. The first he had learned about his recent fatherhood had been exactly one second before every other bloody deity. He had tried to leave with a group of friends, as he had on many occasions, when he'd been met with an invisible force at the door of his domain. It'd flung him backward and slammed him into the far wall. His friends, laughing their asses off, had spread the word of his punishment immediately. He hadn't talked to Hermes or Dionysus since. *The bastards.*

Focusing on the matter at hand, Hades turned his thoughts to who could've fathered his children. The two queens currently sitting on the Three Thrones: Hela and Freya, were impossible choices. Their punishment was to lose their and their partner's right to rule. Given there hadn't been any play of musical chairs, the math simply didn't add up.

The Ladies of the Underworlds could also be discounted given they faced the same consequence Hades did. Not one of them ever failed to escape her suffocating kingdom whenever the chance arose.

As for the minor goddesses, they were, well, minor.

This left the two brothers with a much shorter list of possibilities of who could have mothered Hades' children.

"What's the Raven Queen been up to these days?" Hades asked melancholy as if inquiring about an old friend.

The Raven Queen was their code name for Morrighan. Given all gods and goddesses could eavesdrop on any conversation once their name was spoken, the two brothers had decided to play it safe and come up with a code name for everyone.

"Same old, same old," Zeus replied. "She's hanging out on battlefields, waiting for her feast and generally creeping everyone out. She would definitely have the power to fight a Holy Curse, but..." He lifted a single shoulder and let it fall again. "It's not really her style, is it? Plus, last I heard, didn't she turn you down?"

Bloody gossips.

Zeus let out a roll of thunderous laughter. "Gotta keep

a clear head, brother; can't be letting your emotions cloud the game."

"Given the clusterfuck your mind normally is, I'm surprised you know what clear is," Hades muttered.

"What?" Zeus asked, as if his sensitive ears hadn't heard.

"I said, then what about one of the love or sex goddesses? This sort of thing is right up their alley."

"Sex sure, but to birth a child and break an HBC?" He shook his head. "The sex goddesses would never be able to orgasm until the curse is lifted. Can you imagine the pent up frustration of never releasing? And then times that by all the stars on every plane because your entire being craves sex. I would bet on the queens of the Three Thrones before one of them."

Zeus shuddered and Hades barely hid his wince.

"As for the love goddesses, I've found that they would be doomed to fall in love with the father only to have him always spurn them even if their love was true. It would drive them mad."

"Mad enough to start a war? To hire a bunch of made vamps in an attempt to kill my daughter?" Made vamps who had all happened to be followers of one of the other gods, meaning they hadn't arrived in his kingdom upon death.

Zeus paused as his eyes grew shrewd and lightning cracked around the irises. The human saying of one's eyes were the window to their soul was a bygone of their memories of the Myth and for very good reason. Every creature could have their emotions read from their eyes, even the mighty gods. And the Graeca God of the Sky was not happy with the prospect of a civil war.

"Have you had any obsessive goddesses recently?"

"Nothing more than normal," Hades sighed as he

slouched back in his chair. "Although..."

His eyes narrowed as he tried to recall a memory that didn't want to be found. Black flames curled around the fingers of both hands as he fought the magic shrouding this particular moment. It was fleeting, blurry, and he fought to bring it into focus. Fortunately, Zeus knew enough of his brother's color coding to know when to keep his mouth shut so he could think.

Hip length, strawberry blonde hair bouncing behind ivory shoulders. Warm thighs interchanging with the cool air as she moved up and down, up and down. A necklace gleaming bright and familiar...but it was impossible. How could she have not faced the consequence?

The flames burned the color of dried blood. When Hades finally met Zeus' eyes, his brother grinned like a wolf closing in on its prey.

"I can't see their mother, but the necklace she wore was courtesy of the Valkyrie Gifter."

And just like that, the wolf frantically realized the rabbit he had thought he was chasing, was, in fact, a fully grown dragon. And she was royally pissed.

SEVENTEEN

She still hadn't healed.

It had been two hours since Snuffles had bitten Emma, and the slice across her arm hadn't been that deep. A person with her power should have fully healed by the time they'd made it off the fells and into a small village. But now, a long car ride later, she was still shivering in the backseat, the blanket wrapped around her.

Her – the daughter of two gods. A woman with more power in her pinkie than everyone else in this car had combined.

His eyes going back to the road, Rogan glanced at the welcome sign to Ballina, Ireland. His grip tightened on the wheel.

But if she didn't have access to her powers, if somehow, she hadn't entered her ascension like most did during puberty, then his time with her had been real. The heels hadn't been spelled. She hadn't captured him in some magical illusion that made him want to trust her against his better judgement.

And she hadn't played him into attacking Snuffles, into almost killing a member of his team.

Fuck. That had all been on him.

"You sure it's not just because she's hot?" Jack's words came back to him like a bug one couldn't shake. Rogan had dismissed that possibility so quickly before. In nearly six decades, he'd never been tempted. But now? Knowing she wasn't capable of even healing herself?

His jaw tightened as he pulled into the lot of a hotel. He glanced up at the rear-view mirror. Their eyes locked. Her face was pale. She was still shaking.

Fighting every urge to ask her how she was, Rogan opened the driver's door and stepped out. He walked into reception and booked three rooms for them. Xeno would stay with Emma tonight... Hunter and Jack in another. And then him on his own.

His stomach tightened at the idea of spending the night without her, but it was now undeniably clear he was compromised. Xeno would need to take point and he –

His foot stopped mid-step.

His eyes rose to the car as Xeno and the others climbed out. His mind whirled, a thought rising through the chaos.

In over six decades, he'd never been tempted...

No.

The pull to her had been instant.

Oh Hades' fire.

He had put his entire team in danger, nearly getting Hunter killed, because she'd been hurt...

Fuck.

Emma wobbled on her feet, and he took a step toward her. Her face was still pale, but it held more color than it had earlier. Perhaps she was healing. Perhaps she had good, strong magic but was just trying to hide it?

But he knew even as he thought it that it wasn't true.

She wasn't an evil descendant working with Sebastian, trying to trick him into lowering his guard.

She had never known this world existed until he'd thrown her into it.

She'd never accessed her powers.

The pull he'd been feeling all this time was because she was his bloody lifemate – the literal other half of his soul.

At the start of everyone's first life, their souls were ripped in two by the gods and flung separately into the worlds. Most people never met their lifemate before the true death. There were billions upon billions of people to sift through, maybe trillions once you counted all the different timelines. The fact that he'd found her in her first life... The odds of that were slim but not impossible.

Fuck.

She took a hesitant step forward and nearly collapsed. Rogan was beside her in a second, holding her steady. Ignoring the looks of his team, he scooped her up in his arms and carried her up the stairs. She stared at him, exhaustion and gratitude clear in her eyes as her good arm wrapped around his neck. When she relaxed on a trusting sigh, his grip tightened.

She was his lifemate.

He could feel that truth in his very bones. His soul. And he hated it.

He was going to have to choose between saving her or the Seven Planes. He could not do both. Emma's very existence would kill them all. The gods would go to war. The Royal Courts would want her imprisoned. People would fear her, try to assassinate her as she slept. Rogan would have to quit the Elv've'Norc and take her into hiding. It would be a life constantly on the run from both his old friends and gods alike.

A future with her would be impossible.

He had to accept that.

Shifting her in his arms, balancing her with one hand, Rogan used his other to slide the key card into the lock of Xeno's room. He stepped inside and lowered Emma onto the first of the two beds. Her arm dropped from around his neck, making him feel barren. Crouching in front of her, he gently lifted her hurt leg. The bleeding had stopped naturally, but the wound had yet to heal.

"Xeno," he requested, looking up at her as she closed the door behind them. As an angel, she could heal nearly any wound or sickness. Only those given by gods or specific magical items were outside her ability.

Her lips tight, Xeno glanced at Hunter. She didn't need to explain further. The energy she'd needed to catch him, to save him had drained her. At her peak, today's events wouldn't even have registered as activities, but given how far she'd fallen, any use of her wings set her back for hours, if not days.

Guilt riding him, Rogan forced himself to stand and take a step away from Emma.

He couldn't do anything for her. He couldn't heal her broken heart and mind. He couldn't save her.

But he could save countless others.

Slipping a hand into his pocket, he pulled out a small blue stone with runes of silence and secrecy etched into one side. He rubbed his thumb across the marks, and its magic swept around the room, following the walls, sealing them in. Any noise they made wouldn't penetrate the barrier until the door or window was opened – or one of the walls was broken.

There was a moment of tense silence as his team waited for him to take the lead in this interrogation.

Crossing his arms, locking his hands away from her, Rogan regained the aloof professionalism he was known for. "How did ye contact yer sister on the plane?"

Emma looked at him, her eyes half-lidded under the weight of exhaustion. "I didn't. She did. I suddenly heard her in my head. It nearly scared me to death."

"But ye could communicate back."

"Yeah. No idea how, but yeah."

"And what did she want?"

Her shoulders tensed and she looked off in the distance. The urge to stop the questioning, to hold her in his arms while she regained her strength swept through him like a tsunami. Digging his fingers into his arms, he forced himself to stay silent.

Eventually, she answered on a whisper. "For me to die."

His eyes flew to Xeno's for confirmation. As an angel, she could detect whenever someone was lying.

She gave the slightest nod. *Truth.*

Rage clawing through him, he fought the impulsive need to fight, to defend his lifemate from whatever dared threaten her life – even if it was her own flesh and blood.

"Why would she want that?" he bit out, giving himself something to focus on other than the violent urges inside him.

Emma shook her head. "Because she believes death is better than falling into Sebastian's clutches, and he –" She swallowed, her eyes blinking rapidly to hold back tears. "He wants me."

An image of Sebastian broken and bloody filled his mind. He wanted the bastard to hurt. He wanted him to die by his own hands. If the vampire ever laid a hand on Emma, Rogan would boil the water inside his blood and kill him from the inside out.

"What else did she say?" Xeno cut in.

Hugging herself, her eyes still on him, she whispered, "That she was having a wonderful time in Europe and had met this fantastic guy, who was really hung." She ran a hand through her messy black hair, tugging at the knots. "They were getting married, and that's why she wanted me to come over. The box was just a ploy. They were going to surprise me with the news when I delivered it to them."

She stayed quiet for a few seconds.

The knot in his stomach tightened.

The urge to protect her from her own memories nearly crumbled his resolve.

We need to know what she knows.

"Liz said there were entire worlds we weren't privy to. That we had a lot of power and that Sebastian wanted to help us access it so we wouldn't be afraid. He knew that I had been kidnapped and wanted to help rescue me."

"She say what these powers were?" Hunter asked gently.

She shook her head. "No, just that I have some too."

"What was the coded message?"

Her eyes finally left his and settled on Hunter. "How did you know there was one?"

He smiled softly. "You move every couple of years. You don't have an online presence. You knew there was a coded message she was telling you. How long have you been on the run?"

She swallowed and dropped her arms. "We're part of WITSEC. Our mom rolled on a mafia boss back..." Tears glistened behind her lashes. "Back when she was pregnant with us." Brushing at her eyes, she added, "She never told us who our father was, just that he was dead."

Hunter and Jack snorted, then coughed to cover it up. Rogan glanced at them but didn't say anything. The fact that neither had cracked a joke about Hades being dead was a great improvement on their usual behavior.

Taking a deep breath, Emma looked over at Rogan again. Her eyes were full of desperation and trust. With no one else to turn to, of course she would look at him, but he now knew it was more than that. She felt the magnetic pull of their souls even if she didn't know that's what it was.

He wanted to go to her, to wrap her in his arms and feel whole. He wanted to promise her he'd never let anyone hurt her. He wanted to tell her what a lifemate was, that she was his and he was hers. But being an Elv've'Nor wasn't about doing what you wanted. It was about protecting those who couldn't protect themselves.

His stomach twisting into a knot, his soul screaming at the distance between them, Rogan locked his feet where they were.

Tears trickled down her cheeks. Her breaths started coming faster. He shuffled a step forward, then stopped.

"I l-let her travel Europe alone. I should have...I should have gone with h-her instead of just making a c-c-code." Squeezing her eyes shut, she folded in on herself, crying through broken sobs.

"We'll find her, love," he promised before he could stop himself, his heart wrenching with every shake of her shoulders. "Ye just have to trust us." *Trust me.*

"But she's in trouble...because of me. I should've been there. I...I could've..." She waved her free hand as if she didn't know what to do with it.

Cursing under his breath, Rogan went to her. He cupped her cheek and forced her to look at him. Her lips trembled, but her eyes held his with a fierceness that left him shaken. He knew all too well what it was like to live with the guilt of 'what if.' What if he'd run faster? What if he'd made the choice to go in first? What if he had never gone home that day? Would those people, his mother still be alive?

Pushing his own grief and guilt down, Rogan focused on the pain of his lifemate. "Sebastian is thousands of years old, love. Ye couldn't have done anything to save her. But ye can now."

Tears flowed down her cheeks. "How? I can't even...I can't do *anything*."

Pulling her hands free of his, she placed them palm down on her thighs and rubbed them hard. "All I... All I c-c-can do is get us...thrown out of a plane. I just... I just... I make more *trouble*."

"Actually, Rogan got us thrown out," Jack offered helpfully. She choked on a sniffle.

"And you have magic," Hunter added. "Just look at your leg and arm."

She froze, as did Rogan. Their eyes dropped to her leg at the same time. Flawless skin stared back at him. *How?* She hadn't healed at all in the car ride here, but within a few minutes, the bone-deep bite had healed. And her arm...

He glanced at Xeno, looking for answers. A lifemate's bond had no effect on one's ability to heal.

The angel's lips were tight. She gave a subtle shake of her head. She didn't seem to know what was going on either.

Turning back to Emma, Rogan continued softly, "Ye can help by telling us what ye know about her situation. Was there anything else she said?"

She sucked in a sharp breath, her face red and splotchy. Wiping at her eyes, she took a few moments to breathe. But when she started to shake harder, Rogan wrapped an arm around her and pulled her against his chest. "Just breathe, love. Ye've got this. We'll get her back."

Leaning into him, she pressed her face against the

crook of his shoulder. The wetness of her tears seeped through his shirt. She spoke against his chest, her words muffled and broken. "She mentioned a wedding. That means all eyes are on the bride, and considering I had her box...she wanted me to look in it." She pushed further into him. His arm tightened as if he could shield her from all her pain. "There was something in the box, something important, and I just...I never looked."

She shuddered. A sob vibrated against his chest. "She said, 'I love you.' Liz never says, 'I love you.' I think she's going to kill herself."

Swearing, Rogan wrapped both his arms around her. He didn't care that he was supposed to be keeping his distance anymore. He didn't care that his second-in-command would question his ability to lead them on this mission. All he cared about was his lifemate crying in his arms. The utter pain and helplessness he was feeling.

"Everyone out," he said softly.

"Rogan –"

He glanced over Emma's head at Xeno, his eyes hard. Digging into his pocket, he tossed her the other two hotel keys. "Ye are in with Hunter tonight. See if ye can't figure out who her parents are. Jack, find us some wheels." His eyes landed on Hunter. "Call Tegan to see where Galvanor is. He should've been here by now." The man's telepathy would've led him right to them regardless of where they were.

"What about Cer– Snuffles?" Jack asked as he pocketed the key Xeno gave him. "What if he turns up?"

"Then we pray he's not too pissed at me when he arrives."

EIGHTEEN

Snuffles was bloody furious when he finally dragged himself onto land. Zeus had struck him with a lightning bolt as he fell, flinging him far into the Atlantic Ocean. His other two heads had yet to recede, and, dripping wet, they snapped and snarled at each other with promised growls of revenge.

They were going to rip that blasted elementalist apart limb by fucking limb, starting with his cock.

Shaking the water from his coat, Cerberus turned his three noses to the sky and howled. Picking up the scent of his prey, he dashed through the rain with thundering steps. His teeth flashed dangerously when he reached the other side of the small island.

Ireland sat in the distance, and without breaking stride, Cerberus bounded into the frigid, rough water. His desire for revenge multiplied with every wave that splashed him in the face.

Snarling, he imagined each head biting into Rogan's pathetic, flimsy flesh.

NINETEEN

What the fuck was she doing here? She should be out there, hailing a taxi to the airport, running to her sister's aid. Liz was going to kill herself, and Emma was just *here.* In the arms of a man she barely knew. Crying like the useless coward she was.

Because there were *vampires* now.

And *gods.*

And *Cerberus.*

And a man who made her feel safe despite it all.

She let out a broken laugh. She couldn't even feel safe without feeling completely overwhelmed. How the fuck was she going to save her sister?

Squeezing her eyes shut, Emma struggled to control her breathing. But on the edge of each breath, her nightmares crawled toward her, digging their sharp claws into her mind, dragging her away from this reality.

And she almost wanted to run toward them.

Because the pain of being stabbed and the guilt of killing some imaginary child was nothing to the absolute agony she was going through.

"It's going to be okay, love." His arms tightened around her. She wanted to push them off and pull them closer at the same time. She wanted comfort while expressing her anger and frustration and helplessness. She wanted to believe it was all going to be okay even though she knew, right below the surface of her consciousness, that it would never be okay again.

Liz was in the hands of a sadistic monster wanted by some fantasy special ops team.

She was being tortured, beaten and starved at the very least going by the bruises on and haggardness of her cheeks.

She was going through Hell and Emma was...Emma was *here.*

In the arms of a man who wanted to throw her sister in jail for life, as if she hasn't already been through enough.

Liz would never recover from this.

And Emma would never recover from letting her down.

Choking down her grief, she placed her hands on Rogan's chest and shoved. "Get off me."

He'd shifted away as soon as she'd spoken, and the absence of his body left her chilled.

Sniffling, she pressed the bottom of her palms into her eyes and breathed.

She did not have the time to cry. Liz needed her.

Sucking in a great big ragged breath, she asked, "How do you... How do you kill a vampire? Garlic?" She winced at how stupid that sounded to actually say aloud. "A wooden stake through the heart?"

He nodded. "Aye, if ye can get a wooden stake to pierce Sebastian's heart, that'll do." He smiled softly. "But a knife would work better. Easier, aye."

Heat filled her cheeks. "It doesn't have to be wood?"

He shook his head slowly. "Anything hitting our hearts will do, or ye can sever it from our chests. Ye can also cut off our heads, burn us with fire, poison us, infect us, and kill us a thousand other ways."

For the first time, hope started to fill her chest. She grabbed onto it with both hands and squeezed it hard. "You killed those vampires with water?"

He dug into his jacket pocket and pulled out a small vial. Holding it up to her, he let her look at the clear liquid for a second. It had a tinge of teal to it. "This is holy water, and it only works on made vampires. Sebastian is a born one. It won't do so much as give him a rash."

"Holy water... Does that mean –" She lowered her voice. "That God's real?" And the devil? And hell? And angels? Her heart twisted. Could she pray for Liz's survival? Could she ask an angel to guard her? A merciful god to listen?

"Nay. He was created by the SCU as a way for humans to forget about the Seven Planes."

Her head swarmed. "Oh... Wait." Her eyes widened. "The SCU as in the Special Crimes Unit?" They were in the news quite often. If the FBI or CIA or MI6 or any other government organization couldn't solve a big crime, then they called in the SCU. They specialized in serial killers and high-intelligence criminals. They went all around the world. *How has no one ever noticed?*

He nodded and she felt as if she'd been splashed with cold water.

"Holy fuck. They're just operating out in the open?"

"Aye. They keep our world a secret. They'll clean up the mess we made at the hotel, wipe the minds of any witnesses."

Her mouth dropped open. "They can do that? Like 'look into the light'?"

His brow furrowed. "I'm unfamiliar with that phrase, so I can't say."

"You've never seen *Men in Black*?" *Of course he hasn't, you dimwit. He's an alien, remember?*

Is he an alien?

She opened her mouth, then closed it again. She had way too many questions to go down that road right now. Breathing out strongly, she asked, "Can we call the SCU now? Can we get them to save Liz?" Tears burned her eyes, but she was too burned out to create enough water for them to fall down her cheeks.

"Nay. The SCU is well trained, but Sebastian is nearly five thousand years old. He and Rakian almost destroyed Earth the last time they were here. Even with their advancement in technology, the SCU wouldn't stand a chance." He paused. "We also have no idea where he is. Sebastian's been in hiding for nearly three and a half thousand years. He came out a few years ago." His jaw tightened. "We've been trying to grab him ever since."

That hope Emma had felt died a horrible, twisted death. They'd been hunting him for millennia, and they'd never caught him. *Oh God. I'm never going to see Liz again.*

Her stomach twisting, she wrapped her arms around herself. Her eyes lingered on her leg. "Can Liz heal?" she asked softly.

"Aye."

She didn't know if that made it better or worse. If Liz tried to kill herself, would she know how to do it? Or would she blissfully think she was dying only to wake up healed, stuck in the nightmare all over again?

She closed her eyes, but she was dried out of all her tears. Her lip wobbling, she sucked in a ragged breath. "Tell me what I can do."

His weight shifted on the bed. She tensed, expecting

him to touch her, but he never did. "Ye get some sleep."

"I don't want to –"

His finger touched her lips. She shivered as she fought the sudden urge to open her mouth and suck him in. Or to flick her tongue out and taste him. The silence stretched between them, and through it all, she could hear his breathing. Short and quick and ragged just like hers. Her heart pounding, his finger still on her lips, not daring to open her eyes, she asked, "Rogan?"

A groan was pulled from his chest. The pressure on her mouth intensified, pushing on her bottom lip. She parted them ever so slightly, needing this bit of comfort, this distraction he was offering. And God did it feel so right.

She touched her tongue to the end of his finger, tasting the salty roughness of his skin. Shuddering, she sucked him further into her mouth. Desire pooled between her legs, and she pressed them together. Her fingers tightened against her palms.

"*Fuuuck*." That pulled out groan had her salivating. The push of his finger had her leaning forward, wanting more. *Needing* more. Her body an electric circuit of sensitivity, she ran her tongue down the underside of his finger.

She wanted him to touch her. She wanted him to make her forget that her life was a hellish ball of flames. That Liz was most likely being tortured. That she might never see her again. She wanted him to make her forget about her guilt and the agony and the frustration clawing at her.

Leaning forward, almost desperately, she reached for him.

Her hands touched a hard chest. Splaying her fingers out, she slipped under the leather fabric of his jacket. As soon as she started to move them south, his other hand grabbed her wrist, holding her still.

"Emma –"

She didn't want him to talk. She didn't want him to remind her that, although better than Sebastian, he was still the enemy. She just wanted him to distract her. To quiet the thoughts running through her head at a million miles an hour.

Pulling her head back as his fingers left her lips, she brought her foot up off the ground and swung her leg over his lap. As he cursed, she opened her eyes and pushed him down on the bed, his legs over the side, her on top of him. She hesitated for just a second, feeling the bulge pressing against her thighs, seeing the battle in his eyes.

His hands were on her hips, his fingers digging in, and neither of them knew whether he was trying to get her to stop or holding her there.

Grabbing the hem of her shirt, Emma pulled it up over her head. He sucked in a breath. His grip tightened. With his eyes on her breasts, which were cupped in red lace, his cock hardened.

She shifted on top of him, pressing into it. His back arched. His head fell back. His eyes closed briefly.

She rocked her hips again, her lips parting as bolts of electricity, of togetherness, of a connection terrifyingly intense shivered through her body.

The pressure built inside her.

Placing her hands on Rogan's chest, she started to ride him, not quite ready to take off his clothes. Or any more of hers. His hands moved to her ass. His hips rocked up, causing her to gasp in between little pants as he rubbed against her clit.

The lace of her bra felt like too much against her skin. The fabric separating her ass from his hands felt way too thick. Making a noise back in her throat, she lowered her hands to the hem of his shirt and pushed up. The feel of skin on skin made her groan.

His harsh breathing filled her ears as she ran her nails up his chest. Soft hair tickled her fingers. She moved her hands toward his sides and stopped at the bump of his nipples.

She rolled them in between her fingers as she rocked her hips faster. Harder. Wilder.

She was getting so close.

She just needed –

Leaning forward, she wrapped a hand around the back of his head and pulled his mouth to her chest.

His lips closed around her lace-covered nipple.

Moaning, she sagged against him. Holding him to her, she pressed harder against his cock. His hands squeezed her ass, then rose to her shoulders.

The straps of her bra were pushed down.

The air kissed her breasts.

And then his lips trailed across her, his tongue licking everywhere but her nipple.

A cry of frustration bubbled up from the back of her throat. Wrapping her fingers in his hair, she yanked him where she wanted him.

At the touch of his teeth around her bud, she arched her back and cried out. His hand rose to her free breast, palming it as he licked and bit at her other one.

Shuddering, Emma pressed one hand on the mattress beneath them, holding herself up as her legs started to shake.

Panting heavily, she rocked her hips, dug her fingers into his hair, and let herself go.

The orgasm ripped through her, picking up her very soul and throwing it toward the heavens. Stars twinkled inside her, the energy and explosion of a thousand suns rocking her to her core.

The air whooshed across her face as she was suddenly

rolled onto her back. Rogan hovered above her, his lips wet from their kisses, his bright blue eyes on hers. Holding her gaze, he trailed a finger down her stomach, to the waistband of her pants.

She sucked in a breath.

He slipped his fingers inside.

As she struggled to keep her eyes on him instead of rolling them back in her head like she wanted to, he trailed a path down the matching red lace, to the wetness between her thighs.

Her breath hitched.

He paused.

And then he was pushing the fabric aside and sliding his fingers down between her lips.

Her hips arched off the bed. Her eyes fluttered shut.

The tremors of her orgasm still vibrated through her.

Running his finger up and down her slick labia, he leaned down and kissed her.

Slowly.

Softly.

His tongue slid against her lips with every slow breath. His mouth rubbed against hers.

And it felt like being cherished and cared for. It felt like three little words that was way too early to say, especially when they were supposed to just be fucking to get rid of her stress, her frustration, her shame.

Tears burning her eyes, Emma turned her head. *What am I doing*?

The guilt she'd hoped to forget came crashing back a thousand fold. A tsunami of it flooded through her system, overriding all else. She had found pleasure while her sister was only finding pain. She had made out with the man wanting to throw her in jail, not as a ploy to get him to trust her so she could escape but because she'd simply wanted him.

What kind of sister was she?

"Hey." At Rogan's soft words, she broke apart, shaking and crying and hating every part of herself.

What the fuck was she doing?

Rolling off her, Rogan wrapped his arms around her shoulders and pulled her to him. Her mind screamed at her to push him away, but her heart, her soul, her sheer brokenness called to the comfort of his touch. "It's okay," he murmured. "Everything is goona be okay."

But it wasn't.

Because she had no idea what she was doing.

She had no idea how to save her sister.

All she ever knew was how to fuck things up.

It should have been her that had been taken, not Liz.

Not sweet, feisty Liz who deserved the world.

Oh, Liz, she cried. *I'm so sorry.*

I'm so fucking sorry.

TWENTY

Hunter paced around his and Xeno's hotel room, a bluetooth-like device curved around his ear. It was made of a black metal found nowhere on Earth, and it had the ability to transfer one's thoughts across the Seven Planes. He was dying to figure out how the mechanics of it worked given Xeno's simple explanation of, "It's magic," hadn't been enough to sate him.

Unfortunately, he doubted he'd have time to take it apart and find out for himself anytime soon. He hadn't had any time off in the last five years, and with the upcoming shit storm...

He didn't need the power of telepathy to know Tegan's answer if he put in a request for time off.

Not that he wanted any. The Elv've'Norc was his life. And before that, he'd been in the SCU. And even with their 'mandatory holidays,' he'd constantly found ways to get around taking any. He'd pissed off his old boss so much she'd actually drugged him to sleep for three weeks, and his sister had been the one to administer the drink.

He should have known something was off when she'd smiled sweetly at him, but he'd been concentrating too hard on the files of a case.

A case they had managed to solve without him, much to his annoyance, especially since they'd then brought up that little fact every time he'd tried to wiggle out of taking a holiday.

Smiling at the thought of his old SCU buddies, Hunter thought about calling them, but then thought better of it. His sister would talk for fucking forever, and he only had enough energy to put up with one crazy person tonight.

Snickering, thanking the gods Delentia, a sightseeing goddess, couldn't read his thoughts despite her ability to see every timeline – past, present, and alternative – he thought hard about calling her. As the device started ringing inside his skull, he glanced over at Xeno.

She sat on the bed, her legs crossed, her breathing even, her eyes closed. He thought about wrapping a blanket around her, knowing her skin would be cold given her soul no longer occupied it. She'd spirited off to the skies of Halzaja, where all the angels lived. After being banished due to her fall, her physical body was no longer welcome there.

His chest tightened as he thought about all she'd been through. Walking over to the other bed, he pulled off the blanket, then wrapped it around her shoulders. His hands lingered in front of her as he held the blanket to her. His eyes roamed her face, taking in all the details he'd long memorized. The long nose. The high cheeks. The blonde hair framing her face in soft curls – the only soft thing about her.

He knew every pixel of color in her golden eyes, knew every flash of emotion that flittered across her face, and none of it was soft.

Cold and jaded, she kept everyone at a distance.

A distance he was desperate to close.

Sighing, he stepped back and headed for the chair on the other side of the room. He settled into it, his eyes on Xeno as the rings in his head continued.

Die, spermin! Die! High-pitched, feminine laughter suddenly vibrated through Hunter's skull, followed by the shrieks of something dying, the wet slurps of what was either a mouth or the sound of a blade squelching through flesh, and the mad cackling of a sightseeing fury known as Delentia the Incarnation of Madness. He shuddered, knowing she was on one of her hunts.

Although they had been friends for the better part of three years, he still didn't know the details of her hunts. But after hearing some of the stories circulating behind her back, Hunter counted that as a blessing.

Hunter, buddy! How are you? Enjoying the angel yet? You know she totally has the hots for you!

Hey, Del. I'm okay. I survived a plane crash with only a dislocated shoulder, so can't complain really. Xeno's same old distant Xeno, and if she heard you saying that, she'd probably never speak to me again. Although he'd thought it with a slight laugh of his own, Hunter feared it was probably true.

It had taken him years to get her to talk to him outside of mission commands. Whatever had happened to her, ran deep. He knew angels were stoic and aloof rather than the jovial and charming race his kind usually imagined, but Xeno's self-erected walls were an anomaly even for them. Though he didn't know why her wings were deteriorating, it didn't take a genius to know she'd suffered something truly life-twisting.

Nonsense! She wouldn't upset me like that. I hate, absolute hate, *being in the middle of – Hey, rabbit face, you want it, come get it!*

Knowing Delentia would be distracted by her hunt for a while, Hunter returned his attention to the angel in question. She still sat cross-legged on the bed, her sun-colored eyes closed. Her ivory skin was now free of all the cuts and bruises she had picked up during their fall. Thankfully, her ability to regenerate wasn't declining nearly as fast as the state of her wings. Hunter wondered what would happen when she finally lost them and made a note to ask Del that when she got back, if she ever did.

The sound of laughter filled his mind once more, and he quickly pulled his attention away from his comrade. Despite her constant distractions, the goddess had a notorious temper if she was ever ignored herself.

Hunter, babe! You gonna tell me what's up or not? Do you know how rude it is to keep a lady waiting?

My apologies, Del. For the slight, I offer you a lock of my hair upon our return.

Hmmm...okay! What are friends for if you cannot harvest their hair, am I right?

As always. He hid his trepidation with a smile that lightened his thoughts.

There were a thousand rumors for why the sightseeing fury collected people's hair and not one of them was soothing. Some claimed she could use it to tap into everyone's soul and force them to do her bidding for as long as the hair stayed fresh, with the definition of 'fresh' changing with each telling. Others were adamant she had found a way to use it as a window into one's existence. With their lock of hair, she was able to spy upon people day and night, thus ensuring her ability of foresight stayed strong. A few even swore they knew a friend of a friend whom had suddenly died without any sense nor reason not long after handing over snippets of hair. One minute they were completely healthy, and in the next, they were dead; only their bald heads spoke of whatever evil Delentia had managed to cast upon them.

But whatever the truth was, everyone agreed that to deny Delentia a lock of hair was suicidal. Not only would it guarantee a torturous life and then a torturous death, but also a torturous afterlife. She was a fury of the underworld, tasked with torturing whatever pitiful souls deserved it, with 'deserved' having whatever definition she decided. In all of her millennia of existence, there had never been a case of her getting bored.

I would like to know where Sebastian the Ancient Destroyer is holding Elizabeth the Descendant, if there are any weaknesses of Sebastian the Ancient Destroyer's we can exploit in order to retrieve the Scrolls of Atlantis, *and which gods or goddesses, if any, are supporting Sebastian the Ancient Destroyer in any way, whether it be in deed or thought.*

After a cackle that chilled his bones, Delentia began singing in a deafening shrill. *By the neck, by the neck; what a bastard of a wreck!*

Fuck, I did not phrase that request correctly, Hunter thought to himself. He tapped his fingers along his thigh in apprehension, hoping he had worded the other two well enough for an actual answer.

What he left for what he wants or what he wants for what he left! She tuuuuuuurns moooooortal!

Click.

Hunter scrambled to write down her exact words before he could forget them. To miss or replace a single phrase could make her answers meaningless. And though he believed he had messed up the first question, he wrote her answer down anyway in case it wasn't as obvious as it seemed. Del loved her abstract answers almost as much as she did torturing her enemies, which being the daughter of Allecto the Unceasing in Anger, she had much love for. Luckily, Hunter had an insatiable love for puzzles. It was one of the reasons he had been picked as the first and only human to be a member of the Elv've'Norc, much to his parents' pride and his sister's annoyance.

With everything written down correctly, the agent then focused his thoughts on getting in touch with Tegan Jólfrson, the head of the Elv've'Norc. No sooner had the thought formed than his boss' deep voice filled his skull.

Half-asleep, he growled, *This better be good, agent.*

Well, sir, that depends on your definition of good. Is all hell about to break loose a good thing?

The heavenly meadow that had once held so many joyous memories for Xeno now looked desolate and bare. The clouds used to roll out beneath her feet in a beautiful sea, their wispy tendrils swirling around her ankles in a low hanging mist. The flowers in bloom had been a gorgeous mix of oranges and pinks, streaking across the ground like the kiss of a sunset. A large tree grew out of the cloud base, and as the mist had parted and formed again, she used to catch glimpses of its roots digging deep and wide.

The place was still beautiful on a physical level, but the glow that used to envelop it was long gone from Xeno's soul. Now the clouds looked angry, the flowers wilted, and the tree long rotted – just like the poisonous state of her wings and heart. The message was clear: she didn't belong here anymore, and despite what Hunter thought, she would take great pleasure in never returning.

"Xenosmilus."

She turned around at the flat sound of her full name,

her face carefully masked to hide the sharp jab of pain. There was a time when this man had only ever called for her with joy on his lips. It seemed he too had put such foolish times behind him.

"Gabriel." She inclined her head as she greeted him just as coldly. When she straightened, she made sure to meet his detached golden gaze with one of her own.

But where Xeno had thought she would find only stark indifference, two drowning pools full of sorrow awaited her. Gabriel's once proud shoulders now sagged with a weight too heavy to carry. The mouth that had been so quick to smile was now frozen in an eternal frown. The urge to sooth away his worries, to help shoulder the crushing burden he had been born to uphold, was almost too strong to ignore.

Almost.

"Is there any news about which goddess broke the Holy Blood Contract of which we speak?"

Gabriel regarded her with piercing eyes, his face empty of the overwhelming tiredness from before. No doubt, it had only been a ploy to try to get her to lower her defenses. The realization almost made Xeno lash out at him in anger, but she was careful to keep her torturous desire in check lest she be kicked out of here. Again.

"Come on, Gabriel," she pressed. "Whoever it was birthed twins, and we've been ordered by their father to protect the elder. I need to know."

His eyes sharpened to steel. Where others would falsely think they now had his full attention, Xeno knew the truth. She had spent centuries learning to read his emotions, and unlike with her, his tells hadn't changed.

"He does not know?" Before she could answer, he let out a guttural laugh and gave a shake of his long dark hair. "He does not know you're here. Yet."

So maybe he could still read her after all.

She mentally scowled at the flutter of joy that thought sparked inside her, then jumped on it with both feet. Up and down. Up and down until she had squashed it back into oblivion.

"Do you know or not?" Her voice was soft, angelic, and told nothing of the rage eating away inside her. His actions eleven years ago were unforgivable. Every second she spent in his presence made the dagger in her heart twist deeper and deeper. One day, she would be able to take it out and return it, but that day was a long way coming.

"Show me your wings."

Her eyes widened and her jaw dropped – both only slightly but enough for Gabriel to document her clear surprise at his request. She couldn't help her gaze from zeroing in on his own wings. Black, beautiful, complete. Held with such obvious pride behind him that it made her throat fill with acid.

"Your wings, Xen."

His voice was gentle, caring almost, and when combined with her old nickname... She would not let him pity her.

With her jaw clenched, she slowly unfolded her broken wings. She refused to allow the pain, either physical or emotional, to cast a shadow over her features. She kept her chin high, and he matched her false bravado with a careful mask of his own. Whatever disgust or pity he felt for her, she was glad she wasn't able to see it.

Gritting her teeth, Xeno pushed past the breaks that had not yet healed until she was fully extended. Even then, her left one touched the ground. Despite her desire to lift them as proudly as Gabriel did his, she could not.

Feathers had been dropping from her for over a decade.

What few were left were twisted and skewed due to the evil in her heart. Additionally, she had suffered gashes and fractures in the fall. Though her body still recovered quickly enough, her wings no longer did. Gaping wounds offered a window into her broken bones and swollen tendons. Blood matted the feathers and stained the skin. What wasn't already stained red was blanketed in bruises.

Nevertheless, Xeno stood tall underneath his cold gaze. He had done this to her; he could damn well feel the guilt of it.

"You have mere years left."

She gave no acknowledgement to his claim. She had already guessed she was only two to three years away from becoming a fallen angel. Gabriel walked around her to see more of the mattered mess, and she barely fought the urge to snap them shut in shame.

By the time he came back around to face her, only a single minute had ticked by, but a whole moment had passed between them. Feeling the raw burn of it, Xeno pulled her wings tight against her back. She glared at him in silent demand for an answer to her previous question.

Surprisingly, he actually complied. "The mother has to be one of the sex goddesses. I've been told Elizabeth is cursed to follow the orders of whoever beds her. I suspect it will be the same for Emma."

He watched her carefully as he delivered the news, but Xeno had long since buried the memories he was looking for.

Knowing Gabriel wouldn't reveal anymore information on that matter, she asked instead, "Is it permanent?"

A solemn nod. "For descendants, the punishment is eternal. Elizabeth will never be free to fight Sebastian's commands."

At this, Xeno hid her frown. She had seen how Rogan

treated their captive. He might be too blind to see it himself, but Emma was his lifemate.

When a creature of the Myth was born, their soul was ripped in half by the gods. Some believed it was fear that had pushed the deities to make this decision; others that they had simply found pleasure in the turmoil of their creations. Those that had lived since the beginning, however, knew the truth.

The mighty male gods had been trying to impress their female counterparts. Once it had become obvious their powers alone couldn't woo a goddess, they had attempted to make a romantic gesture. Typical male theatrics.

But though its origins weren't serious in nature (unless one asked the gods who had created it, as the art of wooing to them was very serious) it could never be taken as a joke. There was a reason the phrase, 'don't threaten a lifemate' was the Myth's much more vicious alternative to the humans' 'don't rock the boat.'

If Rogan harmed either Emma or her loved ones, it would destroy him.

Fortunately, Xeno didn't have that same restriction. "Then she cannot be saved."

Neither of the two angels pretended her words had been for Elizabeth alone.

TWENTY-ONE

Elizabeth paced the large hallways of her luxurious prison. Given her inability to leave the castle's main building, the need to chain her up in the dungeon was unnecessary. In some cursed way, Sebastian had stolen her freedom of choice three months ago. Despite having grown up in WITSEC, Elizabeth had been too naive, too trusting, and too dumbly in love to take any precautions to protect herself.

Though even if she hadn't pursued the monster with the angelic face, what could a mere human have done against a vampire of his strength?

No, not a human, she corrected herself, but one who had been just as vulnerable.

Elizabeth didn't know what she was anymore, but she was far from weak. If she could just resist Sebastian's commands, she would be able to kill him with a single touch. Ever since she had come into her wretched powers, she had been able to take a life with as little ease as she took a breath. Just a single touch of her right hand with the thought of him dying, and he would collapse never to wake again.

Unfortunately, his first command to her had been to never harm him. His second had been to protect him from all threats, including from herself. And Sebastian's word was law.

Elizabeth wondered briefly if she would be forced to kill her sister should Emma do something brash, but quickly dismissed it lest she fall apart. Later, she would try to find a way to save her twin. Right now, she needed time to prepare herself for the horror that was to come.

Sebastian had ordered her to convince Emma to come to them voluntarily and on her own. Using the overly protective nature her twin had been suffocating her with ever since their mother had died, Elizabeth had managed to slip in a code for danger without triggering the barriers of her curse. Getting Emma to visit voluntarily didn't mean she had to come unarmed or ignorant. And if her sister just so happened to tell her protectors beforehand... maybe they could save them both.

Though who am I kidding? Elizabeth would simply be forced to kill them. Just like she had those people a week ago when Sebastian had ordered her to steal an ancient book at all costs.

The memory of that night made her sick to her stomach, but its contents didn't come up this time. Since the cut in her side wasn't healing, she had to change its bandage every few hours. With every unwrap of her wound, Elizabeth had been forcing herself to remember her every vile action. She wanted to memorize every face she had twisted in pain. Every set of eyes she had forever closed. After a while, she had grasped onto their faces like a lifeline.

She would not forget the men and women who had sacrificed their lives trying to stop her; she would not let them die in vain even if she had been the one to sentence their deaths. The five people who stared at her every time she closed her eyes and redressed her laceration were a main part of the reason she kept fighting. As ironic as it was, Elizabeth owed them her life, and she vowed to their souls that she would find a way to kill the sadistic fuck controlling her.

Somehow.

But first she had to survive the upcoming torment of an enraged vampire.

As if pulled from her thoughts, Sebastian materialized in front of her. His chin was smeared with fresh blood, but even that was not enough to mar the beauty of his features.

His skin, though pale, didn't portray a sickly patient. Rather it glowed from his latest feed. His eyes were a dark brown that many would confuse with the sweet warmth of chocolate instead of the true poisoned soul they hid. His clipped hair whispered of ancient royalty, but instead of making him seem stiff and aloof, it had been styled to give an air of rumpled disarray. It made him look as if he was a prince who had just risen from a vigorous round of morning sex right before a very important meeting. And if that wasn't enough to lure unsuspecting prey, he had a strong pointed jawline that belied an innocence he hadn't had since birth. If even then.

Naive Elizabeth with her desperation to finally feel the love of a man, hadn't stood a chance.

"My lord."

She dipped into a low curtsy, giving herself time to hide the overwhelming fear his presence always caused.

"When can I expect our new guest?"

Elizabeth swallowed in a pathetic attempt to hold on to the truth, but as always, his hold on her was unwavering. Her loyalty to him was complete.

"I don't know, my lord. My connection with her was interrupted. I think they hurt her to sever it."

Sebastian studied her with such cold venom, Elizabeth felt the icy hatred freezing deep inside her veins. The tips of his fangs started protruding from his lips, and she barely stopped the shiver from vibrating across her skin. His eyes, now dark with hunger and rage, fixed on the erratic pulse at her neck. Nauseated, she tensed at the pain soon to come.

Like a cat playing with a mouse, he purred, "And did she sound convinced before then?"

"I believe she will come, my lord."

"Why? And answer honestly, my dear." His voice was the very definition of saccharine, and Elizabeth feared he already knew of her betrayal.

Still, she found her lips parting and uttering the words that would damn her. "She'll want to save me. From you. A sadistic fuck who makes death seem appealing."

The corner of his lips slithered up, a tell tale sign he was getting off on this little exchange. Elizabeth only just managed to stop herself from being sick all over his fancy, aristocratic suit.

"My clever, clever Liz." A cold finger crawled down her cheek, leaving a trail of goosebumps in their wake. He wrapped his hand lovingly around her throat, his thumb pawing back and forth over her rapid pulse. As much as she didn't want to show weakness, she couldn't help the shiver of fear raking through her. The obvious fact that he delighted in it only made her shake harder.

Fighting to keep her horror under her mask of courage, Elizabeth hurried to give him a reason he would accept.

"She would've already suspected something wasn't right, my lord. If I told her everything was fine, it would have given her pause."

His thumb stroked her in an unbreakable rhythm, as if he hadn't heard a single word she had uttered.

But then he released her and turned away with such a casual air of indifference, Elizabeth tensed in nauseous apprehension.

"Of course. It had nothing to do with trying to alert the Elv've'Nor holding her."

"My lord –"

He backhanded her hard across her mouth.

She closed her eyes as she took the next hit. The ones that followed left her crumbled up on the floor in a puddle of blood and saliva.

"So tell me when can I expect them!" he commanded in between kicks before reaching down and yanking her up by the neck.

"My lord, p-please." She grabbed his hands but wasn't powerful enough to claw him off her, his second order keeping her from hurting him.

His grip tightened until she couldn't breathe.

The world darkened, pinpointing on his face.

His fucking angelic face.

His smile was the last thing she saw before her head sagged forward, unconscious.

A sharp kick to her kidney jolted her back to painful awareness. She came to gasping and cradling the bloody mess at her side.

As he raised his foot again, she fought to remember the question he'd asked before he'd strangled her. He didn't like repeating himself. *When can I expect them?* "I d-don't...know."

"You lying bitch!" Another kick, this time to her back.

Any harder and he would've snapped her spine. "You would know her plans. You were in her fucking mind, and she has not come into her powers enough to resist."

"I wasn't...a...aware...I could. Still...learning."

He spat on her in disgust, but she had grown too used to his belittling to even care.

"Well then." Sebastian's voice was slick, back to his dangerous purr. "I'll just have to teach you some more, won't I?"

Liz fought back her tears. He might take her body and her words, but he would never take her mind. He would not break her. No matter what more he did, he would not.

She inhaled a breath of determination. On the exhale, she uttered the phrase he currently desired without so much as a clench of the teeth.

"Yes, my lord."

As she fought to ignore the sound of his ruffling pants, Elizabeth focused on the fact she now had a male ally. He had touched her mind right before she'd contacted her sister on the plane, telling her he'd placed something of importance inside her box of memories, something that could potentially save them both.

At first, Elizabeth hadn't believed him. How had he even known she'd planned on getting her sister to help her escape? Once over, Emma would have started to panic when she didn't get picked up at the airport. Then she would've gotten the authorities involved. She would've hounded them until they created search parties. She would've contacted every news outlet. She would've made sure the world knew Elizabeth was missing and that she needed to be found.

She would've saved her without ever being in danger...

But then, the person had told her he knew about the phone, that he had been the one who had left it for her to find. That he had later destroyed it so Sebastian would never know.

And although she hadn't seen another soul for months, she felt many around her and a great deal more below her. Whoever her ally was, it was one of them. Whether human or vampire, she wasn't sure. For though she'd learned to differentiate between the two, not because of their obvious locations (vampires walking freely, the humans trapped in the dungeons) but because of their personal essence, she had nothing to grab onto in her mind.

Around her, vampires called to her on a dismissive level as if they were simple pieces of the background. Humans, on the other hand, were more like luxurious pieces of clothing just waiting for her to collect. She could feel that they were alive, and her new deathly powers were drawn to them much like a moth to a flame.

But in her mind, her powers were restricted. She could not discern anything about the male who'd claimed to be her ally. She could only trust him blindly. And although she feared it was another one of Sebastian's tests, she couldn't help but hope.

A brutal grip dug into her hair. Before she could be wrenched up off the ground, a feminine voice made Sebastian release her.

"The three are here."

Not wanting to draw attention to herself despite her burning curiosity, Elizabeth stayed curled up on the floor. She peeked up from beneath her bloody lashes to discover whomever had dared interrupt. Sebastian did not forgive easily.

The brash (or stupid) newcomer was a striking woman of Asian descent. Her thick black hair was twisted up in a stern bun. Her eyes matched the same tint of Sebastian's, but where his were an art piece of cold cruelty, hers held menacing calculation. Her strong cheekbones curved high beneath her eyes. Her lips, even when pursed, whispered the temptation of a lush kiss...if the woman didn't kill them first.

Elizabeth doubted the woman would even hesitate to do it. In fact, she would probably find pleasure in it like Sebastian did.

When their eyes met, Elizabeth shivered. A brush of *something* coursed through her. Her chest tightened as a stillness washed over her, following an emotion she could not name.

Along with the abilities to kill with a single touch and to sense life moving around her, she'd also been cursed with the ability to sense strong emotions. Given all she had experienced so far had been unwavering rage from Sebastian, nauseous pleasure from the vampire guards, and devastating pain and loss from those being tortured in the dungeons, it wasn't a skill she'd tried to hone.

Now, though, as this *something* flowed through her, she wished she was experienced enough to know what it was. It was soft like compassion but only in the barest sense. It was hot like anger but only just.

But was that anger toward Sebastian? Her? Or the world in general? Was the compassion for her or herself? Elizabeth already had one possible guardian angel; was she lucky enough to have two?

A sharp kick in her back sent all thoughts of that possibility flying out of her. The woman didn't even flinch. Her emotions stayed still, her eyes not even on her.

As pain radiated through her body, Elizabeth fought back a whimper. She would not give him anything. On the next kick, numbness flowed through her lower half. She knew the feeling well enough by this point to know he'd broken her back. But as awful as it was, she was glad for it. Now, when Sebastian came back from his meeting and punished her for 'making him wait,' she would not feel it.

Lying there on the floor, Elizabeth pressed her cheek against the cold stone.

And waited.

"You dare keep us waiting?" The goddess who spoke was adorned with precious stones and the finest of silks. Even when compared to the other two beside her, she was dressed in a class far superior. Her pristine white dress hugged the fine curves of her upper body before flaring out at her hips in a way that mimicked the delicate bloom of a flower. A single layer of translucent fabric wrapped around one breast and over the flawless skin of her shoulder to trail freely down her back.

The belt that circled her petite waste was molded out of pure gold. Within it were set thousands of shining gems the color of a dragon's breath. Even in the dark gloom of the castle, they sparkled with light to mimic the golden red hue of a fire's warmth. A necklace of equal power and fortune decorated her porcelain neck, and on every finger was at least one priceless ring. A golden band circled both biceps three times, and just as many bracelets dangled on her wrists. Only her face was free of jewelry, but even if not, no one would have noticed.

Her natural beauty could easily outmatch any piece of craftsmanship – even if it was created by the legendary Hephaestus.

Her eyes put the sun's rays to shame in both warmth and color. Her luxurious hair made even the shiniest of golds envious. Her lush mouth made every hot-blooded male and female quiver with the desire to taste.

To say she was striking would be like saying Helen of Troy had the beauty of a troll...after plummeting from a tall cliff and falling onto the jagged rocks below. And that was before the delicate curve of the goddess' neck and the fullness of her curves were taken into consideration.

But warm and delicate, Freya the Vanir Goddess of Love and Beauty was not.

Bowing low, as a peasant would when talking to royalty, Sebastian murmured, "My sincerest apologies to each goddess." Rising, he asked, "To what do I owe for the pleasure of your three's honorable presence today?" He smiled with sincerity, but Freya's acrimonious demeanor would not be swayed.

"The talks of war have begun."

Given the bitterness mirrored in the other two's eyes, Freya was not alone in her wrath. He had expected as much when his blood sister had told them of their sudden arrival. Any time the goddesses were displeased, he paid dearly. The last time, they'd forced him to leave behind a woman of great importance to him in order to prove his devotion to their cause.

But he had an ace up his sleeve this time – something he would find great pleasure in teasing them with.

"Yet you have not been able to read the *Scrolls*, let alone put our plan into action."

At Aine's, the Gaelic Goddess of Feminity's, biting accusation, Sebastian inclined his head in agreement. "I have not. However –"

He paused when Freya made to speak. Though the act in itself was chivalrous, he was secretly ecstatic over her obvious discomfort. Would she attempt to get in one last jab at his incompetence or would her thirst for vengeance be strong enough for her to swallow her pride?

The clench of her jaw as she jerkily motioned for him

to continue pleased him like nothing else.

"However, I have found that those not of the Myth are able to."

"A human is able to read the *Scrolls of Atlantis*?" Freya scoffed in disbelief. "They were written well before they were even created, and they know nothing of our ancient tongue!"

Sebastian shrugged. "At first I did not believe it either, but after three successes, I could not deny it."

"And how did you figure this out when no one else has been able to?"

He grinned at her accidental praise. "I have my ways. Alas –"

He ceased talking once more when all three sets of eyes narrowed over his lack of a genuine answer. He barely managed to hide his satisfaction over watching them squirm.

"Go on," the Vanir Goddess of Love and Beauty bit out behind clenched teeth. Did they know they were much prettier when angry?

Sebastian hid his arousal as he dipped his head in thanks. "Alas, none of the humans I have acquired have been able to understand it."

"But you just said they could read it."

"They can, but it seems that the words are a bit...complex for such simple minds."

"Then find someone who can."

He did so enjoy baiting them with his acts of incompetence. As if his dungeon wasn't currently filled with top-of-their-field scientists and members of the human esteemed MENSA. He had even discarded his many SCU toys to make some extra space. One of them, a delectable female who looked more like a stripper than a genius, was showing true promise. Once he found that kid of hers, he was certain she would spill the secrets of its pages. The goddesses, however, did not need to know that, not without a price – one he would collect in due time.

"Of course." He bowed at the waist. "I shall get right on that as soon as I no longer have the honor of your three's presence."

There was a collection of gasps at his sly dismissal. As dangerous as it was to insult a god, Sebastian knew they would not kill him. Not when he was so close to securing what they so desperately desired.

"You play with the sun, vampire."

Sebastian inclined his head. "I do give my sincerest apologies to each of you. I only want to do what makes you happy."

No sooner were the words out of his mouth than he fell to his knees from the agony of a broken heart. Lucille, the woman he had been forced to abandon, surged to the forefront of his mind. Despite their time together, though, he'd never loved her. She could never fill the empty hole in his heart, the hole that still belonged to someone else.

But when he imagined her wrapped in the arms of another, he was overcome with feral anger. Instinctively, he fought the reality the goddesses were feeding him, but their power only increased tenfold. As the scene with Lucille heated, as the pain in his chest grew unbearable, Sebastian raked at his chest in torturous surrender. His claws dug deep as his tormented soul begged for mercy. Surely, a missing heart would be better than a broken one.

"Whatever makes us happy, you say. Well, this does make us happy."

His fingers dipped into the cavity of his chest as he ripped past bone and muscle.

"So very happy," the other two agreed as his vision began to fade.

At last, Sebastian managed to slice through the arteries holding his still dead blackened heart in place. As he slowly slipped out of consciousness, he offered it up in apology. "Always, my goddesses. Always."

TWENTY-TWO

If only last night had been another nightmare, Emma thought on a groan. With her eyes still closed, she shook off the last tendrils of her actual nightmare. She had dreamed of being stabbed a mere seven times after having dragged herself out of Rogan's arms and into her own bed roughly around two o'clock last night. Though she still reeled from the pain of those wounds, it was a breeze compared to the guilt consuming her.

He's trying to imprison Liz.

And you know, he kidnapped me.

Though for some insane reason that last one wasn't nearly as important.

She had thrown herself at him like a crazed schoolgirl in a desperate attempt to forget everything that had happened. Of course, she had been shot at by people who had turned out to not be the mafia, had survived a horrifying vampire attack, rescued a dog that happened to be freaking Cerberus, had fallen out of a plane only to be caught by a giant eagle that used to be a man, and had learned that she wasn't, in fact, human after all – something she had believed for a full twenty-two bloody years. So was it really any wonder she had wanted to turn off her mind for a moment? Emma had no idea how much more of this she could take.

But she couldn't fall apart, not yet. Elizabeth needed her. If Emma could just hold on to that thought, then she would be able to get through this. Hopefully.

When she finally rolled out of bed, she gave a languish stretch toward the sky. She flexed her arms high above her to help ease some of the tension knotted deep in her back. She might be able to heal quickly from physical wounds, but it seemed she did not have the same skillset when it came to the effects of stress. As she released her arms on a deep exhale, she cracked open her eyes. The sight that greeted her had her freezing with her hands still above her head.

Rogan sat on the edge of his bed, his chest free of the blanket...and a shirt, she noticed with an unwanted flash of desire. The urge to lower her gaze to see if he wore boxers was strong enough to sting her cheeks. His lips curled up in a smile as if he could read her thoughts. The hungry call of his eyes bore so deeply into hers she could almost feel him already inside her. And not just the pumping of his fingers she'd been so close to feeling last night.

She swallowed as the want to finish what she had started beckoned to her very soul, her past and present and future embarrassment be damned.

His eyes dipped to her chest.

Shooting to her feet, Emma crossed her arms and darted to the bathroom. Once she slammed the door shut behind her, she collapsed on the toilet seat and tried to convince herself that she wasn't attracted to a ridiculously attractive man. Her repeated phrase of 'he kidnapped you' wasn't working though. All she wanted was to open the door and crawl onto his lap like she had last night.

And it's not like he actually *kidnapped me,* her little voice said. *The police don't 'kidnap' people, do they? They restrain them.*

With cuffs.

At the thought of cuffs – the fluffy black kind, not the gold string he'd used on her a couple nights ago – Emma groaned.

"You need therapy, girl," she muttered as she stood up and started undressing. She also needed a shower. A cold one.

A very, *very* cold one.

But just as she finished stepping out of her underwear, the bathroom door creaked open in front of her.

Yelping, Emma jumped a foot in the air. As soon as she landed, she dropped down to grab something to cover herself with before straightening.

Your panties? Really?

The towel hanging on the wall beside her mocked her like nothing else. But with both arms now occupied with covering her from view, Emma couldn't grab said towel without flashing one thing or another. "Get out!" she shrieked.

Or stay and take off your clothes...

He slowly brought his heated blue eyes up to hers. "Are ye talking to her?"

"Who?" she asked before remembering the last time he'd banged open a bathroom door on her. Shaking her head, she sputtered, "No."

"I didna sense any water being used for a long time," he said, his eyes dipping again.

She struggled not to squirm. Struggled to remember

what they were even talking about when he took a step toward her.

Her pulse kicked up into her throat and down in between her thighs. She flicked her tongue out to wet her lips. Her nipples started to bud against her forearm.

"It's time to go," he murmured. It was such an innocent phrase, but his voice was deep with lust. "Ye should get dressed, lass. We're to be on the road in ten minutes."

She should have said okay.

She should have nodded.

She should have told him to leave.

She should *not* have looked down at the bulge in his pants to see if he was hard.

Because dear God, now all she wanted was to stay undressed. And for him to stay as she tugged his shirt off and unbuttoned his –

"Get dressed, Emma." His words were low, strained, as if he was fighting the same urges she was.

Her breath came quicker.

Desire pooled slick between her thighs.

The urge to slip a finger inside herself as he watched nearly pushed her over the edge.

Cursing, he bent down and picked up her clothes for her. But when he started to straighten, he found himself at eye level with her lower hand and stopped half-way up. His nostrils flared. His eyes darkened.

And Emma didn't know if she had reached forward of if he had pushed her hand away. But his mouth was suddenly on her and she was backed up against the bathroom sink, her neck arched back and her hand in his black wavy hair.

"*Shit.*"

His lips rubbed across hers, fast and frantic and hot. His kiss deepened as his tongue pushed inside her and his hands gripped her ass, holding her to him. She wiggled back on the counter, finding stability, as she lifted one leg over his shoulder.

His five o'clock shadow scrubbed against her thighs, a strong contrast to the smooth brush of his lips and tongue. As he sucked on her clit, he released her ass with both hands. One went to her pussy to spread her open. The other dipped down to his pants, and then there was the undeniable sound of a zip lowering.

Moaning, she twisted on the counter, trying to get a view as he stroked himself. But all she could see was his arm moving furiously. And then her eyes drifted close as he did something that made her scream.

Twisting her fingers in his hair, she urged him closer as she lifted her other leg and wrapped them both around his head, crossing her ankles.

He pulled his tongue out to lick the full length of her. Then flicked it against her clit. She squirmed beneath him, the sensation sending electricity through her body. Lifting her hips, she silently begged for more.

Sucking her clit back into his mouth, he bit it gently as he pushed two fingers inside her.

She jerked upright against him, her knuckles nearly white, her legs wrapped strongly around his head. He'd built her up so fast she hadn't even realized she was on the edge until he'd sent her crashing over.

Breathing heavily, she clenched around his fingers, vibrating with a feeling so strong it scared her. How could she resist temptation when it made her feel like this?

Every part of her craved him. Every inch of her body hummed with the pleasure he'd made her feel in only a minute, maybe two.

Fuck, she was screwed.

As his fingers slid out of her, she tried to wiggle off the

counter, but his tongue took their place, locking her still as good as chains.

She opened her eyes to watch his arm move. Her lips parted with the need to see him. To touch him for herself.

She tried getting off the counter again, but a knock on the hotel room door caused her to freeze.

"You two ready?" Hunter called through.

Without even lifting his head, Rogan raised the arm he'd had on his cock and reached over to turn on the shower. "Emma's just gone into the bathroom. I'll be out when she's done."

And the way he said 'done' had her squirming all over again. She raised a hand to her mouth, her cheeks on fire, as she struggled to stay silent.

"No worries. I'll let the rest know." There was a pause – in Hunter's words, not Rogan's actions.

His tongue still swept across her, his hand back on his cock, his arm pumping hard as he nibbled and licked her to another round of ecstasy.

Squeezing her legs together, Emma tried to fight her orgasm. She didn't want to come with Hunter in hearing range.

But Rogan was ruthless in his touch and taste. He ate her out like he hadn't had sex in years. Like he was being consumed by a primitive drive he couldn't resist any more than she could. His fingers pushed back inside her just as Hunter said, "Xeno's going to want to talk to you in private."

"Aye." His tongue swept across the top of her pussy. She started to shake. "I'll speak to her soon."

"Okay. I'll let her know."

Her cheeks burned. Emma could hold it off no longer. Jerking upright, she opened her mouth to scream.

But Rogan's lips stole the smothered sound she made.

He tasted strongly of her, a sweet, sharp tang, but she was too turned on to care. As her body spasmed from her head to her toes, she sagged against his chest and wished it was bare.

His arm pistoned beside her, his muscles jarring her as he touched himself. Glancing down, her eyes widened at the sight of his uncut dick appearing and disappearing out of the top of his hand.

Her breath started coming faster again.

She reached down and grabbed him.

Hissing, he released his cock as he pushed it into the loose curl of her fingers. Gripping her hand, he forced her to tighten around him, squeezing hard. Lowering his head, he kissed her again as he guided her hand up and down the length of him.

He looked so much bigger in her hand. She couldn't reach solidly around it like he had and it came out so much further past her fist.

Whimpering, she shifted her hips, wanting, *needing* to know what it felt like. But just as she started to move toward him, he palmed her breast and came all over her thighs.

Panting heavily, he leaned his head down on hers and cupped her cheek with his free hand. His other stayed tight around her fist, holding her against the base of his cock as he continued to shoot out cum.

Thick warm globs landed on her thighs and stomach.

Both their bodies flushed and sated, they stayed there in silence, their breaths the only sound for ages.

Then Rogan released her hand, reached over to the roll of toilet paper and pulled off a strip. He cleaned her up, wiping up from her thigh and down from her stomach, making her shiver every time he got too close to her pussy.

Looking into her eyes, he said, "I'm goona go now. Because if I watch ye get dressed, we're not goona be downstairs in ten minutes."

Pulling back abruptly, he shoved his cock down his pants and walked out the door.

Still sitting on the counter, Emma could only stare.

Fuck.

Me.

I'm so screwed.

TWENTY-THREE

Rogan wanted to hit Hunter so badly his knuckles already ached. If he hadn't interrupted them, Emma's pussy would've ended up tight around his cock. As a descendant, she couldn't get pregnant. As a creature of the Myth, it was highly unlikely she had a transmittable disease. If it wasn't for Hunter, he would've felt heaven rather than just having tasted it.

Licking his lips, Rogan fought back a groan. His cock twitched, rising again despite his recent release.

On the other hand, he begrudgingly admitted, it was probably a good thing Hunter had knocked and warned him about Xeno's arrival. If his second-in-command had caught them, she wouldn't have just insisted she take the lead on this mission. She would've tried to get him thrown off it for being so fully compromised – something he would've done himself not too long ago. This mission was too important to screw up.

But if anyone thought they could separate him from his lifemate now, they were sorely mistaken.

Trying not to picture Emma stepping into the shower and rubbing her hands all over her body, Rogan headed for the door. Making sure the hotel room key was in his pocket, he stepped outside and met Xeno there, having felt her water signature coming toward their room.

"What did ye find out?" he asked. "Gabriel know who her mother is?"

She eyed him for a second before shaking her head. "He suspects it's a sex goddess but not sure which one."

"He say why?" Gabriel and the other archangels were tasked with policing the gods. If they had suspicions, they were most definitely well founded. But he'd asked out of a need to know himself, not because he doubted them.

"Elizabeth's curse is in line with the consequences of what a child of theirs would suffer."

His entire body stilled. Xeno never fed information bit by bit like this. She never pulled her punches just because the person she was telling might be a bit sensitive. Which meant whatever she was holding back wasn't good.

"What is it?" he asked softly.

Her lips tightened. Her eyes hardened. "Whoever they have sex with will be able to control them completely. Whatever they command, Emma and Elizabeth will be forced to obey."

He swore. "So Sebastian's raping her."

She nodded.

"Can it be broken?"

She shook her head. "They are the manifestation of a broken Holy Blood Contract. They'll live with their curse for life."

His blood chilled.

The shower in their hotel room turned off, pulling his

attention to the woman dripping water across the floor as she stepped out.

His chest tightened, his heart squeezing hard as he realized he could've just changed her life completely – again. His lifemate, the woman he was supposed to protect. He could've just robbed her of every ounce of her freedom.

"Does it work on just penetrative sex?" he asked, praying it did. He didn't want that imbalance in their relationship. He didn't want her to be forced to stay with him because she magically had to.

Xeno's eyes searched his face, and he knew the exact moment she knew. But her gaze didn't harden like he'd expected it to. She didn't inform him she was calling Tegan and getting him replaced immediately.

Her face softened, actually softened, for the first time in a decade. "As far as we know." The softness vanished before he could feel relief, replaced once more by a cold truth. "But be careful, Rogan. The Royal Courts *will* see her imprisoned. And if we need to use her to get the *Scrolls of Atlantis*, you cannot hesitate."

Rogan blinked as he searched her face, certain he'd misheard. "Ye are leaving me in charge?"

"For now. You are biased, but not yet compromised. I still trust you to make the right decisions as you always have."

Her eyes spoke of decisions he never wanted to revisit.

Saving the Seven Planes had forced him to make calls that would haunt him forever. Civilians sacrificed for the greater good. Men, women, and children he could not save without damning them all. Actions he had committed himself other than ask them of his team. Nightmares he could never escape...

Nodding sharply, Rogan turned on his heels and

headed back into the room. Just being in the same place as his lifemate lessened the weight on his shoulders, but it also increased it in other areas.

Because he wasn't sure if when push came to shove, which one he would choose.

His lifemate.

Or the entirety of the Seven Planes.

TWENTY-FOUR

Hunter stood outside of the hotel, waiting for Jack to come back with whatever car he'd managed to get his hands on, when Xeno came down on her own. Glancing in her direction, he smiled.

He wasn't surprised when she didn't return it. She hadn't smiled once in the many years he'd known her.

Before he could say anything, a blue van pulled up to them. Jack sat in the driver's seat, his lip split, his left eye bruised. The amount of blood covering his jacket made it look like he'd been the victim of a very bad dye job.

"Yours?" Hunter chuckled, knowing damn well he'd take it as an insult.

Jack scoffed. "Unlike you, I don't see the reason to get hit in fights." He grinned as he held out a flap of his jacket. "It was vamps. Just my luck, I came across a nest last night."

He tried not to look nervous. "Should you be driving then?" he asked.

Even a creature of the Myth felt the effects of fatigue.

Some needed less sleep than others, but Jack had already gone the last two nights with barely a wink due to some personal issue. Being as secretive as he was, no one had bothered to ask. As long as their personal life didn't affect the mission, there was a silent agreement between the five of them to stay out of it – something Hunter himself had banked on a handful of times.

"Probably not, but I think I broke my leg, so I'm not moving again until it heals."

Hunter laughed at the joke full-heartedly, but when his colleague didn't even crack a smile, his good humor slowly morphed into uneasy suspicion. He flicked his eyes to Xeno, but she was already climbing into the backseat without so much as a care. Then again, she did have the advantage of being near immortal.

Deciding the only way he was going to get an honest answer was by seeing for himself, Hunter peeked through the driver's window. He didn't have to ask which leg was injured, let alone touch it to see if there was indeed a break.

"You think? Jesus, Jack! Your bone is sticking out!"

"Yeah... Yeah, I just didn't want to scare you. It should heal by the time we get there."

"Bloody hell, what is Emma going to think? She's not going –"

"Think about what?" Rogan interrupted from behind him.

Hunter spun around to find their leader pulling along a flustered Emma.

"Just look at him." He waved frustratingly at a grinning Jack.

When the trickster flashed his missing and cracked teeth, Hunter let out a stream of curses.

Rogan barely looked at him before ushering Emma into

the car. It was only after she had folded herself in beside Xeno, that he asked Jack, "Ye okay?"

"Yeah, just met up with an old friend this morning."

Hunter scowled at Jack's change in story. But even knowing that today's driver hadn't actually spent all night fighting for his life didn't do much to lessen his fear of crashing. Jack drove like a maniac at the best of times.

"Lycra?" Rogan asked as he headed for the passenger's side. He lifted an eyebrow when he caught sight of Jack's leg, but didn't bring any more attention to it.

"Yeah."

"We still have use of her plane?"

"Plane?" Emma paled and Hunter was glad to see at least one of them had good sense. He hadn't been keen on getting on another aircraft this early again either, but being the lowest member of this team, he didn't have much say when it came to decisions.

"Yep," Jack answered, most likely Rogan's question rather than Emma's.

"Good," the elementalist said. "Get in then, Hunter."

"Jesus." Though he cast his eyes to the sky and gave a worried rub of his neck, he did eventually get in.

As soon as the door shut, Rogan ordered him to teach Emma how to shield her mind against any more telepathic intrusions. Though Hunter suspected it was also to ease his own mind during the drive, he gladly focused his full attention on doing so.

Forty-five minutes and not a single car crash later (though there were a few very close calls in Hunter's opinion), they were standing outside the second private plane they were to board in as many days. During the ride, Emma had gotten the hang of building the mental wall needed – or so she claimed. It was a bit hard to tell for certain without Galvanor here to test her self-proclaimed defenses.

As Xeno made her way to the pilot's seat, Rogan pulled the other two agents aside to exchange new information. He kept an eye on their captive the whole time.

"We have an obstacle on the runway." Xeno's voice was calm over the speaker, making Hunter inwardly grown. The calmer the angel was, the more dire the situation. But though he marched into the cockpit with the others, expecting to see an army, he was entirely unprepared for the threat they ended up finding.

"Bloody hell." Jack winced as he rubbed the back of his neck. "Do not let that thing on."

Hunter shoved him in the shoulder. "Dude, you can fly. Imagine how it was for me."

He was about to request they run the damn thing over when Snuffles lowered his head and coughed up a wet fur ball.

"Ew gross," Hunter said as he shook his head. "Aren't only cats supposed to do that, not dogs?"

A low growl informed him that the distance and glass between them were no barrier to said dog's hearing.

With a toothy grin, Hunter quickly added, "Except for magical dogs of great power and wisdom, obviously."

Snuffle's eyes narrowed on him for a long moment, making his skin crawl. Then he bent his massive black head and grabbed the wet fur ball by its tail.

Horror filled each and every one of his veins as clear understanding crashed into him. Fuck. That wasn't a fur ball.

And double fuck, Rogan wasn't going to order Xeno to run it over. He was going to tell her to let it on board.

Because hanging from Snuffle's teeth was the dead rat that had been left in Emma's box.

The message she never got.

"Jesus Christ," he muttered. "Just shoot me now."

TWENTY-FIVE

When Snuffles dropped the dead rat on top of Rogan's shoes, it came with a large puddle of drool. The amount could only be explained if he had horded every drop for the last hour. Looking up, the dog smiled, his tongue lolling out between his massive teeth. Rogan stepped back and shook his foot, thankful he was wearing boots.

"Oh my God, Snuffles," Emma said. "That is just gross. I thought only cats did this."

Snuffles growled at her, and she darted behind Rogan. His fingers twitched at his sides as he prepared to protect her, losing another plane be damned.

Enough! Hades commanded, his tone brokering on the edge of dangerous. *Its message could be of great use.*

Rogan didn't relax. Snuffles, however, didn't care. Then again, if Rogan was a monstrous hellhound with true immortality he wouldn't give a crap about some pesky elementalist either.

Glancing down at the rat, Rogan noticed it looked as if it'd died in its sleep a mere second ago. There wasn't any decay or obvious signs of trauma. If it wasn't for the drowned rat look of its coat, it could have been mistaken for sleeping.

Shifting so Emma could get a good look at it, he waited for her to say something.

But all she did was stare at it.

"Well?" Xeno demanded after five minutes of silence.

"Well, what?" Emma asked when no one else did.

"What's it saying?"

"Saying...?" Eyes wide, she glanced at it again. The left side of its whiskers twitched. Then the right.

Gasping, she jerked away and brought a hand to her mouth. Rogan wrapped an arm around her, giving her stability as he held her tight against him.

"Maybe it's Morse code?" Jack offered as he turned to Hunter.

"Nope. That just looks like random twitching to me."

"W-what are you guys talking about?" Emma babbled, her voice low and strained.

He glanced at her. "Ye not communicating with it or something? Reading a message from yer sister?"

She paled to the color of death. Of sickness. He shifted her so her mouth was more away from him, but he didn't let her go. He wouldn't abandon her when she needed him.

"I-I th-that's..." Her words were so quiet he almost didn't hear them.

She is unable to raise it, Hades said inside his skull. *I will do the honors.*

Rogan turned around to face her, to prepare her for what she was about to see. She'd already gone through so much and it wasn't going to get easier anytime soon.

"Breathe, love. Yer father's goona raise the rat for us."

She blinked. Her jaw dropped. "My *father*?"

"Aye." She was going to find out one way or another; at least this way, he could distract her with some even more hard-to-grasp news.

"Wait. *Raise* the rat? From like...from like...the...t-the..." Her voice faded away as she dropped her eyes back to the rat.

He rubbed a hand in circles around her back. "Aye."

"And my...father can do this?"

"Aye. And yer sister." *And ye, probably.*

Her face blanched. A tremor shot through her. She jerked away from him, shaking her head. Pushing the bottom of her palms into her eyes, she took a deep breath. "Is that all Liz can do?" she asked softly, the hope obvious in her voice.

"Nay. She can also kill with a single touch of her right hand."

She pulled her hands away from her face and stared at them. She raised the right and turned it back and forth, studying it. "So she can kill Sebastian?"

He stayed silent, not wanting to dash her hopes so quickly. Sebastian had most likely ordered her not to hurt him. As strong as she was, a Holy Blood Contract was stronger. Not even the gods could resist its curse.

Giving him an excuse not to answer, Hades raised the dead rodent. Its tiny ribcage moved up and down as it took its first breath. Emma sucked in one of her own, and Rogan glanced at her, making sure she was okay.

The rat shook itself free of Snuffles' drool, then stood up on its hind legs. Its nose twitched in the air a few times before it dropped back down on all fours and scurried a few feet away. Turning back around, it faced Emma and stood back up on its hind legs. After staying like that for a second, it darted forward.

She jumped with a sharp inhale, but the rat barely ran

two lengths of its body before standing erect once more. It ran back the way it had come, then veered sharply right to run in a straight line about forty-five degrees from its previous direction. Immediately, it swiveled back the way it had come for one length and then darted to the left half a length or so. It stood up once more, then ran back into the center.

Rogan frowned. He waited for Hades to say something, to explain what the fuck they were seeing, but all was quiet inside his skull. Snuffles yawned, then walked away, leaving them to watch the rat do this over and over again in various patterns.

After nearly fifteen minutes of this bizarre display, Hunter smiled wide. Knowing something had clicked in that beautiful brain of his, Rogan didn't question it when Hunter scurried off. He came back quickly enough, pen and paper in his hands.

Hunter watched the rat with as much concentration as before, but instead of looking as lost as the others, he nodded his head methodically. Curious, everyone huddled around him as he began to write, their faces each slowly mimicking his in their own way. Xeno's eyebrows relaxed just slightly. Jack rolled his eyes with a scoff. Rogan looked back at the rat, this time in awe, and Emma gasped in sheer amazement.

"Is your sister a whisperer of rats?" Jack asked as the rat stood up on its back paws and then ran in a circle to convey the letter 'O.' "Or just animals in general?"

"What? No." Emma shook her head. "Neither. She... More animals hate her than like her, and she absolutely detests anything that crawls on its stomach or has more than four legs."

As the rodent ran back to the center, stood, ran down in a U shape, and stood back up at the end of it, Rogan glanced at Xeno. If Elizabeth didn't send the rat herself, then someone was helping her...unless this was a trap sent by Sebastian. Rogan wouldn't it put it past him. He was usually multiple steps ahead of them.

Glancing back over to see the full message on Hunter's notepad, he asked, "What in Hades' name is Geltin?"

"No idea," Hunter replied, his eyes still intently focused on the rat. Two letters later, his face cracked open with a grin. "But Tintagel, now that I do know."

Rogan frowned. "From the fairytales?" Tintagel Castle was the famous home of King Arthur, an imaginary king in a child's story...or a future prophecy, depending on who you talked to. It was hidden in a pocket universe called Merlin's Dimensio, created by the greatest witch himself.

Hunter grinned. "Yep."

He stayed silent, waiting for whatever it was Hunter was about to say because he didn't believe for one second that his agent was about to pin everything on a fairytale.

"I'm not saying King Arthur and Merlin is real," he started, "but there are two places on Earth associated with the myths. One is a castle in the southern reaches of England in a place called North Cornwall. It's a ruin now and only shares the same name."

His eyes sparkled as he glanced back at the rat, which was still running around making letters. "But the other is on the edge of the Lake District. It's a bridge near Penrith, and according to SCU legends, if you can get through the magical barrier, you'll access a pocket dimension."

There was a moment of silence. Then nodding, Rogan ordered Xeno to set the new coordinates. She left swiftly, without a word.

Emma watched her leave before turning to Rogan. "Who's my father?" she asked, her voice shaking just the slightest bit as she steeled herself for his answer.

Rogan flicked his gaze to Jack and Hunter, dismissing them so he could speak to her in private.

As soon as they left to separate parts of the plane, he turned back to his lifemate. *Want to weigh in here?* he asked her father.

When he didn't answer, Rogan mentally cursed.

Last night, she'd been so close to breaking. She had crawled into his bed in order to deal with it all. How much more could she handle before she fell apart?

"Rogan!" she snapped, her eyes hardening, her voice a lot harder. "Who's my father?"

Searching her face, he exhaled slowly. "Hades."

She blinked.

Then shook her head.

Then laughed. Loud and manic. "You're kidding me. You're fucking kidding me."

"Nay. He's your father."

She snorted.

Twisted and shook her hands in front of her.

Started to pace.

"No. No my father is dead. He's –" She stopped and turned to face him on another snort. "He's *dead.* Like, king of the dead, isn't he? God, Mom, you had such a horrible sense of humor." She pinched the bridge of her nose.

Taking a dead breath, she lifted her head on the exhale and spat out at a million miles an hour, "So do all the gods and goddesses exist then? Or is it just the Greeks? How did he meet my mom? How does that even work? Diane was like tiny. Shorter than me." She held her hand out in front of her, leveling it at her chest, palm down.

Not waiting for him to answer, she dropped her arm as more questions poured out of her. "Aren't all gods like super big or something? How could she have possibly have – How come more humans don't know about this? Not the god penis, human vagina thing, but them existing in the first place? And how come Liz has her powers, but I don't? I'm older. I'm not saying I even want them or am jealous of her doing something first, but like, what the hell? How does this even work? Am I..." She stopped, a look of pain and horror and relief crossing her face in quick concession. "Defective?"

Rogan scowled, hating she'd used that word. She was perfect and she didn't even know it. "Nay, lass. Ye're not defective. Younger siblings come into their powers earlier all the time."

But even still, most of them gained their powers during their ascension, which happened during puberty. Emma was way past that point. She should've been able to do something by now.

He frowned as he remembered what Xeno had revealed earlier. Maybe there was more to her curse than just being controlled by whoever made love to her? What if she couldn't fully come into her powers until that happened? A sick feeling twisted in his gut. She wasn't going to like this.

And he wasn't going to like getting it confirmed.

But Elizabeth hadn't popped up on their radar until the attack on Xi'aghn, until she'd fallen in with Sebastian. And by the sounds of it, she hadn't had any powers before then.

"Emma," he said slowly, "now this is goona sound a wee rude, but I need ye to answer honestly, aye?"

Her brows furrowed as she stopped her tirade of questions. "Okay..."

"Have ye ever..." He swallowed. "Have ye ever been with a man?"

Her cheeks burned a hot red, unwillingly giving him

his answer. "T-that is none of your business! You might have – have done things –"

"Emma, stop. I'm asking for another reason."

She crossed her arms over her chest as she waited.

Figuring there was no nice way to say it, he blurted, "Xeno discovered yer sister is being controlled. We think ye may have the same curse."

Her eyes widened, and that look of hope on her face tore at his chest like a caged werewolf on the full moon. He was about to crush it. Crush her.

"I knew it!" she squealed. "So we just have to get her away and – Wait, curse? I'm cursed? She's cursed?"

His lips parted, but though he desperately wanted to soothe away her horror, he couldn't think of anything to say that would do the job. She could never have sex without giving up her freedom. She could never fall in love with someone in case she was tempted to go all the way. She could never let him in.

So under all that pain, Rogan fell back on what he did know: cold, impersonal facts.

"Four thousand years ago, there was another child of the gods born. His name was Rakian, and he was the son of Morrighan and Loki. Alongside Sebastian, he ended up wrecking havoc on the Seven Planes, slaughtering entire villages and nearly destroying my entire race, along with the fey. It took us centuries to stop them. They obliterated one plane completely and nearly destroyed two others, Earth being one of them."

He deliberately left out the role Sebastian had played in Rakian's downfall. No one knew why he'd decided to turn on his ally of half a millennium, mostly because no one had been able to get close enough for that conversation. Immediately after killing him, the vampire had vanished.

"What does this have to do with me?"

"After Rakian and Sebastian was defeated, every clan and species came together to force the gods to sign a Holy Blood Contract. It's a powerful binding they cannot break without being cursed for eternity. Part of the conditions was that their children, called descendants, would also suffer a curse in an attempt to make sure that level of destruction never happened again."

She looked away from him, her hands clenching and unclenching in front of her. Turning her head back to him, she nodded for him to continue.

"Ye and yer sister are descendants. Your father is Hades and your mother is some unknown sex goddess."

She shook her head, but it wasn't wild or panicked this time. It was her slugging through all the information that had been thrown at her. "No, because Diane is our mom. She raised us. She looked just like us. She –" She shook her head again and closed her eyes. When she opened them, she took a deep breath and exhaled. "What does this have to do with my love life?"

He didn't want to tell her. Telling her would mean he'd lose her. Telling her would mean she'd never trust him or any man near her again.

But if he didn't tell her, she'd be vulnerable. Especially if she ended up in Damaculus. His jaw tightened at the thought of her in that twisted hellhole. Regardless of how this mission went, regardless of whether he failed to save Liz and Emma grew to hate him or not, he would not let the Royal Courts take her.

She was his lifemate, and want it or not, she would have his eternal protection.

He scanned his eyes over her face, memorizing each freckle that graced her cheeks, the line of her nose, the spread of her lips. He wanted to remember her like this, before she learned to fear him.

Exhaling strongly, he said, "Yer curse is based on yer parentage. As a daughter of a sex goddess, ye cannot have sex without –" He forced the words past the growing knot in his throat. "Losing yer free will. Ye will be forced to obey whatever they ordered."

Emma paled to the color of sickness.

He wanted to take her hands, to give her a squeeze so she knew she wasn't alone.

Doubting she'd want the touch of any man right now, he clenched his fingers at his sides. "But I think yer powers will not develop until ye do."

He shifted onto the balls of his feet in the following silence. The seconds dragged into a minute, then another as Emma stared at him in frozen silence. Unable to fight the urge to soothe her any longer, Rogan reached for her hand.

Once his fingers grazed hers, Emma's paralyzing shock shattered like a broken mirror.

She jerked away from him, her eyes wide. "Oh my God, is that why you – This morning, you were just – Oh my God."

"Emma –" His chest tightened at her accusations. After everything he had done to try to ease her into this so she wouldn't have new nightmares on top of the old, this was how she thought of him? A cold, calculating bastard who would seduce her so he could make her do anything he wanted?

"Don't Emma me!" She rubbed her hands across her arms, her chest as if trying to erase his touch. "Did you know this morning or not?"

"Is that what ye think?" he asked, his stomach growing heavy.

"Yes! Because you could use me to get to Liz! That's all you want, isn't it? Her and this stupid artifact! You don't give a single damn about me!" Tears burned her eyes.

Lethal frustration burned from his. "I doona give a single damn, do I?" he growled, taking a step toward her.

How could she not feel their bond? How could she not know he'd do anything for her? That if it came to her or the Seven Planes, he'd decided he would watch the worlds burn?

She glared at him, her arms crossed, her chin raised. "Not a fucking one."

He took another step toward her, his eyes locked on hers. She sucked in a breath, her lips parting as the first flicker of uncertainty crossed her pretty face.

She took a step back when he continued his advance. Her breathing changed from that of furious anger to heated desire, but she didn't break his gaze.

Crowding her against the wall, he trapped her in between his arms and just watched her. His nostrils flared as he breathed her in. The smell of the hotel's shampoo made his cock hard as he remembered the taste of her this morning. His tongue darted out to lick his lips. He could still taste her there. He could still feel her hands in his hair. Could still feel her pussy pressing against him as she moaned.

"R-Rogan?"

A wicked grin turned up a corner of his mouth as he cupped her cheek. Her eyes fluttered close as he stroked a rough thumb over her lips. "Aye, Emma. I'm goona show ye how much I doona give a damn."

And then his lips took the place of his thumb, hard and hot and heavy.

His hand moved to the back of her head, angling her into the best position for an earth shattering kiss. His lips rubbed across hers in a tantalizing promise of ecstasy.

She kept her mouth shut for a second, two before

parting it on a moan. Her tongue flicked out greedily for his, but he was gone before she could satisfy her hunger. Her frustrated cry immediately turned into a sound of arousal as his lips found the sensitive spot on her neck. He kissed down the length of it before lavishing her skin with his tongue.

Her head fell to the side to give him better access. Reaching up, he palmed one of her breasts, teasing her through the fabric as he rubbed his mouth over the crook of her neck. Moaning, she dug her fingers into his hair and rocked her hips against him.

He grabbed her ass and lifted her up the wall, pinning her there with his body as his mouth claimed hers. His tongue pushed its way inside, lapping up every moan and sigh she couldn't help but utter.

Her brain might mistrust him, but her body didn't. Her body craved him, was willing to let him do anything and everything he wanted to it.

And gods, did he want to do everything. The taste of her this morning hadn't been enough. It had been over too quickly. He wanted to be able to taste her in his mouth for the entire day. He wanted to be able to smell her on his cock. He wanted to know what it felt like to slide into her wet pussy as she bucked and moaned beneath him.

Dragging his teeth across her bottom lip, he nipped her, then moved back to her neck. Gripping her ass, he lifted her higher so her breasts were at mouth level. Releasing her with one hand, he used it to push up her shirt and bra.

His mouth closed over the erect bud of her left nipple, causing her to arch back as her legs tightened around his waist. He licked his way across her breast to the other, then cupped the one he had just left. As she squirmed beneath his touch, he teased her mercilessly. Her hands dug into his hair. Her body bucked against him. He knew she was getting close. He loved that she was sensitive enough to come just by his mouth on her tits.

When she yanked his head down and arched off the wall, he raised one hand and covered her mouth. Her moans and screams were for him alone. He didn't want Jack, with his stupid fucking hearing, to be blessed with anything at all.

As her scream vibrated against his palm, he lowered her back down the wall. His mouth replaced his hand as she sagged against him, her legs struggling to keep her up.

His tongue rough inside her, he feathered his hands down her body and slid inside her waistband. One hand grabbed her ass, massaging it with his fingers, while the other slipped to the V between her thighs. She jerked against his fingers.

Not waiting a moment longer, he pushed three fingers inside her, spreading her wide. She gasped against his mouth. She squirmed against the wall. Not waiting for her to get used to the girth inside her, he pumped his fingers hard as his palm pushed against her clit. He applied pressure to the outside of her pussy as he curled his fingers to hit that special spot. Relentlessly, he finger fucked her as she screamed into his mouth.

His cock strained hard against his pants.

Releasing her ass, he undid the button and pulled down the zip. Grabbing her hand, he lead it to his thick cock and forced her fingers around him through the fabric of his boxers. She searched for the hole in front and slipped inside.

He hissed when she finally touched him skin to skin. As she pumped him, he fucked her harder. He raised a hand to cup her cheek, then covered her mouth with it as he trailed his lips to her neck and bit.

She spasmed against him, her pussy clenching tight

around his fingers in a pulse that left him shaking. He was so close to orgasming himself.

Gritting his teeth, he fought it back.

Grabbing her hand, he forced her to release him. He pinned her arm to the wall to stop her for reaching back for it. Then he withdrew his other hand and tugged her leggings down to expose her pussy to his view. It was perfectly soaked, her curls of dark hair glistening in the artificial light of the plane.

Gripping his cock, he lined it up to just below her pussy. She sucked in a breath but didn't stop him when he pushed it in between her thighs. The top of it rubbed between her lips as he pumped his hips back and forth. The end of his cock hit the wall. Then drew back and hit again.

Licking his way up her neck to her ear, Rogan caught her bud in between his teeth. "Tell me to stop, Emma." He slid his cock between her thighs, squeezing his eyes shut. He raised a hand to her breast, cupping it as he played with the nipple. "Tell me to stop because of yer curse."

Sharp breaths exited her lips but those words never did. Lost in the throes of her passion, she was struggling to do anything more than rock her hips in rhythm to his.

Growling, Rogan pulled back and reached down to grab his cock. He lined it perfectly up with her pussy this time and pushed in just the tip. "Stop me, Emma."

His body vibrated with his need to enter her. His legs could barely keep him standing. He wanted to sink into her. He wanted to feel her gripping him down to the base, his balls slapping against her ass.

But he didn't want her bound to him.

He wanted to prove to her that she could trust him.

But when she arched her hips, coming dangerously close to sliding down that first inch of his cock, Rogan slammed his fist against the wall and had to use every ounce of his power to pull back.

She whined, the noise coming from deep in her throat. Gritting his teeth, Rogan unwrapped her legs from around his waist and lowered her to the ground. If he didn't stop this now, he wouldn't be able to.

Pulling back, shoving his aching cock back into his boxers, he looked her in the eye. Half-lidded, she stared at him in confusion.

"Nay," he breathed, his chest rising and falling in a runner's rhythm. "I doona have a damn care in the world about ye."

Then with a sharp twist of his heels, he turned and walked away.

Raising his wet fingers to his lips, he sucked them on a moan.

Fuck.

It wasn't just his lifemate who was cursed. This was going to be the death of him.

TWENTY-SIX

By the time they landed at the small airport in Carlisle, a town located twenty-six miles north of their target, Emma was avoiding Rogan with as much vigor as he was her. He'd just informed her she could be controlled if she ever had sex. He had then proceeded to take off her underwear and give her the best two orgasms of her life. All to make a fucking point.

The bastard!

What was she supposed to do with that? Drop to her knees and thank him for not forcing her to obey his every wish and command?

He did tell you to stop him.

Fuck off, she snapped at her stupid voice. What the fuck did it matter if he'd told her that? He'd deliberately put her in a situation knowing she'd be helpless to resist his stupid fucking charm.

Well, no more!

The next time she felt his mouth, it was going to be with her fist. Or a rock she threw at him because a fist would require her to get in way too close to him.

Like shirt ripping off close.

Wrap her legs around him close.

Ride him to oblivion close.

Fuck.

Irritated at herself just as much as she was at him, she forced herself to imagine throwing a rock at his mouth as she walked down the steps of the plane. He stood on the tarmac, talking to the driver of the Honda Civic who had been waiting for them to land. Not an ounce of shame weighted his shoulders. He didn't even glance at her in acknowledgement.

A few hours ago, he'd had his cock sliding between her thighs, and a few hours before *that*, he'd had his mouth there.

But now she was just another thing. Probably another notch in the bed post. Not even worthy of an apology for playing with her. As if her life was okay to play with. As if she wasn't already dealing with enough, learning all about the Seven Planes and the monsters that really existed and knowing her sister was being tortured. No. No, he had to go and seduce her all to show her how much of a 'gentleman' he was. How he was a really 'nice guy.'

The only nice thing about him was his ass.

And his mouth.

And his hands.

Her scowl deepened. Her consciousness could go fuck itself.

You just want someone to be angry at.

She snorted. Oh look at that, at least she wouldn't have to splash out a lot of money on therapists because her stupid voice decided it was qualified.

And okay, Emma admitted as she stomped down the stairs, perhaps it was a little bit right.

She had nothing to hold on to. She had no idea how to navigate discovering she wasn't human and her dead father was actually alive and a fucking god. She had no idea how to save her sister from either a fucking vampire or a lifetime in prison. She didn't know what to do with Snuffles. She'd always wanted a pet, had always loved animals, but he was a freaking three headed dog and guardian of the Underworld. Did he like to play fetch? Did she need to buy him a ball? Or was tug more his idea of fun?

She shuddered, imagining him tugging a pour soul in half. Or thirds, as it would be.

Fuck. She had no idea what she was doing.

Elizabeth would've done a much better job at handling all this. She should be the one with Rogan and them, not Emma. Not useless fucking Emma.

Her eyes skirted to Rogan. The idea of him and Liz together twisted her stomach.

"Tell me to stop, Emma."

The fucking bastard.

Why couldn't he have just answered her question? Why did he have to *prove* that if he wanted to take her, if he wanted to control her, she'd let him? Didn't he know how much that hurt? How much that embarrassed her to know? That she was so out of her fucking depth, she might as well give up swimming and drown?

Exhaling roughly, she ripped her eyes away from him. Her feet touched the tarmac. Her legs carried her over to the car. The driver glanced at her, looked back at Rogan, nodded, and walked off.

"Where's she going?" Emma asked Xeno as her gaze followed the dark skinned woman walking off the runway. Xeno didn't answer, just opened the driver's side door and stepped in.

Left alone with Rogan, Jack already in the backseat of the car and Hunter still on the plane, Emma skirted her gaze around the airport. There wasn't a single other plane in sight.

"She was just dropping off the car," Rogan answered. After a pause, he asked, "How are ye han–"

"Did someone take the rat?" Hunter interrupted, filling the door of the plane with his tall frame.

Heat filling her cheeks, Emma looked down at her feet. The rat had looked so pathetic as it'd run round and round in circles, Emma had known that if she left it behind, one of them would kill it. If not to put it out of its misery, then to stop it from sharing its secrets with whomever found it. Unable to bear the act of any more violence, Emma had stowed it away. If it stayed on the plane, then the only person it could possibly tell was Jack's friend. Despite the injuries Lycra had inflicted on him, surely she was trustworthy enough not to send them to the gallows?

"Emma," Rogan said softly.

She shook her head. "I don't know where it went."

His gaze darted to Xeno, then back to her. And she knew he knew.

When he turned to look at Hunter, she grabbed his arm and tugged. "Please don't," she begged.

His cold eyes made her shiver. Her legs itched to run back toward the plane, but she knew she'd never make it past Hunter.

"It's already dead, Emma. Let it rest in peace."

"It's not dead," she pushed. "It's running around and –"

He stepped closer, his eyes piercing. "It's dead. Hades didn't give it back its soul just like yer sister doesn't give back the souls of those she raises. They're just husks."

"But –" She wanted to be able to save one rat.

She wanted to be able to make one good difference to

someone.

Because if she couldn't save a rat, then how the hell was she going to save her sister?

But Rogan's cold eyes told her she'd fail in this. Just like she failed in everything.

Clenching her fists, she looked away.

"It's behind the couch in the sitting room," he called out.

Her heart tightened as she yanked open the door of the car. Praying Hunter would kill it quickly, Emma scooted in and shut the door behind her. A couple minutes later, she was joined by Hunter. As she shuffled over into the middle seat, she found she couldn't meet his eye.

"It was quick," he murmured. "And already being dead, it didn't feel any pain."

She nodded, but kept her eyes on her feet. What did it matter if it didn't feel any pain when she felt enough for both of them? Liz would've told her to chill out because it was just a rat. She'd always been a softie.

But rat or not, it had once been alive. It had once known pain and hunger and fear.

As the car started, Snuffles sitting in the trunk, she wrapped her arms around herself. Her eyes on the middle console, she practiced building the mental barriers Hunter had taught her. One solid wall made of bricks. A hazy fog that disrupted any incoming communication. And a sun shining brightly, its UV light killing off any lingering invasion.

She practiced this for the entire half hour the drive took, needing to keep her mind occupied, needing to be a hell of a lot stronger than she currently was.

Because she was done whining about not being able to do anything. She was done hating the fact that she was useless and inexperienced.

She had to do something.

And so she built the wall a second time, brick by brick.

She swept the fog through and parted the clouds for the sun to shine.

And then she hid the sun and took away the fog and destroyed the wall brick by brick.

With a slow inhale, she started building it all over again.

She was not weak.

She was not useless.

She was the daughter of fucking Hades.

The owner or partial owner of fucking Cerberus.

She was going to save her sister.

I'm coming, Liz. I promise.

TWENTY-SEVEN

When they stepped out of the car, Emma didn't even question the fact that they were in the middle of a field full of sheep with not a house in sight. She blindly followed Hunter when he walked forward, his steps purposeful and quick across the muddy grass.

Stopping abruptly, he held up his hand like a mime pressing it against something invisible.

She waited patiently, expecting a sudden mansion to appear because why not?

But nothing happened.

The air didn't even shimmer.

Reaching forward, Hunter closed his fist around the air and twisted as if opening a door. Then he took a step forward and disappeared.

Her eyes widened. She blinked. Jack followed Hunter and he too disappeared.

She looked around the field, wondering if there were any farmers watching nearby. What happens if they pulled out their phones and started recording? Would the

SCU get involved or would the news outlets just think it was a magic trick done with a mirror?

"Come on," Rogan said, grabbing her arm and steering her toward the invisible box. "Ye are letting all the heat out."

Digging her heels in, she pulled her arm free. "I can walk." Lifting her chin, she strolled forward.

And just kept going.

And going.

The grass flattened under her feet. The sheep still grazed around her.

Stopping, she turned back to Rogan. "So where are we? An alternative universe or something?"

He shook his head. "We're in the same field. On Earth." He tilted his head to the side. "Ye missed the door. If ye doona enter exactly right, ye won't get in."

"Well, how was I to know?" she muttered, walking back. "You could've told me before I made it halfway across the field."

He grinned boyishly, one half of his mouth lifting. "I was distracted watching yer arse. Ye do a cute little walk when ye're angry."

Heat filled her cheeks. Sputtering, Emma tried to think of a sharp retort but came up empty.

"Come on though. If the door's left open too long, it'll close on ye, and ye doona want to be caught half-way inside it."

Grabbing her hand, he pulled her forward. One step, they were in the field full of sheep and the next, she was in the hallway of a modern house.

"So where are we now?" she asked again, absolutely certain it wasn't going to be in the same field on Earth.

Hunter looked up at her from his position on the bottom step of the stairs. Tucking his shoelaces into his recently taken off shoes, he said, "Technically, we are still on Earth. We're just in a pocket dimension. The SCU has safe houses like this all across the world."

He placed his shoes on the rack beside the door and stood in his mismatching socks. One was blue with black stripes. The other was covered in the colorful animals of a child's cartoon. "Why don't you take off your shoes and then I'll show you to your room? They're fairly basic, but it'll be your own space for the time we're here."

Personal space sounded amazing right now. Bending down, Emma quickly pulled off her shoes, the laces still done up, and placed them on the rack below Hunter's.

She followed him up the set of wooden stairs. Pushing open a door, he showed her a simple room with a double bed in it and a desk by the door. A double wardrobe stood on the other side. "It's not much, but we're not big on having fun. So if there's anything you'd like to have to pass the time, just ask Rogan and he'll pull it out of his jacket."

"What's up with that? His jacket, I mean," she asked, stepping into the room. "Obviously it's magic, but like, can he pull *anything* out of it?"

"Not quite. His pockets are basically portal doors to a room in the Elv've'Norc headquarters. He has a set list of objects: weapons, rations, camping gear, things like that that he takes on every mission. For special missions, he'll add certain items to the room before we depart. A charm's been placed on the room so that when accessed through his jacket pockets, he'll grab whatever item he's thinking of."

"And if I wanted something other than what he had in there?"

"Then he'll pull out a notepad and write down his shopping list. One of the agents in administration gets a ping every time he accesses it. If they see a note has been added, they will do the shopping. It normally takes them a few minutes to a few hours to get everything depending on the rarity of the item."

"And how big of an item can he take out?"

He grinned. "He pulled out a king-sized mattress once. Basically, if he can get it to fit in the room, he can pull it through the portal."

"How?"

He shrugged. "I haven't figured that out yet, but one of these days, I will."

"So can he bring me some clothes?"

Hunter nodded. Opening a drawer, he pulled out a notepad and a pen. "Just write down your sizes and style preferences. There's a basic toiletry set in the bathroom, but if you want anything specific, just add that too."

She wrote down a request for four sets of clothes, all loose fitting shirts and pants that allowed for flexibility. Her cheeks heating, she glanced up at Hunter. "Will anyone read this other than Rogan and whoever does the shopping?"

His grin shot up to his eyes. "Do you mean me?"

She nodded.

He placed a hand over his heart. "Dragon's honor, I won't peek."

She chewed on the inside of her lip as she studied him. Was it worth the potential embarrassment just to get back at Rogan?

Cupping her hand around the notepad, she scribbled down her request. Her cheeks heated. Ripping the sheet off, she quickly folded the piece of paper into fourths and handed it to Hunter.

He raised his hand, his eyes shining, his teeth full across his face. Pinching the piece of paper, he held it in the air, not yet taking it from her. "You know," he said slowly. "If you really want to mess with him, add a rose to the list."

"Hunter!" She wanted to die. "You said you wouldn't peek!"

He shrugged. "And my curiosity is going to kill me one day." He rolled his lips together. "But I can't resist poking the guy. He's always so freakin' serious. You're good for him though. I've never seen him more on edge."

She snorted. "He's on edge?"

"Oh definitely. I think the last time he had sex for actual pleasure was about..." He cocked his head to the side. "Six, seven years."

Her eyes widened. Her mouth fell open.

He shrugged. "Probably longer. Given how uptight he is, he's probably still a virgin."

She worked her throat as a flush burned across her cheeks. "He is most definitely not inexperienced." Eyes widening even further, she slammed a hand across her mouth.

He chuckled. "I'll be sure to pass on the compliment."

"Don't you dare!"

"You're right. Given how loud you were, I'm sure he already knows."

She dropped her head in her hands. "Oh my God, just kill me now."

He laughed. "I'm joking. I didn't hear a thing. Jack might've; he has the hearing of a fucking bat, and Xeno can probably sense your essence on each other –"

"Oh my God, please stop talking."

"Okay, okay, but now that the cat's out of the bag, what's the harm in adding to that list?"

Peeking out from between her fingers, she looked at the list still folded in his hand.

She hesitated for just a second and then grabbed it. Unfolding it on the table, she picked up the pen and added a couple more items.

Her face hotter than the sun, she kept her eyes on the floor when she handed the note back to Hunter.

"I will deliver this personally and report back on his reaction," he promised.

Oh my God.

"In the meantime, try to get some rest. I'll bring dinner up for you later."

She nodded. Despite having not done much physically today, she was absolutely exhausted. As he left the room, she crawled onto the bed. But just as she laid down, she bolted upright and rushed for the door.

But she was too late. The lock had clicked a second ago. Twisting the knob, Emma kicked at the door. "Dammit, Hunter! What are you doing?"

"I'm sorry. Rogan's orders."

"The fuck!" She banged on the door with her fist.

"I tried to talk him out of it, I swear."

"Rogan, you coward!" she shouted loudly so he'd hear wherever he was in the fucking house. "If you want to lock me up, have the balls to do it yourself!"

Hunter chuckled. "Oh, you two are made for each other. I'll be up with food in a few hours. And don't bother screaming anymore. Rogan will just spell the room so we can't hear you."

Whistling – fucking *whistling*, the traitor walked away.

TWENTY-EIGHT

True to his word, Hunter brought her something to eat a few hours later. He placed the tray down on the desk, dodged the pillow she chucked at him, then shut the door behind him.

By tomorrow, she was a bit more calm. This time, she only squeezed the pillow in her hands, wishing it was his throat. Given his foot of extra height and his sixty or so additional pounds, she wasn't foolish enough to try it for real.

"Looking beautiful, sunshine."

"I'd look better if I could actually enjoy some sunshine."

He crossed over to the window in silence and pulled the curtain back. She refused to look at the rain pelting the glass. It was blowing an actual gale outside.

"If you really want to go outside today, I can probably convince Rogan to let you walk around the field. He read your list yesterday and has been in a mood ever since." He grinned. "If you ask me, it's cuz he's horny as hell."

"Hunter!"

"What?" He snickered. "Isn't that what you wanted, him squirming at your mercy?"

Well, yes, but it was a bit more complicated than that. She wanted a bit of power over him so she didn't feel so helpless. He'd thrown it in her face that he could have her whenever he wanted her. And if they did ever have sex, she'd be enslaved to him.

But more than that, he'd taunted her with the level of his control. She wanted him to be crazy about her like she was crazy about him. She wanted him to go mad thinking about her. So wanted…him to care.

Ignoring Hunter's watchful eyes, Emma dug into her breakfast. Leaving the sausages, she finished her eggs, beans, and toast. "Thank you. That was delicious." When she finished the last bite, she asked, "Any idea when the stuff will get here?"

He laughed so hard she couldn't help but smile. "It came last night, but Rogan's absolutely refused to take anything out of his jacket since then. Probably because he's thinking about the rose toy too much and doesn't want to accidentally pull it out."

She pressed her lips together to hold in her chuckle. She hoped the bastard was suffering as much as she was. "He could be thinking about the crotchless lingerie."

"Or the cuffs."

Her cheeks heated, but she was laughing too hard now to care.

"Well," Emma said once she finally managed to suck in a stable breath, "if you can get me some clothes, that'd be great. These are starting to smell."

"A lady never smells."

She rolled her eyes. "That is so sexist. Of course women smell."

"Oh yeah, women do but not ladies like yourself." His

wink sent her over the edge.

Standing, his smile fading, he nodded. "I'll bring them by with lunch."

Sighing, she nodded. He'd see her before that to take her to the bathroom, but she didn't want to mention it. It was embarrassing enough having him stand outside the door, listening to her go.

When the door shut behind him, she stood up from the bed and started doing some warm up stretches. It was about time she got back in shape. Next came sit ups, push ups, punches, and kicks. Elizabeth was a lot better fighter than her, and Emma had no delusions she'd be able to fight a vampire or any of the other creatures hand-to-hand anyway, but at least it gave her something to do.

Breathing heavily, a glean of sweat on her skin, she placed her hands on her hips and waited for her heart rate to come back down.

Lunch came and went. Hunter gave her a set of clothes, then led her to the bathroom to have a shower. She glanced around for Rogan in the hall, but as always, she didn't see him.

She shut the door behind her, then sagged against it with her new set of clothes held to her chest. Closing her eyes, she took a deep breath, then pushed off the door and started to undress.

As she slid her underwear down her legs, she glanced at the door, half-expecting Rogan to open it. This would be the first time she'd managed to shower in peace if he didn't.

When the door stayed shut, she tried to ignore the disappointment flooding through her. Shaking her head, she stepped into the shower. She reached forward to turn the knob to cold when she realized it was already twisted to the stopper. She stared at it for a second before a stupid smile filled her face.

Rogan was taking ice cold showers. She hoped he was being tormented by the thoughts of her.

She was in the shower. Rogan couldn't help but feel the water sliding over her skin, running down every gentle curve of her body. He tried to shut off his seventh sense, the one of magic, but even though he no longer felt Hunter's presence, Jack and Xeno having already left the house, he could still feel hers.

And it was driving him insane.

He could sense her hands disrupting the droplets of the shower as she rubbed them over her body. She lingered on her neck, her breasts. Was she remembering his touch there? Was she wishing he was in there with her, taking her against the wall?

Shifting in his chair in his room, Rogan kept his eyes on the piece of paper in front of him. Hunter had written down the answers Delentia had given him and handed them each a copy to try to decipher.

He had read them over and over again, yet wasn't anywhere close to a useful answer. 'By the neck,' he and the rest of them had decided meant Sebastian had been choking Liz at the time of Hunter's questioning. Although it pained Rogan to know Emma's beloved sister was being tortured, it wasn't of much use. Even if she was as much of a victim as Cariad's team had been, the Royal Courts would not be merciful in their sentencing.

And neither would Rogan's team.

He couldn't ask them to risk their lives trying to capture her. If push came to shove, he didn't want them to hesitate doing whatever they needed to in order to stay alive. If they pulled their punches from the get go, she'd kill them all. Hunter was human. As trained as he was with every weapon, including his bare hands, he didn't have their strength or speed. Jack was less than a hundred years old. As powerful as he was, he couldn't stand toe to toe with a descendant. And Xeno... She was nearly a fallen. This would probably be her last mission as it was.

His eyes narrowed on the sheet of paper, trying to focus on what the other two answers meant, but all he could see were the water droplets sliding down Emma's skin at the other end of the house.

He shifted in his seat again, sensing the water flowing down her stomach and between her thighs.

His cock strained against the harsh fabric of his pants. His breathing became heavier. When the words on the paper no longer registered in his eyes, he leaned back in the chair and groaned.

This is fucking useless.

Perhaps, if he relieved himself quickly, he'd be able to focus again...

Unbuttoning his pants, he pulled down the zipper and closed his eyes. His hand fisted around his cock as he focused on the water sliding over his lifemate's skin. He could make out the buds of her nipples, the curves of her body. He could feel her rubbing her hands across her breasts, cupping them like he wanted to.

He slid his hand down to the base of his cock and then stopped.

Fuck, he felt too much like a peeping Tom to enjoy it.

Cursing, he released his cock. He had half a mind to go to her and relieve them both. She'd asked him for a dildo and a rose toy that sucked on her clit. She'd wanted lingerie. And cuffs.

He could take them to her. He could cuff her to the shower head, dress her in the lingerie, and use the toys to tease her as she'd been teasing him.

Jack and Xeno weren't here, having left to try to find the way into Tintagel Castle.

It was just him and her. And fucking Hunter. Gods, the guy was cockblocking him left and right these days.

He sucked in a harsh breath and jerked back in his chair as he felt her hand run down her stomach and to her wet pussy. If she stuck a finger inside herself, he was going to lose it.

Focusing on the water coming out of the shower head, he pushed out with his power. He controlled the stream in the air, separating the molecules to make a sentence.

Ye've got my attention. Now what are ye going to do with it?

Emma sucked in a breath as she read Rogan's message. She had one hand frozen cupping herself and the other pinching her nipple.

The water droplets all across her body ran upwards, causing her to squeeze her thighs together. He wasn't just watching. He was here with her.

Fuck. She'd never been more turned on.

Feeling his eyes on her, his magic, she increased the pressure on her nipple. She imagined his teeth claiming it. Digging her nails in, she pinched it harder. The water message dropped from the air, flowing naturally from the shower head once more.

Wondering if that meant he was gone, she paused. The water swirled around her hands, urging her to continue.

Moaning, she pushed one of her fingers inside herself. It wasn't as thick as his. It wasn't as long. But it curled at just the right spot to make her legs weak and her heart race.

The water moved around to her back. Her legs flew out from under her as he forced her to fall. He caught her in the air and lowered her down into the tub until she was lying against the back, her legs pushed up, her knees bent. Then he was pushing her legs apart, opening her up to him. The water flowed down her pussy, slow and leisurely, and she just knew he was learning every inch of her.

Squirming, Emma pushed her fingers deeper inside. Water coated her hand, applying pressure on her knuckles to change the rhythm. She could feel his desire through how fast the pace was. He moved her other hand, using her to play with her breasts.

Rolling her head back, Emma moaned. She lifted her hips, meeting her thrusts, *his* thrusts as she imagined him in the tub with her.

An ice cube formed in the air in front of her face. She sucked in a breath as she watched it lower to her breasts. She tensed in anticipation of the cold. Then jerked when it finally touched.

Her nerve endings sparked from the intense sensation. Gasping, she watched it with wide eyes as it trailed lower, leaving goosebumps in its wake. Her fingers moved faster. She cupped her breast tighter. When the cube passed her belly button, she spasmed in the tub. The anticipation was killing her.

Would he touch her there?

But when it got to the top of her curls, it melted back into water. She jerked upright as the entire area prickled from the semi-pain of the cold.

His touch left her hands.

And then the water in front of her hardened into ice once more.

Her lips parted. Her chest rose and fell in heavy pants.

An ice model of his cock pressed against her mouth.

Shaking, she waited for him to push inside.

Releasing her breast, she lowered her hand down to her clit, rubbing it as she slipped another finger inside herself. She moaned his name as the tip of his cock ran across her lips.

Pushed to the edge of ecstasy, Emma closed her eyes. She pressed down harder on her clit, tensing, ready for that final fall. But then there was a shock of cold between her thighs. She jerked upright when his cock pushed against the lips of her pussy. Electricity arched through her. The intense cold was almost too much. Painful as well as pleasurable.

She wanted him here. She wanted to break his control. She wanted him inside her, as wild and as needy as she was.

Lifting her hips off the tub, Emma begged him to enter her.

But he teased the outside of her lips, numbing it before body-warm water heated it back up again. Squirming, Emma pressed an arm across her mouth and screamed.

The alternating temperatures were driving her wild. It was as if he was really here, holding an ice cube in his mouth as he licked her to the edge of orgasm.

He rubbed the cock against her clit, her labia, her thighs. He had her twisting and knocking the shampoo bottles off the edge of the tub. They clattered against her legs. Rogan righted them again, moving them out of his way.

Throwing her head back, Emma bit down on her arm when he finally pushed his cock inside her. Her thighs squeezed together, holding him in position.

A message appeared in the air. *Fuck, Emma. Open for me.*

She whimpered, the feeling too much to bear. She was

stretched tight, the ice too intense. Or maybe that was just his size.

"Fuck," she breathed as his cock slid in another inch.

Open for me. Take me all.

She rotated her hips, trying to spread herself wider.

He sank in another inch.

Whimpering, she gripped the edges of the tub.

His cock started to slide out. Her knuckles turned white as the sensation rocked through her. He slammed back in, slightly further than before, and she gasped his name in pleasure.

He pumped inside her, going deeper and deeper every time until he was finally in all the way.

She tried to close her thighs, wanting to wrap her legs around him, but he pushed them apart, keeping her open.

He used her hands to cup her breasts, to squeeze them like he wanted to. When he wrapped water around her fingers to pinch her nipples, she moaned his name.

And then again when he slid his cock back out and then in.

He picked up rhythm. Lifted her hips. Palmed her breasts. And then placed another ice cock near her lips. She panted against it, and it slid in, numbing her mouth so she could swallow it deeper. As it knocked against the back of her throat, the cock in her pussy moved faster.

He took her in both holes, riding her hard and fast in each. He slid against both set of her lips. Her tonsils and tongue wrapped around one while her pussy gripped the other. He pushed so deep, so fast, so rough.

Crazy.

Wild.

Feral.

Knowing he was as swept up in this as she was, the pressure increased inside her. Her legs started to shake.

Her thighs quivered, and her hands squeezed her breasts hard.

Jerking up off the tub, she tried to scream but couldn't make a noise around his cock.

And still they pumped inside her, building her back up before she even had the chance to come down.

Writhing, Emma was helpless to the second wave.

And the third.

And the fourth.

It wasn't until the fifth that he finally left her body. Exhausted and spent, she couldn't move her legs, let alone stand. So he helped her to her feet. Lifting her out of the bath, he wrapped a towel around her.

Get dressed. Hunter's starting to get suspicious.

Too sated to even care, Emma stumbled back to her room without shame.

TWENTY-NINE

"Morning." Hunter's teasing tone caused her to groan.

"Please don't." Emma pushed her head further into her pillow as yesterday's shower and last night's activities came back all too clearly. She would've liked to claim her weak decisions on alcohol. Or boredom. Or some femme assassin seduction shit. But the truth was, she just wanted to make him crazy about her. So she'd snuck the ice toy out with her on her way back to her room, and Rogan had stayed with her nearly all night.

How she didn't have an ice burn was beyond her.

She groaned, really, really hoping Hunter didn't ask.

Personal boundaries, he did not seem to have a respect for.

"So..." he said slowly as he placed the tray of food down on the bed. "How's your p–"

She jerked upright and swung her pillow into his face. "Don't you say it!"

Laughing, he stepped away, his arms raised. "Weird reaction to have when I was asking how your drawing was coming along, but okay." His eyes twinkled with delight.

Blushing over her outburst, Emma tried to shrug it off. "Oh, yeah, that. It's..." She glanced over at the desk. The ink drawing in question was a half done scene of a man (*cough, cough* Rogan) being eaten by a giant spider. She'd only drawn him and the two fangs piercing his torso so far, but his face, twisted in agony, told of his impending doom.

"Yeah...I've lost motivation for...that." Picking up her fork, she dug into the eggs. "Probably not going to finish it."

"Because he made you orgasm like six, seven times last night?"

Leaning forward, she coughed on her breakfast and whacked her chest. "Uh...w-what do you... I don't know... Uh..." Swallowing past the lump in her throat, she grabbed the glass of orange juice and downed half of it.

"I knew that shower you had was too long."

Her eyes watering from the heat of her cheeks, she refused to look up at him.

"Fuck my curiosity, but how the hell does that even work? Does he use, like, water tentacles or something?"

"Hunter! Get out!"

"Oh, come on. Getting anything out of Rogan is like prying teeth from an alligator. Yes, you might be able to get a grip on one with pliers, but you'll lose your whole fucking arm in the process."

"Oh my God. Send Jack in for now on with my food. Or Xeno."

He placed his hands over his heart as if wounded. "You don't mean that."

No, she didn't. Despite how much embarrassment he caused her, she loved his company. "Yes, I do."

He dropped onto his knees and held his hands up, his fingers entwined as if in prayer. “Please tell me what I can do to get back in your good favor. I’ll do anything. Anything. I swear.”

Laughing, she swatted at his hands. “Alright, alright. I’ll forgive you if...” She hesitated, working through what it was she wanted. She doubted he’d let her out, and given Rogan wasn’t giving her anything she asked for (well, outside of a certain area), asking for material items was pretty useless too. Somehow, she doubted Hunter had the time to go out shopping for art supplies or books to pass the time.

Finally deciding on what she wanted, she smiled. “I’ll forgive you if you spar with me.”

He quirked a brow.

“I’ve taken some lessons. Growing up in WITSEC with a paranoid mom...” She blinked. Had her mom even rolled on the mafia or had that all just been a ruse to keep them hidden from all this? From their father? From Sebastian? Or the WALL?

Deciding it didn’t matter right now, she continued, “I know a bit of krav maga and kickboxing. And I can shoot a bow.” At a non-moving target only thirty feet away, but he didn’t need to know that.

He smiled, but it wasn’t an enthusiastic one. It was an “I’m so sorry, but Rogan is never going to go for that” one.

“Please?” she begged. “I want to know how to do something other than build mental blocks.”

Rising to his feet, Hunter kept his eyes on her. Hope bloomed over the fact he wasn’t automatically shooting her down. “Or a book on defense against vampires and werewolves or whatever?” she tried. She’d take anything at this point. Just something to not make her feel so useless and helpless.

Digging into his jacket, he pulled out a throwing knife. "Do you know how to use one of these?"

She nodded. She knew *how* to use it. Hold the non-stabby end; poke people with the stabby end. She just wasn't very good at it.

"Alright then," he said with a shrug. Holding the knife out to her, hilt first, he said, "Take it."

She smiled so wide her cheeks hurt. Grabbing it, she breathed, "Thank you! If you can bring me a target, I'll love you forever."

He grinned and bowed his head. "Of course. Anything to make you happy."

Whistling, he turned from the room.

Giddy over finally being able to do something, Emma placed the knife down beside her and scoffed down her breakfast.

Afterwards, she opened the cupboard, stood on the other side of the room, and threw the knife hard at the backside.

When it embedded deep to the hilt, she smiled.

Hell yeah.

She wasn't so helpless after all.

She completely ignored the fact that the knife was sticking out of the wall, nowhere near where she'd aimed.

"We need to use her." Xeno's words caused Rogan to still. He'd known this decision was coming, would have brought it up himself days ago if it wasn't his lifemate they were talking about.

How many times had he used people as bait? Men, women, and children? Although he had yet to lose a civilian this way, it was always a dangerous roll of the dice.

Glancing between then, Hunter said, "We've only been here a few days. Give me a few more to find whoever it was Sebastian left."

"He's left a lot of people to die over the years," she said, her cold eyes on Rogan. "There's no way for you to know who she meant."

"It might not even be a person," Jack added. "And if he left them to die, they're probably dead. I fail to see how us giving him back a corpse is going to help."

Rogan couldn't either, but he didn't care. He wasn't using Emma. "She stays out of this."

"She's already *in* this," Xeno countered. "She was born into it and you know it. She will never know a life free of danger. Or one of peace."

Aye, he knew. He knew that after saving her from Sebastian, he would have to save her from Tegan and then he'd have to save her from the Royal Courts. And it would not stop there. They'd be running for the rest of their lives.

But at least then, when they were finally caught, she would not be imprisoned in Damaculus on her own. He would be right there with her, rotting in the hellhole so dangerous not even guards roamed inside it.

"She might not even be what he wants. Delentia might have been saying we need to give him world domination or a way to read the *Scrolls of Atlantis.*"

"There isn't a way to read them," Jack said.

"Not known," Hunter corrected, "but there has to be a way. It wouldn't have been written otherwise."

Xeno stayed quiet; whatever truths she knew, she kept to herself. She might have vowed to give her loyalty to the Elv've'Norc, but she was still an angel. Whatever secrets they wished to keep, she would take to her grave. And given how powerful the *Scrolls* was believed to be, a pure creation of the gods, Rogan doubted she would ever speak. Some knowledge was too dangerous to share.

"Emma doesn't have any powers. If things go wrong, she won't be able to protect herself."

Xeno's eyes hardened. His chest tightened. He didn't want to hear what she had to say, but ever so softly, she spoke. "You know there's a way to change that."

"What way?" Hunter asked in the heavy silence. "She wants to be powerful. If you know a way to –"

Rogan rounded on him. "Nay. I will not curse her to be with me."

"Curse?"

He shook his head, not wanting to voice what Xeno was hinting at. He didn't even want to think about having sex with Emma just to turn her into a weapon.

"Hunter, just keep searching for whatever or whoever it is Sebastian left," he ordered. "And ye two, find a way into Tintagel Castle. Sebastian isn't going to be holed up inside it. He'll have left a trail somewhere. Meeting adjourned."

He walked away before Xeno could say anything else. A restless energy ate at him. He rolled his shoulders as he stalked through the house. He wanted to go out for a run, but his feet took him to Emma's room.

Standing outside it, he gritted his teeth. If he opened this door, there was no going back. It's why he'd forced himself away. Why he'd locked her up here in the first place. She'd shown him on the plane that she wasn't strong enough to resist their bond. And if he tasted her one more time, he wouldn't be either.

Fuck. He'd almost taken her freedom away on the plane. The bond between them had pulled so tight, reeling him in, reeling them together that he'd had to avoid her for the rest of the flight.

And in the car ride, he'd spent every aching minute forcing the blood back out of his cock so he didn't get a boner.

He should walk away.

He had to walk away. For her.

But her voice came through the door, wrapping around him like a silky robe and rooting him in place. "Hello?"

Fuck. Closing his eyes, Rogan clenched his hands into fists. He wanted to knock. He wanted to just open the door and barge in. But what would he say?

He didn't want her to think he was just here for sex. For a way to get rid of the restless energy driving him crazy.

He could give her the clothes she'd ask for... That was a very good reason to be here. "It's Rogan," he said.

Her small gasp had him grabbing the door knob. His knuckles turned white. *This isn't a good idea.*

"Rogan?" Emma said his name like a prayer. Like a woman down on her knees, begging for something she desperately wanted.

"Aye." He shut the door behind him, closing them in. His eyes ran hungrily down her body. She was wearing a loose blue shirt that dipped to the top of her breasts and a pair of black slacks that hugged her hips. A hatred lit up in his chest, feral and sudden. He hated that Hunter's hands had been on the clothes she was wearing. He wanted them off her. He wanted her clothed in the items in his jacket. Stepping toward her, he reached a hand into his pocket. "Take off yer clothes."

Her eyes heated as her lips parted. "What are you doing here?" she breathed.

"I've brought ye what ye wanted." He pulled out the lingerie she'd requested. It had been burning a hole in his pocket for days. It was about damn time, she wore it.

"You actually..." She swallowed. "You actually brought it?"

"It is what ye requested." He stopped in front of her, not touching. "Now take off yer clothes, love." He ran his knuckles down her cheek, holding the crotchless teddy in his fist, then threaded his fingers through her hair to cup the back of her neck, pressing the garment against her. "Unless ye want me to help?"

A smile beaming across her face, she nodded slowly.

He brought his thumb across her lips, stroking before applying pressure. When she opened her mouth for him, he pushed inside. His cock hardened when she wrapped her tongue around him. Lowering his eyes to her shirt, he reached for the hem with his other hand. He pulled the fabric up slowly, revealing her belly button, her ribs, her breasts cupped in a white bra.

His eyes narrowed as a growl erupted from the back of his throat. Hunter had picked this one out for her. He'd seen it, had his hands all over it.

Removing his thumb from her mouth, he yanked the shirt and bra up over her head. After throwing them across the room, he grabbed her ass and lifted her in the air. She wrapped her legs around his waist. He leaned forward and fell onto the bed with her. Moving down her body, he pulled down her slacks and underwear together, not wanting to see the evidence that Hunter had seen them too.

Her legs hanging over the bed, she pushed up on her toes when his breath skirted across her pussy. Her fingers grabbed his hair. He reached down and slid her legs into the teddy. Pulling it up her thighs, he waited for her to lift her ass. As soon as she did, he leaned down and kissed her.

She jerked beneath his mouth. The lacy fabric rubbed

across his five o'clock shadow. Digging his fingers back into her ass, he lifted her to the perfect angle. His lips rubbed across her as he kissed her like a lover. His tongue swept up between her labia to her clit. After circling it, he flicked it hard, then pulled it in between his teeth.

Her thighs swung inward, pressing against his head, holding him there as she arched off the bed on a moan.

Pinning one arm across her waist, he held her down.

Gods, he had missed the taste of her, the feel of her, the sound of her moans as he pushed her to orgasm.

Her nails scratched against his scalp.

Her legs wrapped around his head.

Pushing against his arm, she writhed beneath him, her hips rotating to chase that high.

Growling low in his throat, absolutely obsessed with the taste of her, Rogan pushed her higher. He dug into his leather jacket and activated the sound runes, wanting her to scream his name but only so he could hear.

Licking the full length of her, Rogan slipped his tongue inside and pressed his nose against her clit.

She arched again.

He could feel her pleasure building inside him as if it were his own. She wanted him to stay where he was, his tongue in this exact same spot, and he wanted to do anything to please her.

Keeping his position, he thrusted into her, in and out as he rubbed his lips across hers. The tension built inside him, drawing tight across his entire body. And when she orgasmed against his mouth, he shattered along with her.

Groaning, Rogan rested his head against her thigh and took a moment to just breathe her in. He was cradled by her body, by the new feeling of warmth spreading through him.

When her legs relaxed around his head and her heavy

breathing reached his ears, Rogan crawled up her body and finished dressing her in the teddy. Her breasts pushed up in front of him, fully supported and fully exposed.

Taking a moment just to appreciate them, he ran his fingertips over the perfect mounds. Circling to her nipple, he ran his finger over it, then pinched it with the help of his thumb. Slowly lowering his head, he took it in his mouth.

Her hand held him close.

Her lips breathed his name.

Palming her other breast, he squeezed as he licked. He pinched her nipple as he bit. He worshiped her body until he was so hard he was certain a mere brush of her hand would cause him to come.

Kissing his way up her body, he lingered on her neck. She was sensitive at the base of it, and as he pleasured her, she writhed on the bed beneath him. Her hands tugged at his pants. Her hips thrust up to meet him. Keeping his cock away from her, he pulled the rose toy out of his jacket. He pressed it over her clit.

Once it sealed around her, he turned it on the lowest setting. She sucked in a breath, and he moved up to her mouth to kiss her, wanting to swallow her moans when he made her come again.

She whimpered against his mouth as he played with the settings, slowly increasing the suction. Breathless, she arched her head back. He feathered his kisses across her check. Digging her hands into his back, she held him tight and screamed his name.

He held her through her orgasm, his heart expanding through his arms and seeping through his hands. He was absolutely crazy about her. He never wanted this moment to end. He never wanted to live a single second outside of her presence.

Rolling them over, positioning her on top of him, he yanked her knees to either side of his hips. She gasped when she rocked against the hard length of him. He wanted to be inside her. He wanted her breasts in his mouth as he pushed inside that very first inch.

She tugged frantically at the front of his pants. Digging her hands inside his boxers, she fished him out. When she angled his cock toward her pussy, hovering right over the end, he bolted up to grab her breasts.

Doona!

Squeezing his eyes shut, he turned his head to the side and flinched away.

"Rogan?" Her concern cut at his heart. She wanted him to explain to her what was happening. She wanted to know how she could help. He could feel those desires inside him as if they were his own.

But they weren't.

Shaking his head, he grabbed her hips and rolled her off him. Throwing his legs over the bed, he bolted to his feet. *What in Hades' name is wrong with me?*

He didn't hear any of Emma's questions over the crashing waves in his skull. Opening his eyes, he caught a glint of metal on her desk. His brows furrowed. The need to crawl back into bed ate at him, but he was distracted by the knife in his vision. Hunter's knife.

What the fuck is it doing here?

Rogan shook his head, trying to fight through the fog holding him. Something wasn't right. He needed distance from her, but gods, did he not want to go. Every inch of his soul was demanding he stay, that he entered her as she so desperately wanted. He turned to her with pain and anger in his chest. When she recoiled as if he had struck her, he knew his feelings had seeped into his eyes.

"Rogan, w-what's –"

But he couldn't listen to her words. Shoving his cock back inside his boxers, Rogan jerked open the door in desperation, practically falling through it as he sought to escape her clutches. He slammed it shut behind him, his entire body shaking. It was as if he was having a fit of withdrawal.

His legs heavy with lead, Rogan pulled himself away. His heart begged him to go back to her, to do everything and anything to make her happy. He lurched down the stairs with no specific destination in mind. Only the need for distance urged him on.

"Rogan? What the fuck man?"

"Check the parameter!"

"Clearing the ground floor."

"Will take the second."

"Nay! Stay away from her!"

He struggled to make sense of what was happening, but all he could think about was going back up to her. He wanted to fall back into Emma's bed and take her with wild abandon. Emma was his lifemate, his regardless. He was filled with the primal desire to mark her in some way, to let anyone and everyone know she was his and his alone. This need was driving out every other thought he could come up with.

His eyes landed on Hunter.

The bastard had seen her underwear.

He'd been in her room.

Growling low, he pulled on the magic of his water.

Stumbling back, he forced himself to drop his arms, to fight the magic driving him mad.

Clutching his head, he crashed into the wall. The pain helped clear a bit of the haze, and Rogan was vaguely aware of Xeno walking toward him. Her strides were sharp with purpose. Her hands hung loosely at her sides, but there was something about them that put him on edge. He dodged to the left, but it came out more as a stumble. As her fist connected with the side of his jaw, he toppled to his knees in surrender.

The following undercut knocked him out cold.

THIRTY

The throbbing pain was the first sign he was awake. Raising a hand to his head, Rogan covered his eyes, trying to block out the light banging around in his skull.

"Want to tell us what happened?" Jack's voice, a bit too loud, caused him to flinch away as it added to the pain.

Squinting, Rogan blinked against the harsh light until he could open his eyes completely.

Jack sat in front of him, his forearms on his knees as he leaned forward with a grin. Xeno stood in front of the only door, angled toward him, her arms crossed so she wouldn't have to move much to blast him with a beam of angelic light.

When he didn't see Hunter, his eyes narrowed. If the fucker was with Emma, he was going to –

"Hey, now, easy there, boss." Jack stood up with him, his arms raised. His easy grin never fell, but something lurked behind his green eyes. Something dark, something dangerous.

A warning.

"What happened?" Rogan asked. "Where's Hunter?"

Xeno pushed off the door frame and walked toward him. "You don't remember? You attacked him."

He winced. And then he stilled, horror gripping his heart as he imagined his friend dead. "Did I..."

"No, I'm fine," Hunter shouted from the hall. "Xeno's just being Xeno and not letting me in."

Rogan's eyes flicked to his second-in-command's. If she was that worried about Hunter, Rogan must have done something bad. *What in Hades' name happened?*

Pinching the bridge of his nose, he tried to think past the pain taking up all the space in his mind. *Emma.* He'd ended up in her room. They were about to have sex. *Shit.*

"Emma?" he rasped, praying to gods that never listened that he hadn't cursed her.

Xeno's words were like a balm across his shoulders despite the iciness of her tone. "She's fine. Hunter locked her room when you came down."

Hunter in her room. He growled at the image. His fingers twitched as he instinctively searched for a water source. Shaking his hands out, he took a step back. "What the fuck?" Had he really just tried to attack Hunter again?

His eyes turned back to Xeno, searching for answers. Her entire body was relaxed, but her eyes were glued on his hands. "Tell me the last thing you remember." It wasn't a suggestion.

Rising slowly, he walked behind the couch, wanting to put as much distance between him and Hunter as possible. Whatever was wrong with him, it seemed to be centered around him.

"We had a meeting about using Emma as bait." His eyes narrowed on Xeno. She'd been the one to suggest it. Another growl clawed at his chest. His fingers twitched. Fighting whatever it was happening to him, he forced himself to look away.

"And then?" she pushed.

"I went to Emma's room to give her the clothes she requested." He stopped, his eyes flying back to Hunter. "Ye gave her a knife."

Xeno and Jack turned to look at him too.

"Is that an innuendo," Jack asked, "or were you actually that stupid?"

"Why'd you do it, Hunter?" Xeno demanded, her voice low and dangerous.

Hunter looked between them in bafflement, as if he really didn't understand why they were asking. "Because she wanted it."

"Did she want anything else?"

"A sparring partner and –"

"If ye hurt her –" Rogan snarled, taking a step toward him.

Hunter scoffed. "Me?" His eyes narrowed. "You're the one who locked her in her room."

"Uh, guys?"

"I did it for her own good so I wouldn't activate her fucking curse." His fingers twitching, Rogan ignored the water in his jacket and locked onto the source in Hunter's blood. It had been decades since he'd controlled another person's body, the first and last time, having ended in the death of a person he loved. But Rogan would tempt it all again, he would suffer through all that pain in order to protect his lifemate.

"What sort of bullshit is that? You don't have the power to curse someone."

"It's not my curse, genius. It's the bloody Holy Blood Contract, or are ye too stupid to understand it's not just the gods that are bound by it?"

"Uh, Xeno, are we stopping them yet, or..."

"So what curse does she have then?" Hunter demanded.

Rogan glared at him. It would be so easy to kill him before anyone realized. Xeno, as much as she'd try to stop him, couldn't react faster than he could cause a blood clot in Hunter's brain. The bastard had seen her underwear. His hands had been all over them. "If she has sex," he growled, "she'll be forced to do that man's bidding just like Elizabeth is being forced by Sebastian."

Hunter's jaw twitched, his eyes hardening into steel. "You'll treat her like Sebastian?"

"Jack!"

Rogan jumped backward as Hunter lunged forward, a knife glistening in his hand. A beam of light stole his vision, but he didn't need his eyes in order to kill. Raising his arms, he started to manipulate the blood in Hunter's body, but a heavy blow across his face caused him to lose his grip. Turning his attention to the new threat, Rogan pulled a whip of water from inside his jacket. He swept it out in front of him, hardening it into ice as it sliced through the air.

"Dammit, Rogan! You almost took my head off!"

Something shattered to his right. A body hit the floor, then rushed toward him. Feeling Hunter's waterprint, Rogan shifted the whip into a flurry of knives and sent them rushing toward his target.

Hunter shouted in pain, but he was drowned out by the feminine scream coming from the floor above.

Whipping his head toward the stairs, Rogan ran for his lifemate. A huge body barreled into him. The roar of a dire bear assaulted his ears. Teeth snapped by his head, and claws sank into his arm, nailing him to the ground.

Grunting in pain, Rogan twisted his fingers and sent a knife of ice into the bear's eye. Roaring, Jack rolled off him.

His vision slowly returning, Rogan was able to witness Xeno aim a blast of energy at Hunter. The man crumbled to the ground and didn't move. Rogan smiled.

He took a step toward him to finish him off.

"Rogan!"

Pivoting on his heels, he raced back for the stairs.

A knife slammed into the back of his leg, dropping him to his knee. Growling, he reached behind him and pulled it out. Just as he was about to throw it at Xeno, the fucking bear tackled him again.

The knife skidded across the floor, knocked away by a massive paw. Opening his mouth, Jack clamped it over Rogan's hand.

Yelling in agony, the elementalist raised his other arm and shoved his fingers into the gaping wound in Jack's eye. Snarling, Jack smacked away his arm, but he also released him and rolled away.

Before Rogan could finish him off, he caught sight of Xeno disappearing up the stairs. His heart in his throat, he chased after her, wincing with every step. Blood seeped down his leg and into his shoes. It dropped onto the floor from his arm and hand, from the wounds Jack had given him.

"Emma!" he shouted as he jumped up the last five steps. His heart dropped at the sight of her open door. If Xeno hurt her –

Bellowing, he crashed into the room, a whip of water by his side. And then froze, skidding to a halt by the door.

Emma stood in front of Xeno like a human shield, her arms pinned to her sides, her face panicked. A knife glistened across her throat, steady in its threat.

"You know my reflexes are fast enough," Xeno warned.

He gnashed his teeth like an animal, but forced his whip into a puddle of water at his feet.

"R-Rogan?" Emma's cracked voice tore at him. He wanted to save her. He wanted to protect her.

He took a step forward, but stopped when the knife shifted across his lifemate's throat. Snarling in frustration, he clenched his fists, imagining they were around Xeno's throat.

Her lips by Emma's ear, Xeno spoke softly, like a mother would to her ill child. "Calm down, Emma. This is your doing, and he'll relax if you do."

"W-what?"

"You've come into your powers, and Rogan is reacting to your fear. So I need you to calm down and tell me what started this all."

Rogan shifted on his feet, trying to figure out what to do. Xeno was a lot faster than him. She was a lot stronger than him. With age, came power, and she was older than his entire race.

"I-I don't know," Emma stammered.

"Untrue. What made you upset, Emma? Everyone was fine a few minutes ago. Rogan was up here. Hunter had given you a knife. So what changed?"

Tears rolled down Emma's cheek. A whine released from the back of Rogan's throat. He formed his whip of water, then released it again, knowing Emma would die before he could even swing it.

"Look at him, Emma. He's not himself. You need to release him."

Emma's eyes burned into his, and he took a small step forward to comfort her.

"I d-don't know h-how to do...that with a...a knife at my throat."

"I'm not going to hurt you," she said louder than all her other words. "But this knife is insurance against Rogan. I can't drop it until you release him."

"Then tell me how."

"Build the mental barrier Hunter taught you. Find your calm behind that wall."

She took a shaky breath and smiled at him. It was weak and a lie, but it eased the pain in his chest. His lifemate was strong. He could feel her strength inside him, her desire to breathe evenly. Sucking in a deep breath, Rogan held it for her.

He breathed out for her, calmly, gently, all the while holding her gaze.

"You're doing great, Emma. You'll be free in no time."

The tension in his shoulders started to ease.

His heartbeat slowed as he breathed in tune with his lifemate.

"That's it."

But just as the fog in his brain started to clear, someone shoved into his shoulder, trying to get past him. Rogan slammed his elbow back and up, hitting Hunter's solar plexus. The man dropped to his knees on a wheeze.

Emma screamed.

Whimpering, Rogan stilled, hating that he had caused her fear.

"Think about a future with him, Emma," Xeno ordered, her words sharp and commanding.

He pulled on his water, only to release it on a shudder. Emma's desire slammed through him. She wanted to build a future with him. She wanted to run into his arms and let him hold her. She wanted to see his home, meet his family and friends. She just wanted him back to how he used to be. Calm and in control.

His breath leaving him on a shudder, Rogan dropped to his knees. He squeezed his eyes shut, fighting through the last tendrils of the fog controlling him.

Reality hit him like the fist of an enraged berserker.

Pain shot up from all across his body. There was a sharp moment of confusion as he tried to figure out how he'd gotten here and what had happened. The last thing he'd remembered, he was standing beside the couch. But then he noticed Xeno sheathing a knife, and the guilt of all his memories hit him like a dire bear's paw.

Before he could apologize to her, as well as thank her for keeping Emma safe, his lifemate flung herself into his arms, stealing all his attention.

He held her tightly against him, shaking from the feel of her skin. She was safe. She was okay. Trembling, he pressed kisses into her hair, then lifted her chin and claimed her lips.

She kissed him back feverishly, desperately, her tongue sliding along his like the taste of heaven.

But then she was pulling back and staring at the wounds all across his body. "Will you heal?" she asked, her voice shaky with emotion.

He nodded. "Aye." He would physically, at least. But the knowledge that he had attacked his team, his friends. That he had lost control of himself enough to stab Jack in the eye and nearly break his vow to never control the water in another person's blood again. Those acts, that guilt would stay with him forever.

Looking over Emma's head to Xeno, he said, "Thank ye."

She nodded without a word, but he heard her threat nonetheless. If Emma didn't get her powers under control and soon, his second-in-command was going to make sure this never happened again...one way or another.

THIRTY-ONE

Emma paled as she stepped into the living room and surveyed all the damage. The couch was flipped over backward. A vase was shattered as if it'd had a grenade dropped down the middle of it. One of the curtains was ripped by the claws of an animal, and the railing hung by only one point. The bookcase was splintered into pieces and numerous books littered the floor, their pages twisted and crumbled.

"That was one hell of a party."

She jerked back in horror, one hand going to her face when Jack sat up from behind the couch. A gaping wound had replaced his left eye, leaving it bloody and open.

"Maybe stay off the meth next time, eh, Rogan?" Jack grinned through broken teeth as he strolled past them stark naked.

Her lips moved wordlessly before she could find the words she was looking for. "I'm sorry."

The trickster glanced at her, his grin widening. "Don't be. That was the most fun I've had in a while."

He disappeared down the hall and into the kitchen before she could think of anything else to say.

Guiding her into the room, Xeno flipped the couch back upright and then gestured for her to sit down. Emma didn't feel like sitting, but she wasn't about to argue, still remembering the cold feel of Xeno's knife on her neck.

Her eyes on Rogan, the angel said, "Until she's fully calm, you and Hunter need to stay away from her."

She tensed, not wanting to be left alone with the angel. Her arm outstretched, she nearly reached for Rogan's hand, but feeling the shift in the room, she dropped it again.

Desperately, she started building the wall again inside her head. She would not be the reason these people died.

Blinking, Rogan shook his head. "Aye." He turned to Emma, his face blank, his tone soothing. "No one's goona harm ye, love. I'll never be far."

He dropped a light kiss on her hair, then stepped back. With strained strides, he left the living room alongside Hunter.

She was quiet for a long moment, her eyes on the empty doorway. Hushed voices reached her ears, but she couldn't make out what they were saying. She hoped Jack and Rogan could really heal from that much damage. Hunter looked scratch free, but he'd shared that same glazed look with Rogan.

Turning back to Xeno, she took a deep breath and clenched her fists in her lap. "What's happening to me? What happened to them?"

Having removed the books that had been tossed onto the armchair, the angel placed them horizontally on the floor. She sat down on the edge of the seat and leaned forward, her arms on her knees.

"You caused Rogan and Hunter to try to kill each

other."

A hand flew to her mouth. She was going to be sick. "But Hunter doesn't have any wounds." She'd said it with desperation, wanting to believe the accusation was not true.

"That's because I knocked Hunter out while Jack tried to keep Rogan away from him."

Flinching, Emma curled back into the comfort of the couch. She looked down at her hands. They felt the same as always. Her entire body did. Wouldn't she have known if she'd been using magic?

"Talk me through the moment Hunter gave you that knife."

"Nothing really happened. I wanted to leave the room, but he wouldn't let me, so I asked for a knife to practice with."

"He wouldn't let you leave?"

Emma frowned. "Of course not. He was following Rogan's orders."

"Did you actually ask him to let you out?"

"Well, no –"

"But you asked for the knife."

She nodded. "Why? What does that mean?"

Xeno stared at her in silence. Digging her fingers into her thighs, Emma tried not to panic over what she was about to hear.

"What do you want from Rogan?" Xeno asked.

"What? What does that –"

"Answer the question."

A heat blared up her cheeks. She didn't want to voice what she wanted. That was personal and scary.

But deciding Xeno was scarier, she mumbled, "The idea of being controlled by whomever I have sex with is fucking terrifying. I just wanted..." She rubbed her hands against her legs. "I just wanted him to love me, so that...so my curse wouldn't be so bad."

She started to squirm, not liking that pathetic truth hanging in the air.

"But he left when you were about to have sex?"

Her entire face burning, Emma could only nod.

"You're not the daughter of a sex goddess then."

The slightest bit of hope filled her chest. She looked up. "Does that mean...does that mean I won't be cursed if I have..."

"No." The word was clipped and final. "You and your sister will share the same curse. But this means, Hunter and Rogan weren't fighting because they both wanted you. They were fighting because that's what you wanted."

"No, it's not!" Emma hated violence. And she liked them. The last thing she wanted was for them to hurt each other.

"But it is. You wanted out of your room. Rogan was keeping you locked in, so Hunter attacked him. You want Rogan to love you. He got jealous you were spending so much time with Hunter. They both fed off your desires, Emma."

She shook her head, trying to make this make sense. "But how? I don't have any powers!"

"You didn't have any powers," Xeno corrected as if she was talking about the weather. "But you're starting to pulse. When someone powerful hits their ascension, their magic is too strong for them to control, so they expel the excess from their bodies until they're capable of holding it all in."

Her stomach twisted. "So this will happen again?"

Xeno nodded.

"How do I control it?"

"You can't control a pulse. If you try to keep the magic

inside you, it'll kill you. All you can do is try to shape it into something less harmful. Given they're feeding off your desires, when you feel the pulse happening, be mindful of what you wish for."

"That's it?"

"It's a start, but I have no idea how far your powers will reach. If previous descendants are anything to go by, at the peak of your pulsing, you could affect an area about the size of England."

"So this was only, what? A percentage of my power?" She looked around the living room, horror eating at her gut, gnawing on her intestines like a greedy little demon. She didn't want to cause this much chaos. She didn't want these powers.

"Yes," Xeno answered. "In a few years' time, you'll hit your peak."

"*Years*?"

She nodded. "On average, a descendant pulses for four or five years. You'll hit your peak sometime about a year from the end."

"Oh God." Why was it that every time she thought things couldn't get worse, they always did? "Rogan and I haven't had sex," she blurted. "He said my powers would not come until then. But we haven't. So maybe...maybe Sebastian caused this? Maybe..." She trailed off at the shake of Xeno's head.

"That was his assumption when he thought you were the daughter of a sex goddess. But you're not, Emma. Your mother is a love goddess."

She jumped to her feet, needing to move. What Xeno was hinting at, that she was coming into her powers because she was falling in love, was something she wasn't yet ready to admit.

Her hands twisted in front of her as she tried to break

down all the new information into sizable pieces. She didn't have the luxury of being eased into all this. The flow of information was fast and it was hectic, but it was her life now. Either she learned to swim in the current, or she'd be washed under and drowned.

Taking a series of deep breaths, she turned back to Xeno. The woman was cold and distant, but at least she gave her honest answers. "If my powers are activating without the need for sex, does that mean my curse will too?" Could Rogan control her even now?

The idea of that clung to her like a sickness. Bile threatened her throat.

"Perhaps, but I do not know enough to say."

Biting her lip, she nodded. "Will I be able to raise the dead then, like Liz can?"

"There's never been a case of descendant twins. I don't know if you'll share her powers exactly or if you'll develop your own."

She tried not to let the frustration of not knowing eat at her. "So what happens now?"

"You'll probably have a few days between your pulses. Maybe even a couple weeks. We won't be able to track your cycle until you have four or five of them. Until then, everything will run like normal."

Ha. As if anything would ever be normal again.

Emma was glad to see the kitchen looked completely normal when she walked in. Clean and tidy, it was a sight for sore eyes. As were the three men sitting around the table, chatting amicably with each other.

"Thank the godsf Snuffles left this morning," Jack said, taking a bite out of his sandwich. It was a full baguette filled with so much meet, cheese, vegetables, and sauce that she had no idea how he'd managed to fit it in his mouth. "Can you imagine –" He stopped, his eyes on her.

Rogan rose to his feet as Hunter twisted in his chair to look at her. Placed in the spotlight, she froze.

"I'm so sorry," she whispered. "I didn't know I could do that."

Crossing to her in long strides, Rogan took her hand and ushered her to the table. "It's okay, love. Jack's been claiming for ages, he could take me on in a 1v1. At least now, he'll shut up about it."

Speaking around a mouthful of food, the trickster snorted. "I was trying not to kill you. I was effectively fighting with one hand behind my back."

"Uh huh."

"Just admit it, Jack," Hunter cut in. "You got your ass kicked."

Throwing a napkin at his face, Jack teased, "Says the guy who got knocked out with one blow from Xeno."

"Hey! She knocked Rogan out too earlier." He rubbed his jaw. "And I didn't want to hit her back."

"Because you couldn't."

"No, I could –"

"Oh, could you now?" Xeno's soft, light voice caused them all to freeze.

Then Hunter shot to his feet so fast he knocked over his chair. As Jack laughed his ass off, Emma smiled. She was happy to see they weren't too hurt despite the ugly wounds they were sporting.

"I've gotten in a couple shots during our sparring," Hunter said, a smile lighting up his face.

Xeno stared at him in silence.

His grin widened as his gaze moved to Emma. "It might have been after she'd pinned me to the ground, but I'm still counting them."

"Perhaps I should ask Xeno for lessons then and not you," Emma teased.

"Ouch." Clasping both hands over his heart, Hunter leaned back.

"If ye want to learn to fight," Rogan murmured in her ear, "I'll teach ye myself."

She flicked him a glance. His eyes were serious. Her breath caught.

When her chest tightened, she looked away. If she fell in love with him, she would lose everything.

But it'll also make you stronger.

Strong enough to fight Sebastian and save Liz.

Oh God, was she really thinking about this? With him? Her eyes flicked to Rogan beneath her lashes. Was she really thinking about giving up her freedom to a man she barely knew? Anything and everything he desired from her, she'd have to give – no questions asked, regardless of what she wanted. For Liz to go through this with a monster as twisted as Sebastian...

And that's what Emma had to focus on. For despite what little she knew of Rogan, he had to be better than Sebastian. *No.* She knew for a certainty that he was. He had protected her, refused to take advantage of her, and he made her feel...safe. Despite everything, Rogan made her feel safe.

She had been abducted into a monstrous world that housed a panic attack around every corner. Gone was her quiet life of keeping her head down and hiding from the mafia, of believing she was normal, human. She should have felt utterly and devastatingly alone and yet... Emma felt safe. She trusted Rogan to keep her safe. Because that is what he had done.

She could do this.

I have to do this.

He was her one chance at survival in this fucked up world and –

Her chest ached. Her throat worked past the knot forming there.

And I trust him. Pure and simple, she trusted him not to abuse her curse. She might be stupid rushing into this; she might regret this decision in six months' time or sooner or later when they fell out, but it didn't matter. Because right now, he was her best option, and she had already learned that she did not have the luxury of time.

Sebastian was searching for her, and if he got her before her power kicked in… If he got her and activated her curse himself…

She shuddered.

Glancing over at Rogan, who was talking to Hunter about something Sebastian had lost, she squeezed his hand beneath the table.

He turned to her in an instant, halting the conversation mid-sentence. Leaning his head to hers, he asked, "Ye okay?"

She nodded. "How's your leg?" She glanced down his body and winced. "And the rest of you?"

"I'll heal."

As the conversation around the table started up again, she asked softly, "Is there anything I can do to help?"

The corner of his mouth kicked up as his eyes dipped to her lips. "Are ye asking to play doctor?" When his gaze slowly lifted back to hers, they scorched a path right to her pussy.

Her lips parting, Emma shook her head. "No. I was genuinely asking…" She trailed off when he pulled her hand to his leg and placed it palm down. Dragging it across his muscled thigh, he stopped just below the one place she really wanted to explore.

He leaned in, his breath hot against her ear. "Because I could do with a full body exam."

Panting, she dipped her eyes to the tent in his lap. Her cheeks enflamed, she dragged her gaze back up and then glanced around the table.

She couldn't. Not with them all here.

As if feeling her desire for privacy, Hunter stood up and nodded at Jack. "Let me take a look at your eye in the command room. Don't want to freak Emma out." He flashed her a teasing smile. "She might have a sudden desire for me to kill you just so she won't have to look at your ugly mug anymore."

Eyes wide, Emma choked on air. "I would never, Jack. And I'm so sorry about –"

He waved her away. "Stop apologizing. Watching you two" –he waved at her and Rogan– "is making me want to gauge my other eye out anyway. Let me just grab another sandwich and then we'll be gone."

Another?

"Transformations require a lot of energy. Shifters and tricksters always eat enough for three, but Jack –" He winked at Emma, and she closed her mouth, realizing it was hanging open. "Well, he's just a greedy little bastard. He eats more than anything I've ever met – including a charybdis, which is literally just a giant mouth."

"I eat less than your mom," Jack said as he opened the fridge and pulled out some ham.

"You mean your dad," Hunter snorted.

Jack looked up with a smirk. "You do realize that was a compliment to both my dad *and* my mom."

Hunter sighed. "Yeah, I realized that as soon as I said it."

Jack spread a load of caramelized onion chutney onto the top side of his baguette, then folded it together. "Xeno, you coming too?" His eyes gleaming, he took a bite of his sandwich. "You took quite a lot of knives in those wings."

The temperature in the room dropped to zero. Chills formed on Emma's skin when she looked at the angel in question. If looks could kill, Jack would've withered on the spot.

"You did what?" Hunter asked softly, turning toward her.

"Oh, yeah, Rogan threw a lot of knives at you – which, by the way, was a complete dick move, Rogan, given he was already down – and Xeno shielded you with her wings. It was disgustingly romantic." He took another bite.

"Xeno –"

"I'm fine."

"Then you have no reason not to let me see them." Hunter crossed his arms, his eyes soft and hard all at once.

Glaring daggers at Jack, Xeno turned on her heels and left the room. Hunter followed after her, his shoulders tense.

Grinning, Jack sat back down at the table and leaned back. Lifting his legs onto the chair beside him, he crossed his ankles. "Gods, Rogan, thank you for hitting Xeno. Hunter is shit at playing doctor."

"Ye do know she's going to skin ye alive one day," Rogan said dryly.

Jack grinned. "That'll still feel better than whatever Hunter would've done to me. I'll just shift into a vampire after this" –he held up his half-eaten baguette– "and I'll be back to normal in a few hours." He cocked his head to the side. "Well, 'normal' being relative."

"Do vampires heal faster than others then?" Emma asked.

"They do if they feed." His eyes ran down her body. "I'd probably heal in seconds if I had the blood of a de–" He ducked his head, dodging the water being thrown at his face. The water changed direction mid-air, soaking him anyway.

"Ye even finish that sentence and I'll waterboard ye."

Jack shook his head wildly. None of the water flew off his head and shoulders. Pinning Rogan with a 'this isn't funny' look, he picked up his baguette and headed for the door. "Oh, Emma, actually, could you do me a favor?" he said, stopping to turn around.

"Of course," she blurted, her eyes on the wounds she'd caused him.

"Could you peg Rogan for us to dislodge that stick in his ass?"

Her cheeks burned so hot her eyes started to water.

Rogan flicked his wrist, pulling all the water off Jack's head and soaking it into his sandwich.

"Hey! That's crossing a line."

Rolling her lips, Emma fought the smile wanting to rise. The tension in her shoulders relaxed. The concern she was making a foolish choice disappeared altogether. Her eyes on Rogan, she knew she was making the right call.

Too soon or not, she was falling in love with him.

THIRTY-TWO

"How long will it take you to heal?" Emma asked once they were alone. "Do you need stitches or..." She trailed off, not sure if she should continue. Although she could stitch a wound with the best of them, having learned from her mom – or whoever Diana really was to her – she was worried the stitches might hinder their magical healing process.

Digging his hand into his pocket, he dug out a foot-sized stick.

A wand, she instantly realized, having seen them often enough in films.

"Of course," she said.

"Xeno normally heals us, but her magic is waning." He flipped the wand tail over end and handed her the base of it. Gingerly, she took it. It was a lot heavier than she'd expected it to be.

"Any creature of the myth can use a pre-spelled wand," Rogan explained, "as long as they know the trigger word for it. This one's a healing one, carved from an ovensi sapling."

Her eyes flicked to all the wounds across his body. "Why haven't you already used it?"

"They have a limited number of spells, and the magic hasn't been customized to our body like it would be if a witch was here with us. Pre-created spells are too generic and can actually hinder our own healing abilities. They're good for an emergency, though, but they can't be used on humans or any pre-ascension children."

"Why not?"

"The magic could kill them."

She stared at the wand, turning it over in her hands, stuck on how something specially made for healing could still kill in this fucked up world. "What's the word?" she murmured.

"Iactus. All pre-spelled wands use it. Ye can get custom ones to react to special words, like passcodes, but ye have to be a member of a guild. It's illegal otherwise."

"Why?"

"Because if one cannot prove what the wand does in court, it cannot be used as evidence, and a lot of criminals were very tight lipped about giving up the word that would sentence them to prison."

"But what about children using it?"

He studied her, his eyes piercing her as if he could look into her very soul. He knew she was stalling, working up to whatever it was she wanted to ask him. Softly, he said, "Wands work by harvesting the bit of magic we all have inside us and focusing it even though we cannot. Children do not have this magic until they hit their ascension." He placed his bloody arm on the table and nodded at it. "Ye can try it if ye want. Just point it at the wound. Ye can't mess it up."

Raising the wand, she took a breath and murmured,

"Ee-act-us."

"Eh-ahct-us," Rogan corrected.

She glanced up at him, then back down at his arm and tried again. Her eyes widened as his muscles and skin started to repair itself. Within seconds, he was healed. Lifting her other hand, she trailed a finger down his forearm. When she reached his palm, he closed his fingers over her hand, holding her and giving her comfort.

Emma threaded her fingers through his, confident she was making the right choice. Her heart beat a steady, sure rhythm as she placed the wand on the table and stood up. Her eyes locked on his, she lowered herself onto his lap, straddling him.

"Emma..." He said her name as if he was hurting.

She ran her fingers through his hair and tilted his head up. Leaning down, she kissed his lips. "I want this, Rogan."

"It'll take away yer freedom." His mouth rubbed against hers. His hands spanned her hips, holding her to him. "Anything I say, ye will be forced to do."

She leaned over to whisper in his ear. "Tell me to come upstairs with you, Rogan."

His fingers dug into her skin, ten delicious pressure points that caused her to rock her hips against him. He hissed in a breath as his eyes closed.

"If ye just want to protect yerself, I can teach ye how to fight with whatever –"

She cut him off by pressing her lips to his again. This time, she slid her tongue inside his mouth, kissing him with all the feelings wrapped up inside her. Pulling back, she asked, "Did that feel like I just want protection?"

"Then why?" He stared into her eyes. His need to make sure she had thought everything through, to understand just how big this was touched her heart.

Because I'm already half way in love with you.

"Because I trust you," she said instead. "You won't abuse my curse."

"Ye doona know me."

Her eyes soft, she cupped his jaw. "I see how your team respects you. They'll follow you anywhere and bad guys don't get that kind of loyalty." She smiled. "I know how you keep stopping yourself from taking it too far between us even though, as you proved, I've been more than willing." She kissed his lips. "And I know you will do anything to protect me – even take on fucking Cerberus."

Picking up his hand, she placed it over her breast. "I want this. I want you."

Groaning, Rogan cupped her in the palm of his hand. No longer holding back, he kissed her. She weaved her hands through his hair. She breathed against his lips. As he built the flames inside her, she started to pant, needing more.

Grabbing her hips, he lifted her onto the table. She leaned back onto her arms as his mouth trailed to the crook of her neck. Pressing her fingers into the wood, she spread her legs so he could move in closer.

His five o'clock shadow prickled through the thin fabric of her shirt as he moved down to claim her breast. She arched into him, one hand lifting off the table before fluttering back down as he shifted lower still.

Quivering beneath him, the anticipation killing her as his lips trailed along her shirt ever so slowly, she struggled not to just grab him and shove him down.

Just as he reached her belly button, he came back up to claim her other breast.

Emma's cry of frustration warred with her moans of pleasure as he bit her nipple through her shirt and bra. Her nails making marks in the wood beneath her, she squeezed her thighs around his chest.

His chuckle feathered across her breath. "What would ye say," he said slowly, his teeth still around her, "if I ordered ye not to come."

She jerked back, with both a gasp and irritation, as he cupped her pussy between her slacks, his palm applying a delicious amount of pressure. "Don't you fucking..." Her threat fell into a moan as he scooted his chair back and kissed her thigh.

"Don't I..." he teased.

But as frustrated as he was currently making her, all Emma wanted to do was smile. Who knew Mr. Serious could make jokes? She wished he had better timing, but her heart melted all the same.

And then so did her body when he kissed her other thigh, so close to where she wanted him.

Unbuttoning her pants, he started to slide down the zipper.

She leaned back on her hands, her head falling back, her hips lifting up.

Watching him lower his head nearly sent her over the edge.

But just as his breath heated her and his lips grazed her...

Jack yelled from somewhere else in the house. "The kitchen is for eating everything but pussy, you heathens!"

Her legs closed of their own accord as the wrong sort of heat flamed through her body.

Oh my God.

Leaning back, Rogan muttered, "One of these days, I'm goona pay a witch to make him mute for a day." He stood up from between her legs, his eyes soft. "Ye still want to do this?"

Yes, but she really didn't want to pass Jack nor anyone else in the hall. Worried Rogan would take her silence as a no, she nodded.

Grabbing her hips, he lifted her in the air. She wrapped her legs around him and buried her head against the crook of his neck, hiding her face from view. As he carried her though the hall, she pretended as if she couldn't hear Jack eating a bucket of popcorn as they passed.

"I'll cloak you two for the rest of our sanity," he said cheerfully. "*Your room*, that is. Don't be having sex in the hall against my door."

Oh my God. Someone, just kill me now.

"Fuck off, Jack."

Laughing, the trickster shut a door. Hopefully, the one behind him.

"He's gone," Rogan murmured, stopping in the hall.

She peeked up warily, not trusting Jack not to jump out at them. "Is he always like this?" she whispered once she confirmed the hall was clear.

"Unfortunately." He grinned mischievously, causing her to melt in his arms. "Want to have sex against his door?"

Giggling, Emma shook her head. "The bastard would probably just open it."

He laughed. "Aye. But we can lock it from the outside."

Rolling her lips in, she shook her head.

"Good call. The last time Hunter had a lass over, Jack banged on their door and made noises along with them."

"He didn't."

"Aye." He kissed the top of her head as he started walking again.

"What did Hunter do?"

Shifting her onto his hip, he opened his door and walked in. "Well, and I quote, he said, 'Well, I wasn't going to stop. It's rude to turn a woman on and leave her hanging.'"

Her heart expanding, she giggled against him. "And the

woman was okay with that?"

"Okay?" Scoffing, Rogan stopped at the foot of his bed and stared down at her. "The lass was winding Jack up, getting louder and louder. Good thing Xeno wasn't there or she would've blasted the lot of them."

He tossed her onto the bed, then crawled on top of her. Her breath hitching, Emma stared into his eyes. They searched her softly, still checking to see if this was truly what she wanted. Touched beyond words, Emma lifted a hand up to his cheek and cupped his face. Leaning up, she kissed him.

He took his time tasting her, his tongue soft and slow and leisurely. She wasn't sure how long they'd laid there just kissing, but it was enough for her to fall in love with him. His kindness, his teasing, his patience – they all pushed her over the edge.

Running her hands down his back, Emma cupped his ass and spread her legs, cradling him in between her thighs. She didn't want to wait anymore. She wanted this, needed this. He made her feel whole and safe and loved.

Squeezing his ass, she arched her hips, rubbing herself against him. The kiss changed instantly. His tongue slid across hers faster, went deeper and more urgently. One of his hands cupped her breast, and she pushed into him, wanting, needing more.

Pressing his cock against the V of her pants, he moved his lips to her neck. She arched again, desperate to have him inside her. Reaching for his belt, she unbuckled it and yanked it off. Tossing it somewhere onto the floor, she attacked his button and zipper. Rogan breathed harshly against her neck when she slid her hand into his boxers.

Shoving her shirt up, he pushed up her bra at the same time she wrapped her fingers around his cock. Groaning, he dipped his head to her breast and swirled his tongue around it.

She arched. She moaned. She closed her eyes, chasing that beautiful high. As she pumped him, she marveled over his thickness. The thought of it being inside her, of it stretching her as she screamed his name made her so hot she started to pant.

She needed him now.

Lifting her hips off the bed, she struggled to push down her pants. But just as she started to wiggle free, he sucked her nippled into his mouth and teased it with his tongue. Tightening her hand around him, she fell back on a gasp.

"Not yet, love," he murmured against her skin. "I want ye to come on my face first."

As he slowly kissed his way down her body, Emma tightened her fingers in his hair and tried to push him faster. She couldn't take much more of his teasing. Prying her fingers free, he murmured against her skin. "Doona make me get my belt."

Shuddering beneath him, Emma wasn't sure if she wanted to move or not. The thought of being bound by him, of being at his mercy... She rubbed her thighs together on a moan. Her fingers twitched in the air as he pinned her arms to the bed beside him. Being tied, though, would mean she would never get to touch him, and by gods, she wanted to touch him.

Finally, *finally* Rogan rubbed his cheeks against her thighs. His fingers tucked into her waistbands and pulled down, taking both her pants and underwear. His tongue traced a path from her mid-thigh to the edge of her pussy before swapping to her other leg. She jerked beneath him, already able to feel him there, kissing her, licking her, claiming her.

She strained against his wrists, wanting to grab hold of his head and pin her to him. Digging her fingers into her palms, she shifted her hips toward his teasing mouth. His breath hit her, hot in more ways than one, and she trembled so hard she feared she'd come before he touched her.

"*Rogan*," she begged, her eyes peeking at him beneath half-closed lashes. Despite how much more frustration it was causing her, Emma didn't want to look away. She wanted to watch as he dipped his head and licked her.

Panting heavily, her eyes glued onto his tongue, she spread her legs wider.

He peppered kisses all around her, blessing everything but her labia.

She wanted to scream. She wanted to weep, the anticipation driving her mad.

She squirmed beneath him, angling her hips. Small cries escaped from the back of her throat as the build up inside her crept so close to the edge.

His lips landed on the crease of her thigh again, so close and yet so far away. And then his tongue flicked out, diving between her labia in one long, slow, leisurely lick.

Squeezing the sheets tight in her palms, Emma arched back and screamed. Her body spasmed, a delicious heat moving through her, building stronger as he moved against her. His tongue and lips had her panting wildly. Releasing her hands, he parted her pussy with one hand and slid a finger inside her with the other.

Writhing, Emma threaded her fingers through his hair and clenched tight. She rocked against him as his lips and fingers brought her back up to the edge. Curling his finger inside her, he brought his lips over her clit and sucked hard.

Bucking, she spasmed again, arching so far off the bed the wind left her when she fell back down. Or perhaps it'd left because of his wet finger sliding out of her pussy and into her ass.

"Gods, ye're gorgeous," he murmured, his words barely audible over her wild cries. "I could stay here all day."

He licked her long and slow as his finger pushed further and further inside her ass. It was too big, stretching her tight, forcing her to feel every section of his finger. His knuckles hit her thighs and she knew he was in all the way. He gave her a moment to adjust before pulling out and pushing back in.

Panting, her legs jello from the latest orgasm, Emma could only lie there as he brought her back up to ecstasy. Bringing his other hand to her pussy, he slipped two fingers inside as he sucked hard on her clit. Brimmed so full, her hands flying up to grab hold of the headboard, Emma shattered all over his face.

Crawling up her weak and spent body, his clothes completely off, he feathered kisses all the way up to her mouth, stopping for a moment to suck on her nipples. His wet fingers circled atop her breast and his tongue followed ever so greedily.

Releasing the headboard, Emma threaded her fingers through his hair and gently held him to her. Slowly, he made his way to her neck, her ear, and then finally her lips, pushing up her shirt and bra as he went. Pulling it over her head, he tossed her clothes on the floor.

Worshipping her mouth in languid strokes of his tongue, he reached between them and grabbed his cock. He rubbed the head between her labia, gliding through the wetness, causing her to tremble strongly against him.

Kissing him feverishly, Emma placed her hands on his ass and pushed down as she lifted her hips.

The tip went in, causing her to arch. Slowly, Rogan stretched her, sinking inside her inch by delicious inch. There was a flash of pain that caused her to jerk, but when he grabbed her hips and rolled her on top of him, she forgot all about it, the pleasure beating it down.

Pressing her hands on his chest, threading her fingers through the soft hair there, she held herself up as she rocked against him. She stared into his eyes as she sat down all the way, his cock hard and full inside her. His hands squeezed around her hips, waiting for her to set the pace.

Her chest blossoming with too many feelings to name, Emma rode him slowly.

Grabbing the back of her neck, he pulled her face down until it was only a few inches above his. He breathed in her air as she breathed in his, his eyes never once leaving hers.

Her lips parting on little pants, Emma rocked her hips faster. His fingers dug into her thighs. And then he was quickening the pace, taking over completely as he held her still and pounded into her from below. Leaning up, he took one of her breasts into his mouth. She cried out. He groaned. And the two of them came together.

Shuddering, she sagged forward and kissed his neck. She'd never felt more whole, more complete than in this moment. And it wasn't just the sex. It was his tenderness and patience and the magic now flowing through her.

She felt good. More than good. She felt -

"Fuck me," she breathed, knowing no other words to explain the full satedness she was feeling.

"If ye insist," Rogan murmured as he rolled her beneath him. Sitting up on his knees with them in between her thighs, he pulled her onto his lap. Kissing her hotly, he straightened his legs out in front of him, grabbed her ass, and controlled the rocking of her against him.

He took her over and over again, in every position, as if he couldn't get enough, as if he was making up for all the years they hadn't had together. Sitting on the edge of the bed with her on his lap facing away from him, he fondled her breasts with one hand and teased her clit with the other.

She sagged against his hands as he kissed her neck, so utterly spent she couldn't move. And still he claimed her, making love to her as the afternoon wore on.

Leaving her breasts to grab her chin, he forced her to turn her head and kiss him. His lips moved slowly and leisurely like his cock and hand were against her pussy.

Panting in little breaths, she came on another shudder, and he groaned as he came too. She sagged forward, her lips slipping away from his.

He held her in his arms for a long while, occasionally kissing her shoulder as sleep slowly started to consume her. Laying her down with him still inside her, he wrapped her in his arms.

Safe and secure, Emma whispered, "I want you to use me as bait to draw out Sebastian."

He was quiet for a long moment, his body still against hers.

Worried he was thinking she'd only slept with him for this, she turned in his arms. Grabbing hold of his soaked cock, she pushed it back inside herself as she threw a leg over his hip and cuddled close. Cupping his face, she looked him in the eye. "I love you," she whispered, her heart hammering as she waited for his response.

His eyes searched hers for a long moment, reflecting back what he couldn't yet say.

"I know it's been fast, but that's the truth, Rogan." Arching her neck, she kissed his lips. "Order me to tell you the truth if you want."

"I would never."

Every part of her melted at hearing those words. Gods,

she loved him with everything she had. Kissing him deeply, she rocked her hips against him. He was no longer hard inside her, having come three or four times already, but she still loved the feel of him.

He grabbed her hips to hold her still. "Are ye trying to drain me dry?" he asked, his words a whisper across her cheeks.

She laughed as he kissed her.

And then that humor died as she felt him harden inside her. Rolling her beneath him, he pulled out, wiped them both dry with the pillowcase they had sacrificed long ago, and slid back in. Looking into her eyes, he made love to her all over again.

THIRTY-THREE

Rogan walked into the command room as the sun started to set, his shoulders tense, his eyes cold with focus. Emma laid curled up in his bed fast asleep, and he wanted to get back to her before her nightmares started.

She had given him everything he hadn't known he'd been missing. The family he'd left behind. The friendships he hadn't been able to keep. The love he didn't deserve. She had looked at him full of trust, believing he was worthy of the gift of her heart and soul – something not even the gods or angels were worthy of.

Something he would trade everything for to keep. She wasn't just his lifemate.

She was the stars in his sky. The honey in the flowers. The balm on his shoulders.

And if Sebastian thought he could take her from him, Rogan would rip the vampire's heart out with his bare hands.

He stopped beside Hunter, who sat in front of an array of top-of-the-art computers, his fingers flying across the keyboard while he talked to someone on a phone.

Though Hunter had been picked from the Special Crimes Unit nearly seven years ago, he still kept in touch with all of the people he had grown up with. It gave him a special network he could pressure into getting things done. And by the sounds of it, he was putting on a Cerberus amount of pressure.

"I don't care what you have to tell them, Poe. I need this search completed tonight. I have billions of files to search through. I need you to get every base to cover a different section. Break it up by years, working back from the present."

He paused as he listened to whatever the person on the other line side. A smile lighting up his face, he glanced at Rogan. "Whoever had yesterday afternoon won. Happy now? No, I'm not giving you Jack's number. The guy's a pig."

Another pause.

"And as his best friend, I know he's a pig. Now get the search going. Have them call me directly if anyone finds any reference to the thing Sebastian lost. Love you, sis. And tell Mom to stop giving my number out to random women."

Rogan wanted to tell him to stop yapping, but he knew this was a delicate part of the bargaining process. Fighting down his frustration, he held onto his patience.

"No, I'm not trading Jack's number for that. I'd rather go on a million blind dates with Medusa than set you two up."

Chuckling, he hung up. Swiveling in his chair, Hunter finally turned to Rogan. "The entirety of the SCU will be running searches tonight. Hopefully, we'll have something by the time Jack's back."

"Where is he?"

"He left to see if he could find any vampires. Thinks they might come out because of tonight's festival."

The fact that they hadn't spotted a single bloodsucker already had put them all on edge. Normally, a town this size was home to around half a dozen of them. With the additional perks of the area's usual cloud coverage and high latitude, there should have been closer to twenty of them roaming the streets.

Which meant Sebastian had either killed them all or recruited them – neither possibility a good one.

If Sebastian's past methods were anything to go by, the local vampires would've been tortured until they morphed into savages beyond all redemption. They'd be mad with bloodlust, completely controlled by the Craving. It would make them stronger and more resistant to pain. They couldn't be reasoned with. They couldn't be saved. They'd barely have any concept of their own selves, their entire personality centering around the need to eat, to hunt, to kill.

Rogan's team was going to have one hell of a challenge once they finally managed to get in.

If we get in, Rogan frustratingly corrected. They could not do anything until they figured out how to break through the barrier keeping King Arthur's castle hidden, a barrier supposedly erected by Merlin himself, the most powerful witch to ever exist. Or come to be. Rogan's teeth pressed together as he was reminded yet again that they were banking this entire mission on a godsdamn fairy tale.

"He remember to take a tracker this time?" Rogan asked, his eyes bouncing between the screens. Every available file concerning Sebastian's five thousand year history was being searched. Even though the vampire had been in hiding for the majority of it, there had been numerous rumored sightings and dealings with him during that time. They all needed to be sorted and cataloged in order to separate the fact from the fiction. The program Hunter was running was supposed to help with that, but it had been running nonstop for the last three days and had nothing to show for it.

"Yep." Hunter enlarged a map of the surrounding area. A red dot moved across the back alleyways, faster than any human's speed. "Oh, Xeno told me to tell you she's speaking with Gabriel again. Now that they know Emma's mother is a love goddess, not a sex goddess, they can redefine the search. And given Hades called Snuffles back, she wants to see if he'll share anything as to why."

There was a war between the gods brewing. The mortals only hope of surviving was picking a side and praying they came out as victors. Rogan's loyalty was to Emma and most likely her father, but he too wanted to know more before he declared their allegiance. "How long has she been gone?" he asked.

"Forty-eight minutes and counting."

His lips pulled into a thin line. Despite Xeno's constant reassurances that she could handle Gabriel, she had yet to come back from a meeting with him unshaken. They'd been together for millennia. Xeno had been head over heels in love with him, never being able to talk about him without her eyes lighting up in a smile. She'd talked about having his baby fourteen years ago.

But then she'd been kidnapped by Sebastian. In those three years he'd had her, he'd broken her completely. The happy, laughing, joking woman Xeno had once been had been murdered. Only a shell of her had remained.

Gabriel had gone crazy looking for her, breaking the golden rules of the archangels left and right. But when he and Rogan had finally found her, he'd taken one look at her broken and bruised form lying curled up on the floor, naked and impure, and he'd simply spread his wings and vanished. Rogan had carried Xeno out himself, stepping over the two feathers that had fallen from her wings.

Gabriel had not once visited her as she'd recovered. He'd never called. He'd never sent a gift. He'd cut himself out of her life completely, abandoning her when she had needed him the most.

If Rogan had been stronger, he would've killed Gabriel a long time ago.

"How are her wings?" Rogan asked, his voice soft.

Hunter's fingers froze over the keyboard. Pulling his hands to his to lap, he turned to face his boss. "I don't think she'll ever be able to fly again. Your knives severed a few of her tendons."

Fuck. He was never going to forgive himself for this. It didn't matter that he hadn't been in his own mind when he'd done it; he *had* done it. That guilt would stay with him forever. She was his friend, and he'd taken the last thing of hers that she had. Gods, she deserved so much better.

"She told me not to tell you." Fury flashed in Hunter's eyes. "She told me to forgive you." *But I won't,* his eyes said.

And so did the guilt in Rogan's own heart.

He opened his mouth to apologize, but Hunter's phone went off and Hunter was quick to answer it. "What have you got for me, Poe?"

His sister said something that caused Hunter to tense. Rogan stilled, his sixth sense tingling with excitement. This was it. He could feel it in his bones. By the time Hunter hung up, they were both wracked with tension.

"She's sending over a file."

He opened it as soon as it arrived. "Damn, that's gotta

be a hoax." He half-laughed, half-winced as they stared at the image before them.

Sebastian stood arrogantly, half his body covered in blood from a recent feast. His angelic face was distorted by the sadistic pleasure of a monster. Beside him stood a small girl that barely came up to his shoulders. She was smiling as she tenderly touched his red lips between his elongated fangs. A small set of her own peeked out of her mouth and her tongue stroked one with clear delight. Sebastian wasn't paying her any attention. Rather, his complete focus was on the person responsible for the memorphoric photo.

"Find her," Rogan growled, his eyes narrowing, his nostrils flaring.

"It'll slow the other search down." Hunter circled the girl's face to do as instructed. "The computer isn't strong enough to run both processes without lag."

Rogan didn't hesitate. "Then pause the other one for now. I want to know everything there is to know about this girl by morning."

"So you think she's not just a fling?" Hunter fished as he halted the other process.

"I know it. Sebastian does not share his kills." And he sure as hell wouldn't have shared this one. Rogan's eyes fastened onto the girl's mouth, or rather, the blood coating it. It glowed just the barest amount, making his stomach clench in revulsion.

"Show me where this file came from." Rogan's voice was tight with barely contained fury.

Hunter pulled up its location on the Elv've'Norc cloud base. Before he could click on the folder, Rogan stopped him with a hard clamp on his shoulder. "Delete it."

"What?"

"All of it."

Hunter hesitated for a just a second before he shook his head and scrubbed the folder from their computer's memory, the Elv've'Norc database, and the program Poe had used to send it to him. It was highly against protocol. If anyone found out they'd done it, they'd lose their badges – if they weren't prosecuted as an example.

"Make sure yer sister doesn't talk," Rogan said. "Give her Jack's number if ye have to."

"You going to fill me in?" he asked as he picked up his phone and dialed.

Rogan's jaw tightened. It wasn't his secret to share. Besides, if Hunter found out it was Sebastian who had tortured Xeno all those years ago, he'd do something stupid. Hunter's loyalty to his friends was his greatest weakness. Rogan shook his head.

Sighing, Hunter told his sister to keep her mouth shut. He managed to not give her Jack's number either. Just as he hung up, a beep sounded from the computer.

"Shit." Dropping his phone onto his desk, Hunter leaned forward and maximized the map of the town again. Rogan stared at it a second, looking for Jack's tracker before realizing it wasn't there.

Cursing, he stalked toward the door. "Send me the coordinates of where it was last online. And keep the search running," he growled. "I still want her found."

Because even if Jack had found a way into Merlin's Dimensio, moving up their timeline to now, Rogan wanted an ace up his sleeve. And if he somehow failed to keep Emma out of Sebastian's clutches, he wanted a high value bargaining chip to get her back.

The thought of losing her to that psychopath for even a minute made his blood boil. If luck was on his side, Rogan would kill him tonight.

THIRTY-FOUR

A FEW MINUTES EARLIER

Their dead hearts waited in hungry anticipation as the sun began to set. They fidgeted inside the castle's walls, their limbs restless even in sleep. The night called to them, awakening their bloodthirst with little jolts of electricity that grew in number and strength. Until finally, they erupted from their beds with the uncontrollable urge to hunt.

Mad with the full power of the Craving, they bared their teeth and attacked anything that moved, including each other. Limbs were ripped off, hearts were dug out, veins were pulled free with sharpened fangs.

Out of the sixteen that had arisen, only five remained. Standing, their nose to the wind, they sniffed and snarled in a fragile truce. Their Master had ordered them to hunt, to bring back a woman who smelled like power and pain.

Picking up on her scent, the five dashed across the grassy lawn, their heightened speed letting them cross it in a matter of seconds. When they neared the bridge leading out of this pocket dimension, their bloodlust had them shoving into each other, snapping with foam across their mouth. The five were now a three. With a single mind, they raced through the darkened streets of the city, their bodies like nightmarish blurs.

They spotted their prey in seconds. Master would be pleased.

Annabelle stumbled down the street, her bloody legs attempting to carry her to safety. The pounding between her temples made all thought impossible. As her head swayed and her eyes drifted closed, she tried to remember the license plate of the bastard who had clipped her going around the corner. But all she saw was darkness greeting her with its greedy fingers.

She opened her eyes with the sheer will to survive, knowing that if she didn't make it to the hospital, she wouldn't live through the night. Her phone had been smashed when she hit the pavement. With Bonfire Night taking place in the center of town, she had yet to pass another soul who could help.

Blood pulsed down her hairline and into her eyes. With shaky hands, Annabelle wiped futilely at it, buying herself only another few seconds of vision. Just another mile and she would be safe. She repeated that line over and over as she stumbled through the streets, completely unaware of how much distance she was actually covering.

A car alarm sounded behind her, and in her desperate attempt to turn around for help, her legs collapsed in surrender. Her hands shot out automatically to cushion her fall. Her broken collarbone couldn't hold her weight, and the cold pavement cut into her cheek.

She whimpered at the onslaught of pain.

Using her one good arm, she tried to push herself to

her feet, but a solid form knocked her back down. *The fuck?*

She screamed when something bit her in the leg. Jerking back, Annabel whimpered and kicked out at her attacker. He didn't even seem to notice he'd been hit. Digging his fingers into her calf, he pinned her leg down as his teeth sank further still. Screaming, she tried to drag herself backward, but a second assailant pinned her down and bit her in the stomach.

She bucked on a shattered cry. She was going to die here. She would never see her parents again. Would never even make it to her eighteenth birthday.

A third man bit into her arm, piercing deep into her veins. Her tears mixed with the blood on her face. The red tinted world around her caved into a pinpoint.

And then it was gone completely.

Jack tensed at the sound of a woman's screams under the gleeful noises and fireworks of the festival. He shifted his ears into those of a bat's as he moved through the alleys, trying to get a pinpoint on her location. When he got closer, the slurping sound of three vampires chilled his blood, as did the tangy scent of copper. Making sure no one was watching him, he dropped into a crouch and shifted.

Pain and warmth hummed through his body as his bones shrunk and reformed inside him. The skin around his mouth hardened and triangulated outward. Feathers sprouted, his feet morphed into talons, and the rest of his body was soon replaced by that of a kestrel.

Opening his wings, Jack propelled himself into the sky. He craned his neck to look at the pile of clothes he'd left behind. Although normal protocol required him to inform the SCU of any abandoned items, he always left them behind for any out-of-luck werewolves and shifters to find. It was a bitch trying to walk around town these days without any clothes on. At least he was able to give himself the illusion of them.

With a flick of his wing feathers, Jack cloaked the clothes from human view and marked them with a special scent. Rising high into the air, he took off toward the screams.

He found a girl lying on the floor with three vampires, two male, one female, feasting on her frail human body. Knowing they could drain her dry in only a few minutes, he cloaked himself and dived. His bones elongated and snapped, shifting as he fell. Dropping to the ground in his human form, he grabbed one of the male vampire's by the back of his head and pulled him off. A knife appeared in Jack's hand – an illusion to him but not to them. His magic would make them feel it as if it were real.

Stabbing it into the vampire's chest, he pulled it out and stabbed again. The monster hissed as it reached behind and tried to dig its sharpened nails into Jack's back. With a burst of magic, Jack stepped back, cloaking himself once more while calling up an illusion that looked like him.

As the vampire ran toward the fake, the other two looked up from their meal and hissed. His illusion pulled two knives from inside his jacket and flung them through the air while ducking a swipe from vampire number one.

Screaming as his knives slammed into their chests, so close to their hearts, the other two jumped onto their feet and rushed him.

Standing off to the side, the real Jack shook his head. The Craving might make them physically stronger and less akin to injury, but it fuddled their brains to a point long past idiocy. Even a witch at the beginning of her ascension could outwit one as long as she kept out of their reach.

He hoped the other soldiers at Sebastian's beck and call were a lot more fun to play with.

Crouching beside the woman, he checked to see if she was still alive. She had lost a lot of blood and had a serious head wound, along with a few other lacerations, but although ragged and shallow, she was still breathing. Her pulse was still strong. If he could get her to Xeno, she would live. But just as he reached forward to pick her up, he stopped and looked again.

There were no bite marks on her.

Now why in the gods' names would they have healed her before attacking him?

Glancing over at the three vampires still dancing with his illusion, Jack groaned as it finally hit them. They were going to take her back. His original plan of taking the woman to Xeno, then coming back to follow the vamps through the portal wasn't going to work. They would just find another victim to take.

Oh, the things I do...

Knowing this might be his only chance of getting into Merlin's Dimensio, Jack stripped the woman of her torn and bloody clothing, trying not to jostle her too much. He frowned at the state her body was in; she looked like she'd been hit by a truck. Really hoping the vampires hadn't done this to her, Jack swiped two of his fingers through the blood on her forehead. Bringing them to his lips, he closed his eyes and tasted her.

The vampires might be dumb as a post right now, but they'd be able to tell something was wrong if she suddenly changed flavor. If Jack wanted to trick them into taking him back through the portal in her place, he had to look and taste exactly like her.

Memorizing the coppery taste in his mouth, he shifted his blood to mimic it. Then he shifted into her form minus the head injury and broken bones and donned her clothes. He lifted the charm off from around his neck, a tracker that had been spelled to stay with him as he shifted, and placed it on the woman's chest. He turned it off, waited a few seconds, and then turned it back on. Hunter would get an alert, and hopefully, they would arrive in time to save her.

He couldn't do anything else for her without risking the mission.

You could kill her quickly.

He grinned despite the chills running down his back.

In a few seconds, he was going to wish the same for himself.

Lying down in his new identity, Jack cloaked the woman so the vampires couldn't see or smell her. Then he flicked his fingers, making the illusion of himself react a bit too slowly to an attack. As he watched himself get his limbs ripped off and his body get tore into with bloody fangs, Jack sighed. Once they were done, they'd come to feed on him, thinking he was the woman. With luck, they wouldn't kill him before dragging him through the portal...

Right on cue, they turned on him.

Fuck me. I need a raise.

THIRTY-FIVE

"Where's Xeno?" Rogan roared as soon as he walked through the safe house's door. The unconscious woman laid dying in his arms. Jack's tracker was held tight in his fist.

A crash sounded in the control room, quickly followed by the pounding of footsteps upstairs. Hunter jumped over the stairway railing to intercept Emma coming out of the living room, a brush and dustpan in her hands.

"Rogan, what –"

"Bring her in here."

Ignoring his lifemate, Rogan ran toward Xeno's voice. If this woman didn't get an angel's touch soon, she wasn't going to make it. He kicked open the door to the control room, and ice ran down his back when he noticed she wasn't alone. Not having the luxury to stop and glare, he hurried over to the table they'd cleared for him. Hunter was going to be pissed when he saw the state of his books.

After gently laying the woman down, Rogan stepped back and looked at Gabriel. The archangel's healthy thick black wings were carefully tucked behind his shoulders, and although Rogan knew it was an angel's pride to leave them showing, he couldn't help but hate the bastard for doing so in front of Xeno.

"We've got this," Xeno said as she stepped over to the woman's body, her hands raised and glowing with a holy light. "Go see Emma. We don't have much time if Jack's made it inside."

His lips tightened when Gabriel raised his hands as well. Xeno should have been able to save this woman from much worse all on her own. If she needed help with something this simple, perhaps he should order her to stay behind when they went in to find Jack and retrieve the *Scrolls of Atlantis.*

But she'd never go for that.

Nodding sharply, he turned on his heels and headed for the living room. As much as he didn't want to do this, he didn't have a choice. Jack needed this. The world needed this. And so did his lifemate.

"Emma," he said softly as he walked over the threshold. She stood up from her crouch, her dustpan now full of broken glass. Hunter placed the books he was holding down on the pile he'd stacked against the far wall.

"Will she live?" he asked.

Rogan nodded.

"What happened to her?" his lifemate murmured, but though her voice shook, it had an underlining of steel. She was ready for this; he could see it in her eyes even though he didn't want to.

"Some vampires fed on her. If it wasn't for Jack, she'd be dead." He held her gaze, needing her to understand the horrors of what she might face. He understood her desire to be a hero, to fight, but war was never kind.

She paled but nodded. "So what do you need me to

do?"

"We've been told we can get into Sebastian's lair by offering him ye, something he wants. He will not expect ye to have any power, though, and if he realizes ye do, this might not work." He walked over to her and took the dustpan from her hands, buying himself time. He didn't want to force her to do anything even if it was for her own good. Emptying the glass into the trashcan they'd brought over from the kitchen, he placed the pan down on the sofa and turned back to face her. "But if he tries to hurt ye, do whatever it takes to escape."

She froze, her eyes widening, and he knew her curse had been activated.

"Rogan, please don't make me –"

"I will not force ye to chose." His chest twisted, stabbed with all the shards he'd tossed out. He knew exactly what she would choose. If it came down to saving her or saving her sister, it would be Elizabeth coming home.

Tears burned in his throat, but he refused to take that choice from her.

"We leave in two hours." He nodded at Hunter, who then left the room. Walking back over to Emma, he cupped her face and kissed her.

It wasn't a goodbye kiss. As his tongue swept around hers and his lips cherished her, he told himself he would see her again. He would hold her again. And they would figure out a way to survive.

Lifting his head, he kissed her forehead, then stepped back. As of this moment, she was an agent. If he thought of her as more than that, as his lifemate, he would get everyone killed. Jack, Hunter, and Xeno would need him to be his cold, calculated self so they could anticipate his moves. And if they failed this mission, if he got anyone else killed, Emma would never forgive herself.

"Are ye ready?" he asked, his voice detached.

Steel in her eyes, she nodded.

Oh, the things I do. Jack sighed warily as she slowly came to on a cold stone floor, still in the woman's body. Despite the lack of lighting, it was easy to discern she was locked up in a dungeon. She'd been in enough of them to recognize the stench of fear and bodily waste hanging thick in the air. As the drafty cold seeped into her bones, Jack cursed the fragility of the human body.

She rubbed at her arms in an attempt to combat some of the chill. For once, she was glad the vampires she'd come across had been completely consumed by the Craving. Not a single one had noticed their prey had been in critical health before they'd reached her. And not a single one had noticed that the woman's previous injuries had healed. Had they been of their right minds, Jack never would have made it into Merlin's Dimensio.

She gradually wobbled to her feet and peered around the cell. Her pathetic human eyes needed time to adjust to the darkness. After a few moments, she was able to make out three solid walls. Realizing the entrance was behind her, Jack gingerly turned around and stumbled over to the cell's door.

Though she was completely healed of injuries, the vampires had nearly drained her dry before they'd stop. They'd then ferried her across the portal too quick for her sluggish mind to understand the mechanisms of the key. Of course, it hadn't helped that she'd already been drifting in and out of consciousness at that point. The woman whose form she'd borrowed never would have made it.

Bracing herself against the cold metal bars, Jack didn't think too much time had passed given how dizzy she still felt. "Hello?" she tentatively called out. "Is anyone here?"

Someone rasped a hoarse reply, but it was impossible to make out their gender, let alone their words. Not wanting to drain whoever it was of the remainder of their strength, Jack stayed silent and waited for someone else to answer. When no one did, she squinted into the darkness, trying to make out the number of cells and which ones had inhabitants.

Annoyed, she wished she could change her eyes into those of an owl, but she didn't know if Sebastian had warded the place to detect any use of magic. She had just started to make out the faint outline of adjacent bars when light flooded down the hall. She squeezed her eyes shut to ease the piercing in her skull. But though Jack couldn't see the visiting vampires, their soft footsteps echoed loudly throughout the dungeon.

When they stopped outside her cell, she tried not to sigh. *So fucking typical.* Acting the part of a scared little human girl, Jack twisted her face into fear, wobbling her lower lip. Her eyes blinked rapidly, and she even got out a sniffle.

"Wh-what d-d-do you w-w-want?" she whimpered as she scrambled back from the bars, deliberately tripping over her feet.

Feminine laughter greeted her ears, and Jack's urge to roll her eyes almost couldn't be contained. So she brought her hands up to her face and forced a few broken sobs out. As she cried into the cover of her palms, she wondered how long she would have to keep up the facade.

The last time she had played the victim, it had taken a whole week for Rogan and the others to come to her rescue – not that she had truly needed saving given she had been there willingly, just as she was now. It was just... captivity got boring *sooo* ridiculously quickly and there was only so many times she could pretend to cry without wanting to scream. Even when faced with torture these days, she had to put on an act so the torturers didn't feel bad. Nothing anyone ever came up with surpassed Jack's dealings with Lycra – and she visited that crazy bitch for enjoyment.

Or, well, she had until three years ago.

At the flare of pain, she pushed it down. One hand pressed against her stomach as the memory refused to leave.

You should've killed her.

Yeah. Yeah, she should've.

"We want to drink your blood." It was such a horrible line ripping her back to the present that Jack's eyes rolled automatically. Luckily, she was still weeping into one of her hands, so the vampires didn't notice.

Jack sobbed loudly as they rattled the lock on her cell. When the door was wrenched open, she added a bit of shaking to the mix. Fighting utter boredom, she noticed her eyes had finally adjusted to the harsh light, so she peeked out from between her fingers.

Two vampires towered above her, both with long black hair and wide, solemn eyes. Their glistening fangs were already elongated in preparation for their feast. Jack fought the urge to glower. Instead, she memorized their faces so she could enact her revenge later if she had the time.

She was not one to be consumed by the need for retaliation, but she would be lying if she claimed to find no pleasure in it. Her job didn't have many perks outside of saving the world, so she found happiness in the darkest corners of the underworld. Lately, it hadn't become that difficult.

Ignoring the pain of that catalytic day, Jack gave a

convincing scream when they reached for her. As the first set of fangs sank into her neck, she allowed herself to fall limp with terror. As her vision began narrowing into pinpricks, she forced herself to stay in character.

She wasn't sure if every vampire here was under the Master's command or what his plans for her being here were. She had hoped the woman whose place she had taken was wanted for something other than a mere snack. But the way these two were drinking started to give her doubts. Before she could collapse into unconsciousness, a venomous voice rang out like a gunshot.

"That's enough. You drink any more and you can tell your master our deal is off, you filthy bloodsuckers."

The vampires hissed and growled, but neither of them sank their fangs back into Jack's flesh. Interestingly, they actually released her and stepped away.

She tried to raise her head to look around at who'd spoken, but the damage had already been done. *Stupid freaking human bodies.*

The darkness claimed her.

Just when it started to get interesting...

Elizabeth! Help me! Emma mentally begged as she ran through the darkened streets of the city. The cold air stung her lungs as she blitzed through the night. Her legs were beginning to burn with the exercise, but she pressed on like her life depended on it.

She drew on the memory of Xeno holding a knife to her throat, the blood dripping down her neck. As she let her earlier fear rise to the surface, she reached out for her twin once more. *You were right! They tried to kill me! Please, help!*

Though having expected it, Emma still stumbled when

her sister finally replied. She quickly righted herself as she continued to run, taking a sharp turn down an alley as she threw a scared look behind her.

Where are you?

I don't know. Close? They're trying to find you to kill you, and when they realized I didn't know anything, they tried to kill me!

Open your mind so I can see where you are.

Completely at a lost on how to do that, Emma tried to relax and hoped that would work. But though her mind knew those behind her weren't genuinely chasing her, her heart thumped with adrenaline. The effort it took to calm down was much more than she had anticipated.

Found you! Elizabeth's voice cracked just the tiniest bit, but Emma heard it and her heart clenched tight. She wished she could tell her sister it was okay to follow the psycho's orders and bring her in. That this was a rescue, but she didn't dare.

We're sending help now. Hold on, Emma.

I can't stop. They're so much faster than me. She took a random corner, hoping Rogan and his team could really track her without needing to keep her in sight. He'd told her he knew her body's water signature, that even if she couldn't see him, he would be there. But she'd been running for nearly fifteen minutes and had not once seen any sign of them. What if she'd lost them? What if she messed up the whole mission?

Trying to keep those thoughts down, she focused on the knife Xeno had held at her throat. She'd really thought she was going to die.

That's okay. Just keep your mind open, Em. I'll lead our guys to you.

Praying everything would be okay, Emma ran in the opposite direction of the fireworks. She'd just passed a

Chinese takeaway when her mind tingled with a different awareness. She gasped in utter shock as her whole body jerked with power. Stumbling to the ground, she clutched a hand to her chest. Her fingers buzzed with a need she didn't understand, but as she climbed back to her feet, it seemed she didn't need to. Her instinct knew what it wanted, and it wanted those two people behind her.

Blocking her mind off from her sister, Emma turned around to face a duo of vampires – both males with blood red eyes and short black hair. Her lips curled up in excitement as the rational part of her receded in surrender to this completely-consuming, primal power.

Kneel.

Surprisingly, they did just that.

Emma's body hummed with an approval that scared her. Taking a step back, she looked at her hands. They shook but not with fear. With desire. With magic.

She didn't understand.

Did she just transfer her curse?

"Damn, girl." Hunter's low drawl of approval caused her to look up in relief. If he was here, so was Rogan and Xeno. Someone could tell her what the hell was going on.

Walking over to her, Rogan grabbed her hands. "Are ye pulsing?"

She shook her head, knowing that if she was, he'd call the mission off. Sebastian wanted her defenseless and weak. If she pulsed in front of him, he might just kill her. "I – I don't think so." She hesitated, realizing it was true. "This feels..." *Like pure power.*

Her eyes on the vamps, she said, "Drop your weapons on the ground and give yourself a wedgie."

The sound of clattering metal was followed by grunts.

"Remind me to never get on your bad side."

Frowning, she turned to Hunter. "Raise your hand."

When he just stared at her, his arms down at his sides, she turned to Xeno for answers.

"Ask them if they're made vampires or born."

"Made," they answered after Emma repeated Xeno's question.

"So Elizabeth can raise the dead...and it seems like ye can control them." His voice hardening, Rogan stepped in front of the two vampires. "Now let's see if ye can get these two to talk."

Wiping her palms on her thighs, she took a deep breath and then stepped forward. She straightened her back and looked down her nose at them, reminding herself that though they might look human, they were monsters hurting her sister. "Tell us how to get to Sebastian," she demanded.

They bared their teeth but answered nonetheless. "You have to be invited into Merlin's Dimensio."

Brief boisterous laughter caused her to jump. Her heart beat so hard it was going to vibrate out of her chest.

"How ironic," Hunter said, "that vampires have to ask us in. You know, because in the stories they're normally the one who has to – Ugh. Never mind. I wish Jack was here. He would have thought that was freaking hilarious."

Still looking at the two vamps, Rogan said, "Ask about the castle grounds and its defenses, if there's an ambush waiting on the other side of the portal, where Sebastian's quarters are, how many –"

Emma cut in, "Answer all of these people's questions immediately." She wanted this over as fast as possible so they could get in and rescue Liz.

The two did as requested, if a bit bitingly. Sebastian, it turned out, had yet to return from his recent expedition (though he was expected at any moment). There wasn't a guard on the other side because those under the Craving would've attacked them on reentry. Within half an hour, the rest of the questions were answered and Rogan's team was invited through the portal.

As soon as they stepped though and into a small wood, Hunter lunged at a vampire with a dagger. He plunged it deep into the man's heart. Emma opened her mouth to scream, but Rogan muted her with a single command. She retched in silence as the vampire fell to his knees and then crumbled away as a pile of ash.

"Will ye tell this one to believe everything I say, Emma?" She shivered at the lack of humanity in Rogan's voice. He sounded so different to the man she'd grown to love.

"We doona have much time."

Swallowing, she nodded. "Y–yes." Locking eyes with the angry gaze of the vamp, she said, "Believe everything he says."

Rogan stepped between them, breaking her line of sight. "Ye found Emma running from us and ye sacrificed yer friend to get away. Ye barely made it through the portal. We were not able to follow." Pulling a vial out of his pocket, he flipped open the lid and moved to stand behind the vamp. Drawing the water out with his magic, he said, "Will ye tell him not to scream, Emma?"

Telling herself all this was necessary, ignoring the fear in the vampire's eyes, she did as requested. Her chest ached. An empathetic sob choked its way up her throat. She wanted to turn around, to not watch whatever it was Rogan was about to do, but she couldn't hide from this world anymore.

"Don't scream." A tear ran down her cheek.

Rogan knelt as he raised the water in the air. After circling his hands horizontally above each other, he shot the top one out. The water slammed into the vampire's back, sizzling upon impact. His eyes rolling back in his head, the bloodsucker fell forward. His fingers clawed into the ground. Emma placed a hand over her mouth as her stomach heaved.

For Liz.

Stopping in front of her, Rogan lifted her chin, forcing her to look him in the eye rather than at the vampire. "Ye will believe what I just told him. Ye will not remember anything that truly happened after ye ran away from the safe house until ye see me again. Once we are gone, the two of ye will believe ye just entered the portal, and ye will then not control another undead until yer life is in danger."

His eyes seared hers for a second longer. He nodded at Hunter, who dragged the vampire over to them. Knowing what she needed to do, Emma stood a couple feet behind the vamp, then reached forward and grabbed his hand as she would've done had they been running for their lives.

With not even a flicker of emotion in his icy blue eyes, Rogan turned on his heels and disappeared through the trees. Xeno and Hunter followed, a gun having replaced his bloody knife.

And then she was being dragged forward by the vamp, her mind frozen in disbelief. The plan hadn't worked. After everything Rogan had promised, after everything they'd gone over, he hadn't even made it through.

Tears burned her eyes as she realized Liz wasn't going to be saved. Worse, she'd just stupidly given herself to Sebastian.

No. Emma bit the inside of her cheek, using the pain to ground herself.

No. All this meant was that Rogan and his team were not going to save Liz.

But Liz *was* being rescued tonight. She'd just have to

do it herself.

THIRTY-SIX

Shoving off the heavy blanket of exhaustion covering her eyes, Jack forced them to open. Her head throbbed as she pushed herself into a sitting position. Dragging herself over to the bars of her cell, she rested her temple against the cool metal.

She tried to peer through the darkness to find her savior, but it was to no avail. These crappy human eyes couldn't see shit. Wetting her lips, she asked, "So who strikes a deal with the devil but doesn't bargain for better quarters?"

An echoing silence filled every nook in the stone walls of the dungeon. Just when Jack didn't think she would get an answer, a snide British voice slithered between their cells.

"Who gets sucked by vampires and can't act for shit?"

Jack grinned. "Hey, those were real tears."

"The only reason you got away with it was because they're dumb as shit."

Oh, I'm going to enjoy my time here. Rogan could take

months for all she cared. Well, as long as the British lass didn't die in that time. Or worse, if she broke down and started crying. Ugh, Jack hated listening to crying almost as much as she hated faking it.

"Maybe," Jack admitted. "So how long have you been here?"

"Long enough not to get attached to the snacks."

Dammit, that was not what Jack wanted to hear. Her sultry, sassy voice? Oh, hel, yeah. The hint that she was going to die in this stupid pit? Not so much. "So what are you then, if not a snack?"

A second of silence. "A prize."

Jack grinned, but then her smile faded when she realized the woman wasn't being sarcastic. *So what is she to Sebastian?* Could she be yet another descendant? Jack had to hand it to him. He had an eerie ability in finding the bastards when no one else even knew they existed. But if she was, surely these cells wouldn't be able to hold her. So was she a member of the SCU?

Aw, fuck. Was Hunter going to get on to her if she didn't save her?

Jack's chest tightened as some thing moved through her heart. "You human?" she asked, keeping her voice light.

She snorted. "You saying there are other creatures out there besides vampires?"

"Oh, yeah."

There was a second of silence before her voice slithered across the bars, half-curious, half-demanding. "So what are you then?"

Jack grinned. "Soon to be dead by the sounds of it."

Cutting through the woods, Rogan, Hunter, and Xeno

headed for the west side of the castle. The dungeons were located here, and they needed to get Jack out before Sebastian returned. Given they did not know the exact location of the *Scrolls of Atlantis,* they needed his cloaking ability to search Sebastian's quarters in the east wing.

At the end of the treeline, Rogan dug his hands into his jacket and pulled out two bottles of fire enchanted with the rays of the sun. They were charmed to explode on impact. Although sunlight wouldn't harm any of the born vampires lurking inside, it would kill the made ones lost under the power of the Craving.

Handing both of them to Hunter, he dug out two more for Xeno and two for himself. Raising his arm, he looked at his watch. "Three minutes, aye," he said, setting his timer.

Hunter and Xeno nodded. "Xeno, ye stay here while I take south and Hunter takes north."

"No," she said, surprising them both. Spreading her wings, she knocked his response back into his chest.

His eyes widened and he didn't need to look at Hunter to know his face looked the same. Xeno's wings, though still bleeding and oozing puss, now stretched out to their full length. The bones and tendons had miraculously mended. Without a word, she launched into the air.

Hunter took a step forward as if to catch her, but she rose without struggle – something she had not done in months.

"I'll take the south." Flapping her wings, she took off like a comet.

"What the fuck did Gabriel do to her?" Hunter finally breathed, hope in his voice.

Rogan, too, hoped she was healing, but he didn't have time to think about it. Every second that passed was another Emma was in danger. Grasping Hunter's arm, he wordlessly ordered him to take off to the north side. The clocks were ticking and despite Rogan's ability to run faster than a human, he needed to check in with Jack.

With his back to the wall, he moved both bottles to his left hand. His eyes scanning his surroundings, Rogan searched the castle with his magic. Picking up on Jack's waterprint, he moved the middle finger on his left hand, controlling Jack's too.

He'd just touched his finger to his palm when his sixth sense flared to life. His head jerking up, Rogan spotted a female vampire dropping right on top of him.

"Liz!" Emma screamed as she struggled against the vampire holding her, desperately trying to reach her sister. Relief flooded her at the sight of her twin, but it was dammed again as soon as she noticed the haggard gaze of her eyes. Elizabeth had always been the vibrant one, her face easy with a teasing smile more times than not. She enjoyed life in all its colors and shades, never leaving something for tomorrow that she wanted for today. Had enjoyed, Emma realized, her heart breaking.

Finally jerking herself free from the vampire's grip, she stumbled through the throne room. Rushing up the stairs to her sister's side, she threw her arms around her and whispered in her ear, "I'm here to rescue you, Liz. I've come into my powers too, and I can control people. But we need to go now, okay? I won't let him hurt us. I promise."

She ran her hand down her sister's arm and entwined their fingers as she pivoted toward the door. She took a step forward, only to be jerked back when Elizabeth didn't move. Her chest squeezed tight with denial.

No, no, no, no, no.

Turning back around, she looked at her sister's eyes. Her glazed eyes full of tears.

A choked cry rose into her throat. "Did he order you to stay or just to stand still?" Needing to believe it was the latter, Emma looked around for a way to carry her sister in her current position.

The vampire laughed below them. "Are you seriously trying to escape already?"

Looking down at him, still holding Liz's hand, Emma tried to push out with her power, praying to the gods that it worked outside of a pulse.

It didn't.

Her gut twisting, she shifted in front of her sister, shielding her. "If you let us go, I can give you sanctuary."

"Sanctuary? What the fuck do I need sanctuary for?" he asked as he stalked up the stairs toward them. "I get to eat whoever I want with Sebastian. I don't have to starve because some stupid fucking council has declared killing 'sentient life' a crime. As if you people are actually sentient. I've seen your politics. There is nothing sentient about your race."

Her grip on Liz's hand tightened. "You won't win this war. The Elv've'Norc –"

"The Elv've'Norc have been trying to kill Sebastian for millennia and haven't managed. This war was won a long time ago. Sebastian was just waiting for the right moment to come again." He sneered as he stopped in front of her and she tried not to flinch. "Your friends didn't even make it through the portal." He lifted his hand to her face. She smacked it away, her heart racing.

His eyes narrowed in on her.

She lifted her chin, taking solace in the fact that Sebastian wanted her alive. He wouldn't allow his lackeys to –

The vampire's hand shot out and wrapped around her throat. Jerking her away from Liz, he threw her down the stairs. She yelped as she hit her shoulder and tumbled head over heels to the bottom. She'd just managed to crawl back onto her feet, cradling her arm, when his hand wrapped around her neck again.

He lifted her off the floor, bruising her windpipe, causing her legs to kick of their own accord. Yanking her forward until their noses touched, he sneered, "Sebastian gave us orders not to rape you, but everything else is free game."

Smiling wide, he opened his mouth to bite her.

Oh, thank fuck. Feeling her middle finger move under Rogan's command, Jack smiled. Soon, she could get rid of this pathetic human body. Better yet, she'd be sinking her fangs into that sassy woman right after, needing her blood for energy. Forget the fear tasting better crap; it was the courageous ones that tasted the best. Better yet, if they were high and the drugs were fully in their system.

She licked her lips.

Soon, my dear tongue. Soon.

Rogan dove out of the way as the female vampire hit the ground where he'd just been. Rolling to his feet, he pivoted and glanced at his timer as he pulled out a whip of water. Two minutes left.

The woman stood up from her crouch, her face easily recognizable in the soft light of dawn. Lamia, Sebastian's last remaining bloodkin, was his most loyal ally. She'd been there when he and Rakian had nearly destroyed the

Seven Planes. She'd disappeared when her brother had gone into hiding. It wasn't surprising she was back, but he'd hoped at least one of the many call ins saying she'd died hadn't been a hoax.

Sebastian had a focus, an ideology, a method to his madness.

Lamia was a mere killing machine, taking orders like the perfect little puppet.

Waiting perfectly still, she waited for him to make his move.

Hunter glanced at his watch once he arrived in position at the north side of the castle. With a minute and a half left to spare, he crept along the wall, peeking through windows to find the best place to throw the fiery cocktails.

He smiled when he found the jackpot. This window didn't just have its curtains pulled shut. It was boarded too. Pressing his ear against the glass, he heard snores coming from inside.

Raising his gun, he waited for the timer.

Xeno landed a bit harder than she would have liked, her wings already sore from that short flight. Gabriel had told her to not push it, that the ritual they had done mere hours ago wouldn't heal her completely, but the pain was rejuvenating. She hadn't stretched her wings like that in months.

Placing the bottles against the wall about ten yards apart, she backed up and checked her timer. She'd just lowered her arm when the smell of burning flesh reached her nose. Pivoting, she brought her arms up, ready to attack.

Barreling toward her were four vampires smoldering from the faint light of the morning sun.

Pulling a throwing knife from the strap on her arm, she flung it into the leg of her first target. Spreading her wings, she launched into the air. Three other knives were thrown. Three other vampires hit the ground, one of their legs sliced clean through.

She didn't have to kill these made ones. She just had to slow them down long enough for the sun to do its job.

Rogan's whip cut through the air before turning into a tornado of knives. Lamia's mien never changed as she dodged left and right, jumping through the air and ducking under his blades. Her speed made her a blur, and Rogan struggled to keep an eye on her. Knowing she was heading toward him, wanting to get close enough he couldn't just fling his blades around, he took a step back.

But she advanced too quickly, and soon she was right in front of him.

She aimed a punch at his face, and he only just managed to pull up a shield of ice. The breaking of her bones echoed loudly in his ears, but she didn't even seem to register it. Her face an utter blank, she aimed a kick at his shin.

He wrapped the ice around her ankle and slammed it to the ground. Pulling more and more water from his jacket, he built the ice up over her leg, then moved to her other one. She kept trying to smash free with her fists, but once the ice blocks were up to her knees, Rogan stopped trying to reinforce them. He had her where he wanted her.

Focusing on his magic, he accessed the water in her eyes now that she wasn't moving and caused it to boil.

Her face never changed.

Her fists just went faster, two blurs chipping away huge chunks of ice.

Stepping back, Rogan increased the heat in her eyes until they exploded. Twisting his hands, he shifted the remaining ice around her legs into an iron maiden and slammed each spike in.

She dropped to her knees as blood dripped down her face.

The timer on his watch went off.

Knowing he wouldn't have long before she was back up again, her 3700 year old blood and magic allowing her to heal a lot faster than he, he grabbed the two fiery bottles and launched them through the windows of the castle.

The dungeon walls shook from the force of multiple explosions going off above. Weak cries rang out from all the other cells but the one adjacent to Jack's. Standing, she transed into a male vampire and ripped apart the bars of his cell. As he strode over to the quiet one, a set of fangs slid down past his lower lip. Fueled by the desire to feed, Jack easily crushed the lock in his hand. Throwing the crumbled metal away, he stalked inside the cell.

At the sight of his sassy savior, he was rooted to the spot. His nostrils flared with a different desire. But it wasn't her attractive looks captivating him. It was the challenging tilt of her jaw as she faced an enemy she couldn't quite see in the low light. With her blonde waves and sharp green eyes, she stood fast under his approach. It was as if she was claiming he didn't have the backbone to actually go through with what he wanted to do.

And Hades' fire, she was right. Because though what Jack needed to do was feed from her to recollect his energy, what he *wanted* was something else entirely.

Reaching forward, he cupped the back of her neck. She didn't shrink from his touch, just lifted her chin even higher to glare at him. A smile curling his lips, Jack yanked her to him. She smelled like sweat and piss, but her soft skin was so tantalizing it shifted something inside him. Something primal. Something powerful.

His fingers tightened around her neck. He shifted his hips so she couldn't feel his growing erection. The last thing he wanted to do was make her think he was about to rape her. A low deep growl erupted from the depths of his being at the thought of the other vamps having already touched her.

I'll kill them all.

Wrapping his fingers in her hair, he tugged her head to the side, leaned down, and sank his fangs into her neck. She spasmed beneath him. Her hand came up to push against his chest, but he placed his hand over it and held her to him.

She tasted like thunder and lighting and something that could shatter his world. A moan sounded from the back of his throat as her blood, the very essence of her, seeped down it. Stepping closer to her again, unable to fight it, he released her hair to wrap his arm around her.

He pulled her tight against him, and when his cock pushed into her stomach, he nearly sank to his knees in front of her.

She tensed for the first time, but she didn't push against him. She didn't try to break free. His lips working at her neck, he drank until her knees buckled and she collapsed against his chest.

Pulling back, he swept his tongue across her skin, healing the two little wounds he'd created. He lingered for a split second, wanting to stay and taste her anywhere she would let him. Reminding himself his team would most likely fail without him, Jack finally eased the woman to the ground.

He stepped out of her cage and flung the door shut behind him. His biceps flexing, he interlaced the bar on her door with the one on the wall, shutting her in. It wouldn't stop Sebastian from retrieving her given his ability to phase, but hopefully Jack would return before he did.

For SCU agent or not, he wanted the woman that tasted like heaven and hell.

Emma screamed as the vampire's fangs scraped across her neck. Kicking him in the balls, she grabbed the top of his head with one hand and punched him in the jaw with the other.

He dropped her on a roar, stumbling back as his knees buckled. Slamming into the ground at the same time as he, Emma cradled her hand, knowing she had broken a few fingers. As tears built in her eyes, she pushed to her feet and rushed him. He was faster than her, stronger than her. Her only hope at surviving this was hitting him while he was already down.

Pulling her leg back, she kicked him hard in the back, right in the middle of where Rogan had shot him with holy water. He arched, his face twisting in pain, his mouth jerking open, but a scream didn't break the air.

She kicked him over onto his front, then jumped on his back with both feet, ignoring the pain in her heart and the sickness in her stomach. When he no longer moved and his breaths came out only as moans, Emma hopped off him and ran back up to her sister.

Desperately, she tried tugging on her again. "Can you

talk to me, Liz? Can you tell me what he ordered you to do so I can think of a loophole?"

A tear trickled down Liz's cheek, but her lips stayed frozen, as did her body.

Refusing to give up, Emma let go of her sister's hand and wiped at her tears. She could figure this out. She just needed to –

Please let this work.

Bending low, she wrapped her arms around Liz's legs and lifted, making sure to keep her twin in the same pose. A strangled cry left her when it worked. Holding her sister tight, she headed down the stairs. She just needed to get to the bridge. Rogan would probably still be there, waiting on the other side, along with Xeno and Hunter. All she had to do was get to the bridge.

What about Jack?

She gritted her teeth as she struggled not to drop her sister. He'd risked his life to get in here and save Liz. She shouldn't leave without him.

But...

Her hands tightened on her sister.

She would save Liz first and then come back for him. Ignoring the guilt over walking away, over potentially leaving him to die in the time she was gone, she headed for the throne room's door.

Lowering her sister to the floor, Emma shook out her arms and took a deep shaky breath. Already, she was trembling from fatigue. The bridge was a good half mile away from the castle's door. She wasn't going to make it.

I am.

Opening the door, Emma looped her arms back around Liz, and lifted. She took a step forward and then another.

One step at a time, they would make it to freedom.

Hunter dived through the window on the tails of his second explosion, one of the charms tattooed on his chest protecting him from the intense heat. Rolling forward into a crouch, he swung his arms out, a gun in each hand, and fired off a round of shots. Four of the vampires trying to rise from the bunk beds lining the room screamed in agony and rage as the bullets ripped through their arms and legs, dropping them back down onto their burning mattresses

Lunching to his feet, he spun as he moved forward, firing shots all around him. Each bullet slammed into the spine of a different vamp, crippling them instantly. They fell to the ground with feral screams. Dragging themselves across the floor, they tried to crawl away from the flames, but the fire was burning too bright now. Within seconds, the vampires turned into ash, their screams quieting forever.

His shoulder leading, Hunter busted through the door and into the hall. He ducked low and took his first breath since entering the castle. The smoke irritated his lungs, making him cough. Running from the room, he headed down the hall. A giant staircase loomed up ahead, leading to the dungeons.

Ignoring all the screams for help echoing out of the cells he passed, Jack ran toward the light at the end of the hall. The stairway would lead him up out of the dungeons.

Raising his hand, he called upon his magic and cloaked himself from the two vampires guarding the other side of the door. He slipped through unnoticed, then shoved a clawed hand into the chest of the bloodsucker closest.

Grabbing hold of her heart, he yanked it free. Her partner never even looked at her, still seeing her standing and alive due to Jack's magic.

Dropping the still organ, the trickster crossed over to the second vamp and did the same.

At the sight of Hunter running toward him, his guns drawn, Jack dropped onto all fours. His bones splintered, his tendons snapped, his mouth elongated, and his eyes turned a bright yellow. Thick fur erupted all across his body, tar black everywhere but his stomach, which was snow white. Growling, he struggled through the pain, his claws digging deep into the stone tiles beneath him.

Lifting his head, a wide block of muscle and bone like that of a staffie, Jack let loose a howl that echoed through the castle. Screams rose up from the dungeons below. The stench of fear came from every direction. Even Hunter reeked of it, and Jack winked at him to know he was going to take the piss out of him later.

Rising onto his back haunches, he towered over seven feet tall. His arms stretched down to his knees. He sniffed the air, his whiskers twitching back and forth until he pinpointed the scent he wanted.

The *Scrolls was* on the fourth floor of the eastwing, its old book smell leading him straight to it.

THIRTY-SEVEN

A FEW SECONDS EARLIER

They were going to make it.

Emma sobbed in relief when she caught sight of the door leading to outside. Her arms shook as she held her sister tightly to her. Liz had not yet made a single sound, had not yet moved a single finger on her hand. If it wasn't for her breathing and the tears on her sister's face, Emma would have thought her dead.

"We're almost the–"

A chilling roar stopped her cold. Her heart lurched in her chest, pounding and slamming against her ribcage in an attempt to flee from whatever had made that sound. Goosebumps rising all across her body, Emma stumbled forward in a panic.

Her feet knocked into each other. Her knees buckled. Crying out as she dropped Liz, Emma hit the ground hard. Tears burst free down her cheeks as her broken fingers snapped even further under the weight of her body. Biting the inside of her cheek, drawing blood, Emma forced herself through the pain. She lifted her head to find Liz, shaken and relieved to see her still standing exactly as before.

Climbing to her feet, she breathed heavily. Her arms didn't want to move anymore, but she forced them up. Praying her body didn't fail her, Emma stumbled toward her sister.

"Fuck, you're an idiot, aren't you?"

Jerking around at the sound of his soft voice, Emma sucked in a breath. The man in front of her could have been a model with his sharp jawline and stylish dark hair. But his eyes would have sealed the deal. Light with amusement and dark with rage, they drew her in like magnets.

"Now watch carefully, Tony, and see what happens when you step out of line."

Everything inside her dropped. Her heart sat heavily in her stomach as her lungs collapsed. She couldn't breathe, her eyes locked onto the little boy she hadn't noticed before. Standing behind the model, his face red and puffy and terrified, he couldn't be more than three or four.

And then it hit her, this fucker's identity. "Sebastian," she breathed, terror and rage boiling inside her.

Shifting in front of Liz, Emma wished with all her might that she would start to pulse.

His eyes narrowed. The corner of his lips curled into a sneer. "I do hope you scream as much as your sister does."

Prowling toward her, he flashed his fangs.

Rogan grunted as Lamia's teeth sank into the back of his shoulder. Belly down on the ground, he slammed his elbow back to try to dislodge her. After he'd thrown the explosives, she'd smashed free of her bindings and jumped onto his back. She had fangs where he only had teeth. She had claws where he had fingers. Aiming for his hands and arms, she'd shredded him to pieces.

Knowing she'd be reaching for his neck soon, Rogan concentrated on the blood pouring out of her eyes and legs and started yanking it out of her body.

Hissing, she jumped off his back. By the time he made it to his feet, she was a blur across the landscape, knowing all she needed to do was get outside of his range.

Cursing, Rogan pulled a ovensi healing wand out of his pocket. He waved it over the bite mark on his shoulder, making the skin too tight but healed, as he headed for one of the holes he'd made in the castle wall. Stepping over the rubble, he slashed a whip through a fleeing vampire's neck. Anyone here not under the power of the Craving was a willing associate to Sebastian's fucked up plans.

"Rogan!" Xeno landed beside him, her wings held out proudly behind her. He wanted to ask her how she was, how she was healing, if it was permanent or temporary, but now wasn't the time. The rage in her eyes told her why she'd sought him out long before she uttered the words, "Sebastian is here."

A growl rose up from the depths of Sebastian's throat as he sank his fangs into Emma's neck. Her blood was too tantalizing, too powerful to be from someone who had yet to go through their ascension. Now aware he was in peril of being killed with a single touch, he clutched her wrists and squeezed. As her bones started to crunch like a packet of stepped on chips, a heavy weight rammed into his back.

Another growl left his lips as he withdrew his fangs and phased. He appeared three feet behind where he'd just been, and kicked the melted back of the moron who'd just attacked him into Emma's crumbling body.

Their cries rang like music in his ears as they crashed into Elizabeth. The tears running down Liz's face made his cock hard.

Oh, I am going to enjoy this.

"Try not to make this easy," Sebastian purred as he reached down to haul the younger vampire to his feet. The man slashed out with his claws, but he was nothing more than a gnat buzzing around Sebastian's ear.

Plunging his fingers into the man's throat, Sebastian wrapped his hand around his spine and ripped it out. Before his body could hit the floor, he pulled his head off with as little effort as a human did a chicken's.

A delightful popping sound echoed around the hall. He smiled. Emma shuddered as she stood on swaying legs. And thicker tears ran down Liz's face.

He licked at the blood coating his mouth. Reaching for the buckle on his belt, he slowly undid the clasp.

"Someone needs to learn their place."

Despite the short distance between them, Sebastian phased to directly in front of Emma just to hear her scream. He nearly groaned when she didn't disappoint. He grabbed Emma's chin with such force he broke her jaw. He squeezed a bit harder until a few teeth popped out.

The panic and pain in her eyes acted like a drug. He ripped at the front of her pants, knowing he would need to be quick. The fucking Elv've'Norc had set half of his castle on fire already and were quickly cutting through his army. He needed to get the *Scrolls* and make his escape, but he couldn't phase with four people: Liz, Emma, the woman in the dungeons, and her child, if half of them were fighting him. As strong as he was, he was only mortal.

For now.

As Emma pathetically tried kicking him, Sebastian maneuvered her backward until she hit the wall. He pinned her legs still with his own, then reached for his cock.

She struggled harder.

Uselessly.

Delighting in her pain, he looked her in the eye.

The gods had taken everything from him, and soon he would take everything from all of them.

But just as he started to position himself, a powerful magic slammed into his body, causing him to release her and stumble back.

Please her.

The words rang out in his very soul, urging him to do whatever it was she wanted. Shaking his head, Sebastian fought her magic with a growl. He stumbled over to the cowering boy and yanked him up off the floor. Knowing the longer Emma pulsed, the stronger she would get, he phased to Liz's side and grabbed her too.

"No!" Emma's gurgled, pained, broken scream, barely understood through her crushed jaw, made him smile. Holding her gaze, he phased, taking her sister with him.

But when he rematerialized, he wasn't in the dungeons as he had planned. Rather, he was back in the hall he'd just left.

Please her!

The vampire stumbled back from the force of Emma's command, his hands dropping from Liz's and Tony's. Reaching up to his neck, controlled by her power, he extended his claws. But even as his ripped into his own skin, exposing one side of his spinal cord, Sebastian's lips curled into a smile. "That was a mistake."

He laughed as his other hand fisted around the intact side of his neck. He wasn't far from decapitating himself, but he was never going to do it. His eyes on Liz, he watched as she took a step toward her sister.

The hall filled with his soldiers and the filthy, blood-covered Elv've'Nor, all ready to fight for Emma's pleasure, and still Sebastian smiled. Blood poured out of his open throat as he chuckled.

None of them could make the distance in time – not before Elizabeth killed her sister with a single touch.

Stop!

Elizabeth begged her body to listen. Tears ran down her face so fast and thick she could barely see. But she didn't need to see in order to kill. Commanded to protect her master from all threats, his will pulled her straight to her sister.

Reaching out a hand, she wished she was the one to die.

"No!" Rogan ran forward, seeking the water in Emma's veins. He pushed down the thoughts of what could go wrong if he messed this up. Pushed down his childhood memories of all his mother's blood ripping out of her body when he'd pulsed and pulled too hard. He had to do anything he could to save her.

But just as he started to move Emma, Elizabeth touched her shoulder. Her mouth moved in a single command. Despite the distance between them, Rogan heard it with heart-breaking clarity.

"Die."

The elementalist roared as he tossed a tsunami of knives at Sebastian, but the vampire merely grabbed Liz and the child and phased, a sneer stretching across his lips. As Rogan's blades sliced harmlessly through the air, he collapsed to his knees and screamed.

THIRTY-EIGHT

"Ye're not taking her." Rogan glowered as he stood protectively in front of Emma's unconscious body.

He had stayed away from her during the five days she had been recovering in the Elv've'Norc healers ward, certain his face would be the last thing she'd want to see when she awoke. Because of his failure, his lifemate had looked into the pained eyes of her twin and thought she was going to die. Because he hadn't been quick enough, Liz had been taken by that sadistic fucker. Because he'd ordered his team to get the *Scrolls* first and foremost, he was to blame for everything that had happened.

And so he had found the strength to stay away.

Until now, when Tegan, the head of the Elv've'Norc, stood in the middle of her room, a golden chain dangling from his fingers and a grim determination set deep into his jaw.

"By the gods, Rogan, she's a descendant," the man barked. "The Royal Courts are going to want her tried."

By the gods, she isn't even awake yet, Rogan wanted to

roar back. She might never wake. The idea was sickening, enraging, so painful he didn't know how to breathe. Each breath felt like a bottle of acid was being poured down his throat. He didn't want to live without her. He didn't want to breathe any air she would never get to taste. And he sure as hel wasn't going to let anyone, not even his boss, take her from him.

"It will not be a fair trail and we both know it," Rogan ground out, his eyes dangerous.

"Of course it will be, but she's a descendant," Tegan snapped, his patience quickly waning. "She's too much of a threat. Cariad is still recovering from what she did at Xi'aghn and he's the lucky one. Are you going to look him in the eye and tell him you won't give him justice?"

"Prosecuting one's kin is not justice! She will be sentenced to Damaculus like a criminal. Tell me, Tegan is this how we are to thank people for helping us now? Ye know there is no difference between her and I. I've killed more innocents, that's for sure."

"Oh, don't give me that. You know there is a difference. By the gods, you're an elementalist."

Rogan's eyes burned with fury. "Ye think I need the reminder? Ye are the one who seems to have forgotten that Sebastian, who is not a descendant nor even a demi-god, was half responsible!"

"This is not a discussion." Tegan's muscles bulged with the first surge of his berserker Rage. Though normally that single action would cause any level-headed being to step down, it only made Rogan wilder with fury.

"Aye, because she's not fucking going anywhere!"

"That is enough! Now step aside, agent. That's an order," he snarled, his fists clenching as he fought to keep his power under check.

"Over my dead body!" Rogan snapped a whip of water

between them, daring him to take a step forward.

Tegan's nostrils flared as his strong jaw clenched tight. "You're proving my case," he said slowly, trying to keep the both of them calm. "She's obviously twisted your –"

"She's my bloody lifemate!"

The tension in the room pulled taut enough to snap. Cursing, Tegan rolled his shoulders and forced down the last of his berserker Rage. "By Hades' fire, man, lead with that next time."

"There won't be another time."

"Of course there won't be. I know how lifemates work."

"Oh, aye? Because yer ability to under–"

"Enough!" Tegan roared as he pinched the bridge of his nose. "Just let me think what I can do. By the bloody, fucking gods, Rogan, you couldn't have just fallen for one of your own?"

The elementalist's eyes narrowed as he ordered his whip back into the vial in his jacket. He wasn't amused at his superior's attempt at humor nor did he forgive him for his brash attempt to take Emma. But if the man said he was considering another option, then he was.

Tegan was a sly bastard who ran his ship with an iron first, but he had never screwed over a single agent for the success of a mission. Trust was paramount to him, and despite the strict hierarchy, the berserker treated them all like family. A very distant family he didn't particularly like, but one he would suffer through the holidays with because that's what family did.

"Quiet!" a shrill voice cut in even though the room had been silent for the last ten minutes.

Every piece of hair stood up on Rogan's neck and arms, reacting to the power radiating off whomever had just showed up behind Tegan.

A small woman stepped into the room with a smile full

of sharp teeth. She stood a mere four and a half feet in height and was clothed in brightly striped socks, a black fluffy tutu, and an overlarge shirt that read 'Peace is for Bitches' with an image of two female pups beneath it. Her red hair was up in pigtails, hanging under the two dark red horns curving out from her temples. Her nose was cute as a button, and her smile lit up her eyes with genuine amusement.

Stretching her leathery wings, she whipped her razor-sharp tail behind her as if it was jibing to a rock song. Beside her yawned a chimera cub that looked beyond adorable despite its status as a legendary monster.

Struggling not to grab Emma and run, Rogan bowed his head in greeting. As did Tegan. Although he'd never seen a goddess in the flesh, Delentia's fashion sense was known worlds wide.

She waved her fingers in reply, her smile stretching further. "The Courts have cleared it, you boneheaded cock measurers. Emma's totally cool to stay out of Damaculus, but only because I pointed out she would seriously fuck that place up. Like, can you imagine all of those high-level convicts working together under her power to escape? Ha! Now that would be a show worth watching."

Rogan stared at her, his chest tight, not quite daring to believe what she'd just said. Her eyes narrowed. Her smile started to slip.

"Thank ye," he blurted, dropping to his knees and bowing again. Her smile back, she waved his words aside and stepped past him to sit on Emma's bed. He tensed but didn't dare try to stop her.

Pulling Emma's face from side to side, Delentia curled her lips and made a gagging sound. "She's not a pretty one, is she?" she tsked.

"No," Tegan said.

Despite his rage, Rogan bit his tongue. Delentia was known to take back her favors as quick as she gave them.

"Shall we leave you two alone?" Tegan asked, making Rogan's stomach drop to his feet.

"Oh, yes!" Delentia cooed. "When she wakes, I want her full attention!" She shoved her face over Emma's until their noses were a mere hairsbreadth away from touching. Delentia widened her eyes to look maniacal.

"She'll wake?" Rogan breathed, his words hoarse with raw feeling.

Tegan tugged on his arm when Delentia didn't answer. "We have to trust her, Rogan, or we'll both end up dead."

The goddess squealed as she cocked her head to one side and then the other. Her wide eyes never left Emma's closed ones. "He's right! I will slice open your necks and drink them like an orc pie! Starting with her. Oh, hey, can you walk Schizmo for me?" She waved at her chimera. "He totally needs to go for a shit right about now."

Left alone with Hades' child, Delentia grinned as wide as her eyes. It was going to be so funny when this bitch woke. As her face muscles started to strain under her fanatical pose, she scowled and raked a talon across the woman's cheek. When Emma stirred, Delentia cackled with crazed delight.

I'm alive.

The realization hit Emma like a semi-truck, quickly followed by the agonizing pain of her injuries. She grimaced as the full assault of it overwhelmed her senses, and she wondered how she had managed to survive at all. When she finally managed to move past the pain, she worked on opening her eyes.

And then she screamed.

Staring back at her, not even an inch away from her face, were two saucer-sized eyes. They retreated as the creature's head lolled back on a high pitched shout of laughter. "Oh, don't be such a baby, baby. You're going to get everyone killed," the monster cackled as she tilted her head forward again. Her eyes peered deep into Emma's soul. Then she jerked away, but only to flash her painted claws in front of Emma's face instead.

"W-who are you?"

"Why, your fairy godmother, of course! Didn't you see my wings?"

Emma's mouth parted as she took in the red leather towering above the creature's head. Her jaw dropped away completely when she noticed the two curved horns.

"F-f-fairy...?"

"Urgh, those are *such* stupid creatures. Always flying about like they have wings and shit. Makes me want to pluck them like ducks, you know?"

Emma swallowed as she cast her eyes desperately around the room, hoping she'd spot Rogan asleep in some chair. When she realized she was all alone, pain cut deep through her soul. Had he abandoned her so quickly? Now that the mission was done, so were they?

Her lips quivered as hot tears threatened to fall.

"I wonder..." Leaning down, the creature licked Emma's cheek.

She jumped with a small shudder at the touch of a rough forked tongue. "W-w-what–"

"The man beyond the grave cannot die, but the man he is claimed to cannot live. Two fates entwined. Three. Six. Nine. All. With your sister at the heart of it."

Emma's eyes widened at the mention of Elizabeth.

Before she could form a sentence, the creature let lose a scream. "Rogan!"

The last syllable had yet to disappear from the air when the door banged open and Rogan surged into the room. His piercing blue eyes landed on her, softening with guilt and pain and shame.

"Rogan," she murmured, her voice breaking with all the emotions she couldn't say. She'd nearly died. She'd failed her sister. She couldn't lose him too.

"Eck," Delentia spat as she turned toward the door. "Lifemates are the worst."

Tegan stilled as the goddess walked toward him with purpose in her short strides. Stopping in front of him, she looked up and cocked her head.

"Sorry the mission failed," she said. "You have such pretty eyes."

He cast her a quizzical gaze. She purred as she batted her lashes. Curious as to what she was talking about, he slowly edged, "But we retrieved the *Scrolls*. The mission was a success."

"Huh." Delentia cocked her head to the other side, her eyes distant. Eventually, she murmured, "So you did."

A feeling of unease settled low in Tegan's gut, but he knew better than to press for more clarity. Only those she dubbed as friends were allowed to ask her any questions, and even they were limited to a certain number every full moon cycle according to Hunter.

As he watched her leave, he wondered if she'd been hinting that the *Scrolls* they had retrieved was a fake? But that was impossible. The magicprint was a perfect match to the one they had on file, and the item wouldn't allow itself to be duplicated. So what –

"Oh, and Tegan, babe?" Delentia flashed him a smile. "Galvanor sends his love." The fury paused as she tapped her chin. "Or was it hate? Eh. It's hard to differentiate between the two when one's being tortured."

Cursing, Tegan paced down the hall, calling up every contact that might have news about his agent.

"Emma, love, I'm so sorry."

She shook her head, hating the pain in Rogan's voice. "There's nothing to be sorry about. I offered myself up as bait. We did the best we could. We just weren't..." She closed her eyes as she worked around the tightness in her throat.

Elizabeth's eyes stared back at her, haunted and full of tears.

Shuddering, Emma reached for Rogan's hand and gripped him hard. As his lips pressed tenderly against her temple, she almost wished he would order her to forget what had happened at the castle.

But she didn't want to forget a single memory of her sister. Who knew if that was the last one she'd ever get?

No.

She would have more. She was going to save Liz. She was going to grow strong, to learn how to use her powers outside of a pulse so that the next time she saw Sebastian, she could force him to release Liz from his command. And then she'd claw out the fucker's throat herself.

"Did you get the artifact back?" she asked, wanting something good to have come from this all.

"Aye."

She nodded. Her throat worked tight as she realized what that might mean. "Are you...leaving now then?"

"Emma..."

She closed her eyes and shook her head. The rawness in his voice was breaking her more than Sebastian's hands ever could.

"Hey," he said softly. Lifting her hand to his face, he kissed her knuckles. "I'm not going anywhere ye doona want me to go. Ye're my lifemate, Emma, and I...I love ye."

Thank God.

Because she loved him too. Pulling him down onto the bed beside her, she mumbled those words against the crook of his neck. He held her for a long moment, silent as she clung to him, her tears wetting them both.

Eventually, she took a deep breath and asked. "What's a lifemate?"

Squeezing her tight, he exhaled slowly. "Long ago, when the gods first gave us life, they ripped our souls in half and flung them far apart. Those two pieces are called lifemates."

"So we're being forced to like each other?"

"Nay, Emma. Some lifemates become mortal enemies."

A giddiness filled her chest, washing away a bulk of her pain. Life might have fucked her over in every hole she had, but at least it had given her this. "And you're mine?" she asked.

He nodded. "Aye." Cupping her face, he kissed her slowly. His tongue slid along hers, filling her entire body with a delicious heat. "And ye're mine."

Mine.

And together, they would survive anything.

EPILOGUE

Sebastian bowed low as he greeted the three goddesses honoring him once more with their presence. The throne room they stood in was dark and in ruins, but their beauty made it radiate with its former glory. Ignoring the pain from being here, in a room so achingly familiar, Sebastian kept his eyes on them.

"We are displeased," Freya sneered, her ferocity making his blood heat with the anticipation of having her soon squirming from his words.

"My sincerest apologies on losing the *Scrolls*, but the other descendant was much more powerful –"

"That is because I am a love goddess, not a sex goddess, you ignorant fool!" Aphrodite snarled, her face twisting in a beautiful rage. "My daughter will not come into her full power until she has felt love. Your orders were to woo her, not rape her when you got impatient. Had you not failed in your task, you would be ruling this realm by now and our plans would be in the works!"

He bowed low in acknowledgment of his mistake.

Though he had started off courting Elizabeth, his plans had fallen through when she had wandered in on him butchering one of her friends. Doubting anyone could win her back from that sight, he had decided to cut his loses. He'd taken her then and there, having bet that even if she wasn't in her full power, she would still be fairly strong. As usual, he had been right.

"Enough," Freya cut in when it was clear Aphrodite the Graeca Goddess of Love was just getting started. "You have overstepped the line one too many times, insulting us with your lack of respect. You have lost the *Scrolls of Atlantis*, stalling our plans for an unknown amount of time. You have no use to us outside of this, so enlighten us on why we should let you live."

His eyes grew cold as he straightened to his full height. He was no longer content to play their fool. "Because I took the liberty of making a copy," he purred.

The three shared reluctant looks with each other. They were uncertain if he was telling the truth or just trying to save his own skin. Then Aine spoke, her voice soft as it always was. "That's impossible. The *Scrolls* will not allow itself to be duplicated."

He gave a casual shrug of his shoulder. "And it did not."

"You're playing with fire, vampire," Freya warned.

He bowed low once more. He was not about to ruin his grand plans over a bit of pride. "I offer my apologies and beg for your forgiveness." Upon straightening, he added, "I found a human with a spectacular memory. Everything she sees, hears, smells, and experiences is remembered. This is the copy that I speak of."

"But she cannot write it down?"

"No, nor can she speak of it. But she understands the words as well as she can read them."

"And can she be controlled?"

Sebastian smiled as he thought of the boy newly in his care. "Yes. With ease."

"Push our plans forward immediately."

He bowed low with a word of agreement. By the time he rose, the throne room was empty. Smiling, he headed for the door.

It was time to put the next stage of his plan into action. It would bring him ever closer to becoming a god. And then no one would be able to stand in his way.

Least of all three idiot goddesses who thought they could control him.

Want to know what happened to Galvanor?

Pick up the next book in the series:
Think of Me Demon

AUTHOR'S NOTE

Hello everyone!

Thank you so much for reading *Elemental Claim*. Rogan and Emma were characters I wanted to write about for years but never did because of life and money and a thousand other things. But then I lost my job and I had a bit of savings and these two just wouldn't leave me alone, so I finally sat down and put their actions to paper.

This is my first book, my baby, and these two will always have a special place in my heart.

I hope you enjoyed getting to know them, as well as the other members of their team. I promise Liz will get her happy ending too.

Many cheers and happy reading,

PS: A special shout-out to the Koala Hospital in Port Macquarie, Australia. It's an absolutely fantastic non-profit that focuses on the conservation of, surprise, koalas. If anyone else can spare any change, please do! https://shop.koalahospital.org.au/

5 REASONS TO SIGN UP TO MY NEWSLETTER

1. Have the chance to end up as a character in one of my books!
2. Have the chance to join either my beta/ARC reader team.
3. Download sneak preview chapters.
4. Get all the latest information about upcoming releases.
5. Get free book banners and other cool promo.

Sign me up now!

https://mirandagrant.ck.page/0e074e4e9c (direct)
mirandagrant.co.uk (sign-up form)

3 REASONS TO LEAVE A REVIEW

1. They give me the strength and confidence to keep writing. The more reviews, the faster I write.
2. Chance to see your reviews inside one of my books.
3. I will love you forever.

Think of Me Demon

Matakyli is a demon warrior princess and one of the guardians to the backdoor of Niflhel. Her death could lead to the dead escaping, potentially bringing about the annihilation of the Seven Planes. So when a prophecy claims she will die by the hands of an ancient vampire, she and her three brothers do all they can to change her fate. But there's only one solution.

For her to live, her lifemate has to die.

Only Galvanor isn't willing to be led like a lamb to slaughter. He's still suffering from his last visit to hell and isn't keen on returning, especially not for another woman. But it's in Matakyli's nature to play with fire and enjoy the heat of its flames.

As she digs into the secrets he wants to keep buried, she discovers a soul worth saving.

But is his worth the cost of her own?

Death Do Us Part

Honey, Does This Taste Like Poison to You?

I've never been a fan of murder. The mess, the smell, the whole hiding the body thing after – it always seemed like way too much work. But trust me, when you're married to Richard Morningstar, that "work" starts to feel an awful lot like "play". The man is a snake and king of the fairies.

A barbarian. A war monger. A sex god. Uh, I mean a...an ex pod? Doesn't matter.

The point is, it's either him or me. Because one of us is going to die, and at the moment, it's *my* execution scheduled in three weeks. So I just have to figure out a way to kiss him – *kill* him – before then, take his throne, and turn his whole nightmarish kingdom upside down. Easy right?

Maybe – if he wasn't my lifemate.

And if my panties didn't drop every time he snapped his stupid fingers.

Burn Baby Burn

Everything is About to Burn

We all know the story. Cinderella's father remarries. She gets a shitty new family. He dies in a tragic accident and she is forced into a life of servitude.

But what happens when Ella's father is brutally murdered and she's sold to the Romans? What happens when she meets a dark fae who tempts her to embrace the embers in her heart? When he shows her the fire she was born with and coaxes those powers to light? What happens when he tells her that she doesn't need a prince.

She needs a crown.

The Little Morgen

She kills without mercy

On her thirteenth birthday, Thalliya watched her entire family get slaughtered. The humans cut off their fins and hung their heads from their Viking ships. Left cradling what few pieces remained of her twin, Thalliya screamed to the gods for vengeance.

Answered by the Goddess of Love and War, Thalliya now guards the seas without mercy.

He fights without fear

Ragnar is hired to take care of the mermaid terrorising the western seas. With seventeen kills under his belt, he thinks little of venturing into the Mouth of Hel. It'll be a quick job with a quick pay…

But when his ship is wrecked and the majority of his crew is drowned, Ragnar realises that it's not a mermaid he's hunting. It's a morgen, a dark mermaid, that's hunting him.

And there's only one way to kill one of those.

You have to get her to fall in love.